Other books by Kirt Hickman

Worlds Asunder

Worlds Asunder
Venus Rain
Mercury Sun
Methane Moon

Age of Prophecy

Fabler's Legend
Assassins' Prey
Host of Evil

Nonfiction

Revising Fiction: Making Sense of the Madness

For Children

I Will Eat Anything
Purple

MERCURY SUN

WORLDS ASUNDER: BOOK III

Even his worst nightmares wouldn't
have conjured "nuclear war."

Kirt Hickman

Quillrunner
Publishing

Published in the U.S.A. by
Quillrunner Publishing LLC
Albuquerque, NM

Printed in the U.S.A.

Cover art by David A. Hardy

Book design by Susan Cohen
Typeset in Palatino10/14

Cataloging-in-Publications Data is on file with the Library of Congress.
Library of Congress Control Number: 2014900028

ISBN 978-0-9851157-3-9

For my son, Ryan.

Acknowledgments

A book like this can't be created by one person alone. It took the tireless effort of many people to make *Mercury Sun* a reality. My thanks go out to all of you.

To my network of critiquers and test readers: Gerry Raban, Laura Beltemacchi, Larry Koch, Kimberly Mitchell, and others. Special thanks to David J. Corwell for catching the things that the rest of us didn't.

To my editor, Susan Grossman, for ensuring that *Mercury Sun* is the best that it can be.

To David A. Hardy and Susan Cohen, for exceeding all my expectations for book and cover design.

And most of all, to God for blessing me with the necessary time and talents.

CHAPTER 1

Zeke Shepherd pulled eight crates one by one from the stacks and placed them on the trailer behind his battery-powered luggage cart. He climbed into the driver's seat and stepped on the accelerator, and the cart hummed to life. His new protégé, Sean Tanner, sat beside him.

Carefully, Zeke steered the rig into the tunnels of Deep West Base. Both men wore pressure suits, their fishbowl helmets sitting on the seats behind them until they were ready to cycle out the airlock onto Mercury's surface.

"What's up for today?" Tanner asked.

Zeke gave him a tight smile. "You'll see."

During Tanner's first month, Zeke had watched the boy closely. Though Tanner's gaunt frame made him seem the type that was constantly burning calories in needless fidgeting and pacing, he was actually the most at-peace, imperturbable person Zeke had ever worked with. Tanner's mantra was, "I can do all things through Him who gives me strength."

Zeke had seen too many things turn out badly for him to share this particular aspect of Tanner's Christian worldview, but he couldn't deny the boy's equanimity.

Once they'd passed beyond the crowded corridors around the Base Administration complex, Zeke opened up the throttle, pushing the cart to its top speed of twelve and a half kilometers per hour, until he came to the end of the smoothed stone. He slowed then and maneuvered into one of the old rough-cut nickel mining tunnels, which they crept along for nearly a kilometer before coming to a round metal hatch that was too narrow for the cart to pass through.

Zeke donned his helmet and activated the comm. "Come on." He picked up one of the bulky crates, which weighed next to nothing in Mercury's one-third gravity, and handed it to Tanner.

Once they'd stacked all eight crates on the far side of the hatch, Tanner snapped on his own helmet.

"Make sure it's fastened tight," Zeke told him. "I don't want any mishaps today."

"Everything shows green."

"Sure?"

"Yes, sir."

"Okay." Zeke gestured to the corridor, dimly lit by half a dozen sparsely-spaced, bare-bulb lights that dangled by wires from the ceiling. He slammed the safety door closed and spun the heavy ship's-wheel handle to seal it.

"We're not going to pump down this whole tunnel just to go outside, are we?" Tanner asked.

"No." Zeke led him at least fifty meters in his long Mercury strides to an airlock that terminated the tunnel. "Always maintain at least two seals between the vacuum of space and the inhabited portion of the base, if possible."

"Got it."

They stepped in, each carrying a crate, and Zeke cycled the airlock.

"We're a long ways out," Tanner said. "I don't think I've been this far from the base proper before."

"You're in for a treat. Our water supply is one of the most paradoxical systems on the base."

∿❨○❩∾

When the airlock door swung open, Tanner stood mute. Mercury's northern pole was supposed to be in constant sunlight and maintain a surface temperature of nearly 450 degrees centigrade, but the temperature here plummeted even inside his pressure suit, and he stared into complete darkness. Though the base itself, situated just south of the northern pole, experienced darkness for eighty-eight days at a time, it was currently in the middle of its solar day. A trip outside should have meant unbearable heat, blinding light, and dangerous levels of solar radiation, which Tanner had experienced only once before, a few days after his arrival. "What is this place?" he asked through the comm. Stars filled the sky above them. "Are we on the surface?"

"Yes." Zeke chuckled. "Because the sun hits Mercury's pole at a ninety-degree angle, it never shines on the bottoms of the craters here. See that?" He pointed to a ring above them, illuminating the rim of the crater.

"Sunlight."

"That's right. With no atmosphere to scatter it, that little bit reflecting off the rim is all that makes it down here. Your eyes will adjust in a minute."

Gradually, Tanner began to make out huge geometric shapes in the darkness before him, rough cubes, light in color. "What are those?"

"Ice. In the absence of air, no light means no heat. The temperature down here is one hundred eighty-three degrees below zero."

"Wow." Tanner's voice was but a whisper in his own ears. He flipped on the lamp attached to his helmet. A veritable mountain of enormous cubes—each three meters on a side—looked as though they'd been dumped into the crater, which measured half a kilometer across. "This isn't natural ice."

"No. There used to be native ice here—it's part of the reason this location was chosen for Deep West—but we've long since consumed it. Now we import it from Europa. This crater is just a convenient place to store it. We melt it as we need it and the water runs down to a drain." Zeke switched on his headlamp and aimed it at the ground beneath them. Some sort of composite concrete lined the bottom of the crater, forming a giant bowl with a grate at the bottom. "From there it enters the filtration system and gets pumped to several liquid storage tanks, ready for use."

"You told me last week that we recycle our water."

"We do, but the yield of the recycling process is less than a hundred percent, so we top off the supply from here.

"The heat lamps we use to melt it need to be replaced annually. That's our job today. Unpack a bulb and follow me up." Zeke headed for a series of ladders affixed to the crater's sloped walls.

Tanner just took it all in for a moment. Overall, he felt pretty comfortable with Deep West's electrical systems—his degree had prepared him for that—but there was so much more: heating and cooling, breathing-air circulation, water…and those were just the systems he knew about. It seemed every day Zeke introduced him to something new.

Tanner set the crate down, extracted a heat lamp from the gel padding inside, and mounted the ladder. God willing, he would rise to the challenges Deep West presented.

◦◦《 O 》◦◦

Zeke lay awake in the blackness of Ana's hotel suite. Only the green numbers on the wall chronometer gave any indication that his eyes were actually open. It was 4:37 in the morning, Universal Coordinated Time—practically the middle of the night, but that mattered little here, deep within the silicate bedrock on a base that never slept.

The slight weight of Ana's head rested on his shoulder. The soft, warm puffs of her breath disturbed the fine red hairs on his chest and stirred his loins.

Ana Davenport was the best woman he'd ever had—not that he'd had many. Still, he could say with confidence that she was truly special. And her presence felt as natural as if the cosmos itself had willed the two of them to be together.

He sighed. That feeling would last until Ana woke up, and not one second longer. Zeke didn't know what he'd do then, or what he'd say.

While he was still thinking about it, an explosion rocked the base, loud enough that the sound seemed to split his skull, overlaid by a deep boom that he felt in his gut.

The room lurched, as though some sub-Mercurian giant had shouldered the whole of Deep West Base several meters toward the south. The light from the chronometer went out, plunging Zeke's world into utter black, devoid even of sound.

Then the emergency lights kicked on, washing the room in crimson. The air was choked with dust. Zeke picked himself up from the floor, coughing.

Ana, eyes wide, sat up in bed, her tiny hand holding the sheets to cover her lithe, naked form. Her mouth moved, but no sound seemed to come from her. Then she screamed. "Zeke!" Her voice was faint, as though it had come from the bottom of a deep crater. She gripped her head, palms on her temples, and squeezed. Her teeth glowed scarlet in the light as she grimaced.

"Ana." Zeke could barely hear his own voice. He rushed to her side, sat on the bed and held her, but only for a moment.

He couldn't stay. Even near the vent in the ceiling, the dust hung stationary in the air. The life support system had apparently gone down. But backup ventilation hadn't kicked on with the emergency lighting. Zeke had work to do.

When he tried to stand, Ana clung to him like a child.

He gripped her slender wrists, pried her hands gently from him, and kissed her forehead. "I have to go."

Ana stared into his face, confused, and mouthed, "What?"

"Life support!" he yelled. "I have to go!"

Ana hesitated for a few seconds, examining the dust in the air. She nodded once, then practically shoved him from the bed.

Zeke scooped up his jeans, hurried into his shirt, and yanked on the door. It didn't budge. He tugged again, harder. Still no movement.

Rather than fight it, he inspected the jamb and hinges. The frame was out of square, the door wedged within it.

Ana, standing now, began to pull on the blouse and slacks he'd removed from her the previous evening.

Zeke hurried past her and flipped the bed over. He dug his pocketknife from the front pocket of his jeans. Using the blade as a screwdriver, he disassembled the sturdy bedframe enough to separate one of its long sides, which he wedged into the crack between the door and the jamb. Leaning his weight on it, he motioned Ana toward the knob. She tugged once and the door came free.

Outside, the hallway was gone. The top two floors of the hotel, or parts of them anyway, had collapsed into the saloon on the lower level.

For a moment, Zeke just stared at the wreckage. Beyond, the entire Plaza seemed to lie in ruin. What could have caused such devastation? Certainly not a quake. Mercury hadn't seen any seismic or volcanic activity for eons. The base didn't have a fusion power plant, so no facilities explosion could have been enough. Even a ship crash wouldn't have done it. This part of the base was buried too deep to feel even a tanker explosion on the surface.

15

Ana put a hand on his arm and snapped his mind back to her. She pointed. Below, four of the hotel's patrons struggled to free a fifth from beneath the debris.

With a nod, Zeke gathered up the bed sheets and tied them to one another, then to the piece of bedframe he'd used to free the door. He stretched the metal piece across the opening and threw the other end of the makeshift rope down. "You want me to carry you?"

"What?" Ana mouthed.

He placed his lips next to her ear. "Do you want me to carry you down?"

She smiled—wry and humorless. "Don't be silly." She motioned toward the rope.

He wrapped it around one wrist and tested his weight on it.

"Careful," Ana shouted.

The eerie quiet in the presence of the obviously noisy efforts of the men below, and the screaming throb in Zeke's temples, gave the ordeal a nightmare quality. As unreal and disorienting as a dream, but as tactile and vivid as any real disaster.

He climbed down the sheets and stepped carefully onto a layer of debris. It shifted, so he whipped the end of the rope away from the wall, off to his left, under an uncertain overhang. From there, he jumped the rest of the way down to a relatively clear section of floor.

Ana descended behind him.

He waited there until she was low enough for him to grab her by the waist, and swung her to the floor. When he let go, she lost her balance and fell. After a moment, she regained her feet and brushed herself off, bleeding from a scrape on her hand. Zeke motioned her toward a hole in the front of the hotel that led, he hoped, to safety.

From there, he climbed over a portion of the fallen roof and helped the four men free an older woman from beneath a piece of the second-floor hallway. If they'd been in full gravity, she'd have been crushed. As it was, she was breathing, but at her age, Zeke held little hope that she would survive her injuries.

As the men carried her out, a faint pounding breached Zeke's dulled senses. A nearby door opened and closed, banging on the doorframe, barely visible through a gap at the top of the piled debris.

Zeke scrambled up and pulled a few pieces of stairway railing aside. A hand reached through a hole that was way too small to pull the survivor through.

Suddenly, a high-pitched whine seemed to split the air.

Zeke crouched on his perch and covered his ears. The sound only intensified. It wasn't coming from without. It was inside his own head—his damaged ears protesting their recent trauma. That might have been a positive sign, but on top of the throb in his temples and a pain like a knife penetrating the base of his skull, the screech was too much. He tumbled from the rubble and landed in a heap on the floor.

∾《◯》∾

Meanwhile, Ana scrambled past the collapsed façade of the hotel. She tried to run her fingers through her waist-length black hair, but they got stuck in the rat's nest of tangles left over from her passionate evening with Zeke. Only then did she notice the scrape on her hand. She wiped the blood onto her slacks. Through the crimson haze of the emergency lighting, she tried to take stock of Deep West's Plaza, a natural cavern formed by trapped gasses when the iron heart of Mercury had cooled. It consisted of one smoothed-stone main street, just under a kilometer long, with buildings lining both sides.

Nearly all the buildings had collapsed, or partially so—like the Sundown, the inn that housed Ana's room. Only the Sharp Shooter appeared to be undamaged.

People had begun to gather in the street. Some wandered as though looking for some way to help. Those with more initiative moved purposefully from building to building, searching for survivors and recovering the dead. Others stood mute, staring toward the cavernous ceiling lost in darkness above them.

Yet these were the lucky ones. An increasing number staggered into view, limping, bleeding, cradling an arm or hand that had been twisted into a wholly unnatural angle. Those too injured to walk were dragged or carried into the street and left there, with their wounds tended by whatever amateur responders existed among the guests of the Plaza.

Dead bodies lay in growing piles on the ground.

Chapter 2

Sometime later, Zeke's ears began to ring again, softly at first, then growing to a fevered whine, as if some essence of himself was whistling through a crack in his sanity. He lifted his pounding head. Someone had moved him to the street, such as it was. Ana knelt by his side, gripping his hand. At least she was okay.

The uncertain glow of the emergency lamps shining from the roofs of some of the damaged buildings around him illuminated house-sized boulders that must have been shaken loose from the great cavern's ceiling.

His gaze drifted to the darkness above. Apparently the ceiling wasn't as stable as the base architects had touted. He shielded out the direct glow of the emergency lights and stared upward for several long minutes as his eyes adjusted to the darkness, looking for any sign of sunlight from the surface. If there was even the tiniest fissure, they were all losing air.

Oh crap! Air! How long had he been unconscious? How much time had he lost? How much precious oxygen had been consumed?

He sat up. A cacophony of activity swarmed around him. Every noise sounded hollow—fake—but not muffled as before. Wounded were being dragged into the street and left, while their rescuers bounded back into the crumbled buildings to search for additional survivors.

Zeke's head still hurt, but not like it had. "We need—" His voice sounded strange, hollow. "We need to gather the wounded," he told Ana. "Move them to the Sharp Shooter."

"I know." Ana stood, barely taller than Zeke was seated.

His head swam in pain. "Get some help. Get them moved. I have to restore the air flow."

Ana looked skeptical. She'd never had much sway within this community, but somebody had to do it, and nobody else was. More than anything, these people needed direction.

"If you're confident and authoritative," Zeke said, "they'll listen."

"*These* people? Do you realize what you're asking?"

Zeke climbed unsteadily to his feet and put a large, reassuring hand on her shoulder. He bent and kissed the top of her head. "Just try. I have to go." He turned then, his initial steps shaky as his inner ear began to recover from the pounding it had taken during the…blast, or whatever it was.

∞《 ○ 》∞

Ana kept an eye on Zeke's muscular form until he vanished into the haze. Then she tucked the tip of her thumb and forefinger between her lips and let rip a whistle that stopped nearly everybody in sight. "Listen up!" She began to beckon those who'd been milling, or just standing, in the street. "If you're not saving a life, gather 'round."

The people continued doing whatever they'd been doing. A pair of women sitting on a bench nearby, covered with scrapes and scratches, looked up, alert. They weren't locals. Guests, then. In fact, the vast majority of the people there were guests. Because Mercury's brief solar orbit offered the most-frequent launch windows to any planet in the solar system, Deep West had become the transportation hub for interplanetary travel. These women were likely waiting for the next ship-launch to some other world.

"Listen to the paragon of sound judgment," a limping man said, gesturing at Ana.

The women looked curiously at her and then at the man. They turned their attention away and began to grumble their misfortune.

"Listen to me," Ana yelled. "We need to gather the wounded at the Sharp Shooter so they can be cared for."

"In a casino?" said another man, loudly enough for everyone in the area to hear. Someone else guffawed.

"You got a—" Ana began.

The man walked away. He'd been a client once, but not for some time.

Ana dropped her voice to a whisper "—better idea?" She stifled a sob, then moved resolutely down the block toward the Sharp Shooter.

One of the local deputies passed her on his way toward the end of the Plaza that connected to the rest of the labyrinthine base. "You going for the doctors?" she asked him.

"If I can reach the hospital." He hurried away.

Ana stopped a man she didn't recognize—another visitor—who was carrying a small girl with a hastily splinted leg. "We're moving the wounded to the Sharp Shooter." She pointed to the hotel.

The man looked twice at her, as if to assure himself that Ana wasn't a child. With a height of barely over a meter, she commonly got that reaction from people who didn't know her.

"She your daughter?" Ana asked.

The man nodded. A woman joined them, probably the girl's mother.

"The doctors are on their way," Ana said. "They can care for her there."

The man nudged the woman and pointed to the casino, and the three moved off in that direction.

From that moment on, Ana focused her efforts on gathering people who didn't know her personally. Her success, however, could be measured only in meager terms. Those who knew her, knew her reputation. Most of the others thought she was a child, due to her unfortunate size, which was the reason she'd left Earth in the first place.

When she mounted the boardwalk in front of the Sharp Shooter, Simeon Tuck, the hotel's owner and Ana's personal and professional nemesis, stood in the doorway with his hands balled on the hips of his immaculate, Old-West style silk suit. Though he was in his fifties, his trimmed mustache and beard showed gray only along his jaw. He said nothing.

Ana frowned. "Move aside, Simeon."

He stared at her through cold, slate gray eyes. "I will not."

"We need someplace to put the wounded. Yours is the only building standing."

"It's for my guests. Lay your wounded in the street."

Her wounded? He had the audacity to call them *her* wounded, as if this was all somehow her fault.

20

"Come on, Simeon." It galled her that she couldn't keep the futility from her tone. Simeon would feed on it, use it like he used everything and everyone. "There's too much dust and chaos out here. They need rest and quiet."

"I'm running a business here." He looked indignant, with just enough insincerity…

Ana made a show of peering past him into the main gambling hall. There wasn't a soul there, not even Kamoku and Manuko, Simeon's personal Polynesian thugs. "Yeah, I can see that. Thriving, are you?"

She didn't even see his hand move, but the slap he struck across her cheek nearly knocked her down. The red lights seemed to dim for a moment and the whole side of her face felt like it had been scorched.

"Go home, Ana. You had your chance to use the Sharp Shooter."

❧❦◖○◗❦❧

Zeke made the mistake of inhaling through his mouth. Dust coated his throat and made him cough. He considered looking for a source of water but decided against it. Even if water was still running somewhere in the Plaza, which he doubted, he couldn't spare the time. With no current to drive the dirt-clotted air to the filters, it just hung there, clouding everything with a ruby-tinged haze.

He jogged down the street, past three broken hotels, a grocer, the dentist, a bakery, and what was left of Higher Orbit, the most prestigious specialty coffee shop in the solar system. Coughs, shouts, wails of anguish, and the occasional scream drifted from dark recesses in the rubble. Let the people milling in the street aid the individuals—Zeke had a larger responsibility. He had to help them all. If he didn't get the air turned back on, every one of them, trapped or freed, wounded or healthy—Ana—they would all die.

When he arrived at the hatch to the main tunnel, the metal safety door was closed, the pressure gasket sealed. Apparently someone had thought to close it since the disaster. It was usually left open. He reached for the comm panel beside it. "Zeke Shepherd to Administration."

After a moment, he tried again. "Zeke Shepherd to Base Administration. Can anybody hear me?"

Nothing. Not even static.

He changed channels, "Zeke Shepherd to generator room." He waited. "Zeke to generator room. Is anybody there?" Still nothing.

Beyond a pair of electric luggage carts sat an emergency closet. Rather than trust the base's integrity, Zeke donned a pressure suit—the only 2XL on the rack—pocketed a flashlight, and strapped a tool belt around his waist.

The manometer gauge for the other side of the safety door read atmospheric pressure, as it should. He turned the big wheel counter-clockwise as far as it would go, then heaved the door toward him. A second door blocked his path, closing off a three-meter-square chamber, a safety airlock between the cavernous Plaza and the rest of the base. The pressure readout for the corridor beyond also read normal.

He sealed the first door and opened the second. Beyond, long stretches of darkness separated the emergency lights. From there, the condition of the tunnels forced him to slow down.

Some of the corridors had been old mining tunnels before Jupiter's moons became a practical source of ore, when nickel mining was Mercury's primary industry. Others formed as natural rifts when Mercury's core had cooled. This particular tunnel had been added later, however, after acoustic surveys revealed the huge underground pocket that now housed the Plaza.

Zeke stopped at one of the major intersections and observed the dust for any stirring that might suggest air circulation or a vacuum breach, but saw none.

He stepped carefully past a section of the right-hand wall that had collapsed. A low groan sounded from somewhere in the depths of the base, as if Deep West itself had been buried alive and now moaned in pain. A trickle of dust and pebbles fell from the ceiling. He waited for it to stop before proceeding.

Farther on, a trio of survivors limped from a side tunnel, down which several cargo warehouses and much of the base's food stores resided. Two men supported the third, whose leg was bleeding.

One of them looked both ways down the main corridor. His eyes focused on Zeke from his dust-encrusted face. "Is the hospital still accessible?"

Zeke activated the external speaker on his pressure suit. "I hope so, but I haven't made it that far yet."

"You came from the Plaza?"

"Yes."

"How is it?"

"A mess, but accessible. If you make it to the hospital, tell them there are hundreds injured in the Plaza who need attention. Many of them shouldn't be moved."

The man nodded wearily, and the three continued down the corridor.

Several minutes later, after Zeke's efforts to reach the generator fuel stores had been thwarted by a number of collapsed tunnels, a group of seven—no, eight—survivors rounded a corner. One man held a blood-soaked rag to his face. Two others dragged a fourth along the floor, on top of a blanket.

"That way." Zeke pointed. "The passage is clear all the way to the Plaza."

The last man in the group stopped. His long, oily hair was covered with dust, as were the company overalls that draped his gangly frame. "That you, Zeke?"

"Oh, thank heavens. It's good to see you, Tanner."

"You all right?" the young man asked.

Zeke's head had begun to clear a little. "Well as can be expected."

Tanner looked at his departing companions, then down the tunnel in the direction Zeke had been headed. "Whatever you're up to, I'll give you a hand. Nobody should be wandering the base alone right now."

Zeke wasn't exactly wandering. In fact, he needed to pick up his pace and he could use the help. He handed Tanner the flashlight and flipped on his own helmet lamp. "Come on."

Two intersections later, he rounded a corner. Their way was blocked by yet another cave-in. "Damn."

"Any idea what happened?" Tanner asked.

"Huge meteor strike is the only thing I can figure."

"Wouldn't we have had warning?"

"One would think."

CHAPTER 3

Major Bill Ryan of the US Air Force Space Command viewed the devastation of Deep West Base from the cockpit of the *Black Panther*, one of four Cover Armed Tactical Spacecraft approaching Mercury. "Take us closer," he told his new pilot, Lieutenant Lindsey Carter, as their CATS came into orbit over Deep West, the joint US/EU base on Mercury. Portions of Deep West might have survived. *People* might have survived. One thing was clear, though. The landing pad and the hangars directly beneath were gone.

Bill thumbed the comm panel and verified that the encryption light was on. "Ryan to McCaughey. I'm going to find out what's left of the base and see if I can secure a place for the convoys to land. You and the others locate and destroy the Mingyun satellites." It was the first time any of them had broken radio silence since they'd left Earth twenty-two days before.

"You got it." Dana's voice sounded like an angel's. Being without her was bad enough, but not to have even heard her voice for so long had been absolute torment. The comm channel went silent for a moment. Then, "Be careful, Bill."

"I will."

"Etre," Bill continued.

"Here," said the captain of the *Jaguar*.

"Watch our backs. It's a safe bet we'll have trouble, but our eyes won't be on the sky—"

"If we see anything, I'll give you a holler."

Bill switched off the comm and spoke to Lieutenant Carter. "Bring us in. Spiral approach, beginning twenty clicks out."

"Shall I hail the base?" she asked.

To do so was standard procedure, but it would require an unencrypted transmission. It would alert the enemy to their presence. "No."

Moments later, the tug of breaking thrusters pulled at the *Black Panther* and she began her descent toward the surface.

"Weapons ready," he ordered Duane Townsend, his weapon's officer, the third and final member of the *Black Panther*'s crew.

"Ready," Townsend confirmed.

The descent was slow and easy. From a distance, the planet surface looked a lot like that of Earth's moon, dull gray and pitted with craters. But Mercury also had frozen ripples that covered large tracts of its surface—the so-called lobate scarps that had formed when the planet, once a ball of molten stone, had suddenly, inexplicably frozen. As the ship drew closer, those ripples resolved into sheer cliffs, fifty to hundreds of meters high. Bill gave them little attention, except for that brief curiosity.

Rather, he scanned the ground for any incoming threats to Deep West. He saw none. Even the Mingyun satellites posed no immediate danger. They couldn't target Bill's stealth ship on radar and the small rocket rounds the satellites fired would never penetrate the buried base.

The Chinese and Russian bases each lay a little farther from the pole, approximately the same distance from each other as they were from Deep West. As far as Bill could tell, both Shenming and Gagarin were quiet. For the moment, the coast seemed clear.

"Twenty kilometers," Carter said. "Beginning our spiral."

Several minutes passed.

Bill monitored their fuel supply.

"Ten kilometers."

The external radiation increased steadily from normal background levels, already high this close to the sun, to four times normal and climbing. The ship's shielding would protect them at even higher levels, as long as they remained inside.

"Five kilometers."

Bill examined the base. A few of the surface structures, little more than concrete bunkers housing elevators to the underground base, appeared to be intact. "Put us down over there." He pointed through the polarized windshield to a flat spot, hidden from direct sight from the Chinese approaches by one of the lobate scarps and not far from Deep West's southernmost surface entrance.

Carter eased the ship down to one of the smoothest landings Bill had ever seen from her. He almost said, "Well done," but kept the praise to himself. This was no training mission. He didn't want her to feel like it was.

Here, the radiation read nearly ten times normal background levels. Fortunately, their pressure suits, designed for use in the Mercury system, included some protection from the sun's otherwise-unshielded radiation. Stil ...

"Unless we want to start growing extra eyes and arms, let's not dawdle on the surface," he said.

After receiving an acknowledgement from both crewmen, he thumbed the switch to pump the cabin air back into one of the reserve oxygen tanks. With that in progress, Bill, Carter, and Townsend each strapped on twenty kilograms of equipment, ranging from tool belts to assault rifles, communication and survival gear, medical supplies, and a duffle bag filled to capacity with hand grenades, smoke bombs, and flash-bangs.

When they were ready, he popped the door seal, deployed the folding ladder, and climbed down in gravity more than twice what he'd experienced on Earth's moon a few months before.

"You two secure the ship," Bill said. "I'll go knock on the door." He bounded to the concrete bunker, nothing more than a two-meter cube with a tungsten-steel door.

White coolant vapor flowed over the controls inside a small hatch. The panel behind the mist was dark, except for a small red battery icon. Apparently the lift was running on emergency power. Yet the panel was live. Bill punched a green button adorned with a down arrow.

Meanwhile, Carter and Townsend draped a camouflage net over the *Black Panther*. Townsend pulled a compression-bolt gun from his tool belt and fired anchors through the corners of the net to secure it to the Mercury stone.

Thirty seconds later, the bunker door slid open, revealing a lift car. They stepped in, and the door closed behind them. The lift lurched into motion, leaving Bill's stomach momentarily behind. The car, which also served as an airlock, filled with atmosphere as it descended.

⊰⟨ ○ ⟩⊱

General Chou, now in charge of China's Shenming Base, stood among his lieutenants, each responsible for a different portion of Chou's resources: his Marauder space fighters, the Mingyun missile satellites, his ground troops, planetary surveillance, and base security. Two administration clerks, both chief petty officers, attended him. Four armed privates served as his personal guard.

When the Chinese military had taken over Shenming five months before, Chou had made only three changes to the control center. First, he'd relocated the civilian administrators to another suite of offices at the far end of the base—he had no interest in the civilians as long as they stayed out of his way. Second, he'd taken down all the aluminite partitions, so he could see every one of his men. Third, he'd removed the chief administrator's desk and, in the exact center of the room, had placed a three-meter-square horizontal display screen, which now showed a scalable image of the considerable damage to Deep West. Too short to reach the center of the touch screen by hand, Chou controlled the display with a long Teflon stick that resembled a billiards cue.

He scanned the banks of computer and surveillance screens around him. The nearest displayed manifests for supply ships that had recently arrived—ships he could observe his men unloading via several surveillance monitors to his left. As his government had done three months before, the supplies for the civilians at Shenming had been shortchanged to allow room for the military troops and supplies Chou needed to accomplish his mission: to destroy Deep West Base and deny the use of Mercury to the United States and the European Union as either a transportation hub or military base—in short, to cut the Western powers off from the rest of the solar system. Specifically, he needed to eliminate any threat to Chinese and Russian shipping, whether to space station *Venus Rain* or any other destination in the solar system.

That threat, a pair of military convoys, was now approaching. Chou had two assets to oppose them. His own fighter support crews were now fueling

27

the first, a squadron of four Marauders. These Chou monitored on a pair of vid-screens to his right.

Because of the weapons ban imposed by the Third Outer Space Treaty, he'd had to smuggle the Marauders to Mercury on a freighter, whose reported purpose had been to recover and dismantle China's missile satellites. These satellites were Chou's second-most important resource. Not only were they still out there, but he'd been using them for the past several hours to eliminate his enemy's orbital surveillance capability.

Lieutenant Wu sat behind Chou, directing the satellites, designating targets, and updating a readout that Chou also watched carefully, a readout of every satellite left in Mercury space. Satellite after satellite changed from blinking-red text—indicating it as a Mingyun target—to light gray, followed by the designator: ELIMINATED.

❧❦(O)❦❧

The mission of the CATS wing was to arrive at Mercury undetected before the US and EU military convoys, assess the threat, and prepare a path for the convoys' safe arrival. Though the CATS had launched at the same time as the convoy, their arrival at Mercury six hours early had been a simple matter of selecting a slightly longer trajectory for the convoy ships.

The second objective, clearing Mercury space of threats, consisted, at a minimum, of destroying the three Mingyun missile satellites China had put into orbit.

Now that Bill Ryan and his ship had landed, the mission fell squarely upon the shoulders of Major Dana McCaughey, second-in-command of the CATS wing.

Her mission specs included the known orbit parameters of every object in the Mercury system on the day before the CATS had launched from Earth. Yet when her ship, the *Snow Leopard*, reached the reported location of her target, the satellite was gone.

She thumbed the comm. "*Snow Leopard* to CATS. Have you guys reached your targets?"

"Yes and no, Major." The voice was Etre's from the *Jaguar*.

"Understood, Captain. Duval?"

"Negative. It's not here."

"All right, gentlemen. Our targets have been moved. We need to map everything in orbit. Position and vector. As soon as we go active, the Chinese will pick up our radar signals. It won't take them long to figure out we're here and what we're up to, so make it quick." Fortunately, with three signals filling the void, it would take more than a few minutes to sort them out and triangulate the source of each. "Allistair—" Dana said to her gunner.

"Already on it."

Dana's radar display began to fill with blips. She entered a command for the computer to begin tracking each object and to calculate a trajectory from the successive radar sweeps. But her readings alone weren't enough. An encrypted signal came in from each of the other CATS. The computer merged the scans and began to refine each satellite's trajectory in three-dimensional space.

The sky should have been filled with blips. Hundreds were missing. "You getting this?" she asked her pilot, Lieutenant Johnny Miller.

"There're some big holes out there. We'll have to run a correlation to see what's missing."

Dana tapped a few keys on her console, and a tabulated list of vectors and satellites began to scroll down her screen. One by one, individual lines turned red—NO CORRESPONDING SIGNAL FOUND. *No!* She felt the blood drain from her face.

At first she refused to believe it, but every US and European satellite in the system, every communications relay, every imaging scanner, every data-collection sensor—in fact, every surveillance system—was gone. Dana turned up the resolution on the radar sweep and thousands of smaller bits of debris filled the void in expanding clumps.

"Bastards have been busy," Miller said.

Allowing for reasonable errors in the resolution of the original orbit parameters, three objects large enough to be Mingyun satellites traveled on vectors that didn't match any satellites in Dana's intelligence report—exactly the number of targets Dana was looking for.

She divvied out the new target assignments, one each to the *Cheetah*, the *Jaguar*, and herself, but it would take time to get there and the convoy now trailed by only five hours.

They had another problem too. This had all begun five months before, when the China Dominion Affair had opened the eyes of Chinese President Li Muyou to the dominant position his Mingyun satellites had given his country in space.

There had been an orbital launch window from Earth to Mercury since then. Li Muyou might have already landed military forces on Mercury. Dana and her CATS teams would have to deal with those as well, until Colonel Davis, commander of the American convoy, could get his marines on the ground and organized.

"Mayday. Mayday." It was Colonel Davis in the troop transport. "We're under fire. Repeat. We are under fire."

CHAPTER 4

At the bottom of the elevator shaft, Bill Ryan and his crew stepped into a surreal world in ruin. The architecture, that which he could discern from the partial structures looming in the dusty haze, looked at least two hundred years out of style, but the clothing people wore was as modern as his own pressure suit. The very air glowed crimson, the color that he, from years spent in a CATS training simulator, associated with mission failure. And that's probably what it meant here. Yet people moved everywhere, alive, thanks to a million tons of iron-rich silicate rock.

Bill popped his helmet clamps, pulled the bubble from his head, and tucked it under his arm. His crew did the same.

"You two all right?" he asked.

"Locked and loaded," Carter said.

Townsend motioned at the chaos in front of them. "Better than most of these folks," he said, which wasn't saying much.

As they headed down the main street, Bill began to discern a pattern to the chaotic bustle. Some of the survivors moved with a purpose, but there didn't seem to be a leader. They worked more like ants than like people.

Not far from the lift, a stocky man in a green shirt stopped them. He gestured at Bill's rifle. "Who are you?"

"US military." At the moment, that was all Bill was willing to say. The Air Force Space Command patch on the sleeve of his pressure suit revealed that much.

"Military?"

Several men nearby looked his way. They'd been digging by hand to clear debris from the front of a collapsed store, searching for survivors...or loot.

"What the hell is the military doing here?" the first man asked. His shirt was a sick off-brown in the red lighting.

"Ain't that illegal?" yelled a man near the storefront.

One of his buddies crossed the street to Bill, his forearm wrapped in a bloody strip of cloth. "You guys have any idea what happened?"

Bill ignored the question. "Who's running the show down here?"

The man with the injured arm shrugged. "I'm not sure anybody is."

Another yelled from across the road. "I heard Ana was trying to get people organized."

"Little Ana?" said the man in green. "The hooker?"

The other raised his hands defensively. "That's what I heard." Then to Bill, he said, "People are gathering at the Sharp Shooter. Big building down the street on the left. You can't miss it."

"Thanks." Bill nudged Townsend's shoulder and pointed.

The road itself was flat, smooth stone, not cobbled together but a single piece of bedrock. Though it was wide enough for regular cars, the only vehicles he saw were small, like the electric luggage cart somebody was using to pull wreckage from a Laundromat. In another building, men were using a small forklift to raise a section of the fallen roof.

A sharp whistle pierced the air and Bill looked over.

"You there," a man yelled. "Give us a hand."

Bill hesitated.

"Hurry up, man," the worker called. "There's somebody under here."

When Bill turned to help, Townsend grabbed his shoulder. "We've got a mission here."

Bill shook off Townsend's hand. "We can't just leave him there. Come on." He trotted over.

The building had been a restaurant, or maybe just a soda fountain. Two men were trying to lift an industrial refrigeration unit that had fallen onto a third in the cramped space behind the counter.

"Grab that." Bill pointed to one corner of the refrigerator.

Townsend complied. With a grunt, the four of them managed to lift it.

Carter dragged the man out from underneath by his shoulders.

The victim, a young guy, maybe sixteen or seventeen, was pale as moon-light. One of his legs had been crushed, the foot twisted at a sickening angle. But he was breathing

"We've got to get him to the Sharp Shooter." One of the workers reached for him. He pointed to his buddy. "Grab his legs."

"Wait." Bill gripped the man's arm. "You lift him like that, you'll probably kill him."

The man stared defiantly into Bill's eyes. "You got a better idea?"

"Yeah. I do." He tapped Townsend with the back of his hand and pointed to a booth that was long enough to seat six.

Without a word, Townsend strode over and inspected the underside of the table. He pulled a power drill from his tool belt, fitted a nut driver to it, and went to work. Within a minute, he'd detached the tabletop from the supports to which it had been bolted and brought it over.

The workmen slid the injured man onto it and carried it into the street. Bill and his crew followed. They stopped when the crowd around the Sharp Shooter became too dense to carry the makeshift stretcher through.

"Wait here. I'll see what's going on." Bill shouldered his way through the crowd to the entrance, which boasted an intricately carved door that appeared to be, of all things, real wood.

A man with dark brown hair and beard, tinged the color of blood by the emergency lighting, blocked the entrance. "Line them up out here. There's more room. The doctors can get at them." He looked down the street in the direction opposite from that which Bill and his crew had come. "If they ever get here."

He spoke, Bill thought, to a child, a girl who stood little more than a meter tall. She turned to a grown man next to her. "Go see what's keeping the doctors."

The man ran off as though he'd been instructed by his mother.

"We need the tables, Simeon. And chairs." She pointed with her chin toward the building's interior. "And the air's got to be cleaner in there." Her voice didn't sound like that of a child. She carried herself with very much an adult presence, despite her size. And she spoke with authority, as if she expected obedience. She was, without a doubt, a woman. "Little Ana," the man down the street had called her. Now Bill understood why.

"You want to put the wounded on top of the slot machines and roulette tables?" the man asked.

"We'll move the tables if we have to."

Bill marched up to the door. He stood at least ten centimeters taller than the bearded man and leaned in to loom over him. "Step aside."

The man measured him, his eyes moving from Bill's own down his flight suit to Bill's feet, pausing momentarily on the rifle slung over his shoulder and the pistol holstered at his hip, and then back to Bill's eyes. "Who the hell are you?"

Bill presented the patch on his sleeve. "United States Air Force. We're commandeering your building."

"Like hell you are."

"Simeon, is it?" Bill said.

"Maybe."

Without taking his eyes off Simeon's face, Bill swept the man's feet out from beneath him. Simeon's eyes went wide, arms flailing, as he crashed to the floor in a heap.

Bill grabbed a fistful of Simeon's shirt and dragged him out of his own casino with one hand. With his other, he motioned Little Ana inside.

"Careful," she said. "He's not one to cross."

◈⟨O⟩◈

Colonel Davis, the overall commander of the Mercury mission, watched the international grand-championship speeder race, the Dakota 10k, on the vid-screen in the small lounge at the aft of the US troop transport. The ship, officially designated the *Virgil Grissom*, was affectionately called *"Gus"* or *"Gus the Bus"* by the hundred and fifty US marines to whom it had been home for the past twenty-two days.

Seventeen of Davis's men had also crammed into the lounge, which was designed to accommodate maybe eight passengers. On the screen, thirteen rocket-propelled cars sped around the custom-built track, moving so fast they actually left the ground on the straightaways, touching down only on the heavily banked curves.

Up for grabs was an unopened liter-size bottle of butterscotch bourbon that one of Davis's men had smuggled aboard. When Davis had discovered the contraband, he had verbally reprimanded the soldier. Though he could have put a formal citation in the man's personnel file, such a serious charge as smuggling alcohol during an active combat mission would have prevented the corporal from ever achieving officer rank. To Davis, that seemed a bit extreme.

Instead, everyone interested threw his name into an EVA helmet. Everyone, that is, except Davis himself and Corporal Stevens, the man he'd caught with the bottle. Then Davis drew seventeen of the names, one for each speeder in the race. As each name was drawn, the soldier selected the speeder of his choice, excluding any that had already been chosen. The winner would claim the bourbon, with the stipulations that it not be shared with Stevens and that it not be opened until the convoy had landed and Davis had declared the military situation stable.

As punishment, Stevens would watch his precious contraband go to somebody else. And the race, the fastest automobile event ever conceived, would provide Davis's men with some spirited entertainment, a much-needed diversion during the final hours of their journey.

Because the Dakota 10k was the fastest, it was also the most dangerous land-vehicle race ever run. As the marines watched, the number-four speeder hit one of the banked turns a little too high. The rocket-car slammed into the asphalt and skidded.

Private Weems, who'd bet number four, flew to his feet with a scream, losing control in the meager artificial gravity provided by *Gus*'s steady deceleration.

Pieces flew from the speeder in a shower of sparks. The car shot past the top of the banked curve and tumbled like a rolling barrel, at least fifty meters off the ground, its tail a fountain of flames.

The *Virgil Grissom*'s lounge erupted with cheers and laughter as another competitor dropped out of contention.

Within three rolls, the gyro system onboard the number-four speeder slowed the vehicle's roll, and just as the dome of the cracked cockpit faced upward, the ejection seat spewed the pilot another thirty meters into the air.

35

His parachute popped free and billowed, and the pilot began his gradual descent to the ground. He waved to let the crowd know he was okay.

The camera and commentator snapped back to the action on the track.

That was the fifth pilot out of the race. Twelve cars and seventy-eight laps remained.

Just then, a voice came over the intercom. "Colonel?"

Davis thumbed the TALK switch. "What is it?"

"You asked me to notify you six hours before we reach Mercury orbit."

"Yes, I did. Thank you." That notice meant the CATS would be moving into position, and that good ol' *Gus* was entering a potential combat zone. Davis clicked off the intercom and then the vid-screen.

A loud moan ensued.

"It's time, fellows. Suit up." He grabbed the bottle of bourbon. "We have a few hours before we'll be ready for descent, but I want everybody to suit up now, just in case. Then, if your speeder is still in the race, you can come back. Otherwise, I want you strapped into your seat."

Davis went to his own locker, stowed the alcohol, and donned his pressure suit, which combat regulations required each soldier to wear when approaching hostile territory. That done, he took his place in the command chair, just behind the pilot and navigator.

One by one, the voices of his men began to come over the EVA comm system, acknowledging the readiness of themselves and their gear. Davis turned the volume of that channel down so he could hear any incoming transmission from the CATS.

Thirty minutes passed without incident, aside from two more speeders dropping out of the Dakota 10k. Davis looked back down the main corridor to make sure the two eliminated marines returned to their seats as he'd ordered.

They were halfway down the aisle when a hole the size of a one-man escape pod was blown out of *Gus*'s rear, starboard quarter. The decompression klaxon blared. As the rip expanded, the side of the lounge vanished. The men inside and at least a dozen others were swept into space.

"Hard over!" Davis yelled. The ship canted to one side. "Damage report."

"Assessing."

Just past the windshield, which now had a hole in it the size of a softball, the freight ship *Aries* exploded.

"Davis to fleet. All ships, evasive maneuvers."

He gripped his seat against the gale and trained his eyes on the radar screen. It showed clear all the way to their destination. Not an enemy in sight.

As one, the freighters of Davis's convoy lumbered through a pre-designated burn. Their nimble fighter escort spun away and began a search pattern for stealth enemy ships.

"With the exception of vacuum integrity, vital systems are intact, Colonel," a crewman reported. "Thirty-two men missing."

Davis clenched the arms of his command chair.

An unnatural vibration shuddered through the hull as maneuvering thrusters labored through the course change. Davis increased the resolution of the radar scans. The sweeps, now frustratingly slow, came and went with no sign of incoming Mingyun rocket rounds.

He turned up the resolution again, now losing some of the scan's range. On the next sweep, he saw them. A brief peppering of a dozen or more signals that whipped past before the radar sweep came around again. Most of the fleet had moved out of the way, but one ship, the *Taurus*, veered off at an unassigned angle.

"*Taurus*, what's your status?" Davis queried.

"We're hit," the freighter's commander reported. "Damaged contained. We'll know more shortly."

Davis thumbed over to the long-range channel. "Mayday. Mayday. We're under fire. Repeat. We are under fire."

"Hang in there, Colonel," Major McCaughey replied from the *Snow Leopard*. "The Mingyuns have been moved. We're in route. In the meantime, you'll need to maintain evasive maneuvers."

Great. After the fight they'd endured to escape from Earth, the fleet didn't have enough fuel to maintain evasive maneuvers.

CHAPTER 5

Bill thumbed the comm link in his ear. "Ryan to Davis." A pause. "Major Ryan to Colonel Davis. Come in."

No response.

"Ryan to *Snow Leopard*. McCaughey, do you read? Over."

Nothing.

With base communications down, his own link apparently wasn't sufficient to transmit through the kilometer of rock between himself and the surface.

Somehow he'd have to get a signal out before the convoys achieved orbit.

Beside him, Simeon climbed to his feet and brushed off his suit. He stepped toward the Sharp Shooter, but Carter and Townsend blocked his way.

"Can you contact your base director?" Bill asked him.

Simeon fumed, his nostrils flaring.

"I asked you a question," Bill said.

Simeon straightened. "You're nothing more than a street thug in a uniform."

Bill motioned again for Ana and the wounded to move into the casino.

She glanced warily at Simeon before doing so. Behind her, two men helped a third, limping, through the doorway.

"Sit him down over there," Ana told them. "Then help me clear the tables."

"Be careful with those, Ana," Simeon yelled into the room. "I'll charge you personally for any damage."

Bill stepped past Carter and stared into Simeon's eyes, their faces mere centimeters apart. "All right. Here's the way it's going to work. In less than six hours, this place will be overrun by US and European troops. Like it or not, Deep West is now a military base, the command center for a mission that will likely get ugly before it's all over. And I don't have time for the local big fish to try to throw his weight around."

Simeon showed no sign of backing down.

"You can either cooperate, step aside, or get shoved into a corner."

"Is that a threat?"

"It's a fact. Now, can you or can you not contact Director Anderson?"

Simeon hesitated. "I've tried. I can't reach anybody." He didn't sound distressed or disappointed by the fact.

"Thank you." To Carter and Townsend, Bill said, "Let him go."

His crew members stepped aside. Instead of going back into his hotel, however, Simeon marched off down the street.

Bill went inside. The whole interior of the place had been ornately decorated with marble and woodwork. Most of the floor space was broken up by blackjack, roulette, and craps tables, all large enough to use as beds for the wounded. Ana stood on a chair and cleared off a card table, sweeping the cards and thousands of credits worth of chips onto the floor with no more regard for them than for used cocktail napkins.

Bill stepped up to help her. "Who is that guy? I mean besides the owner of this fine establishment." He rapped his knuckles on the edge of the table. Again, real wood. "He's got money."

"And friends. And power." Concern showed clearly in Ana's eyes. "For all intents and purposes, Simeon is the mayor, the sheriff, and the loan shark of the Plaza. Every gun on this station, to one degree or another, works for him."

Bill unslung the rifle from his shoulder. "Not anymore." He turned to find a place to shed his EVA gear.

"Just make sure you watch your back," Ana said as he walked away.

Bill and his crew threaded their way through the chaotic maze of wounded who had suddenly crowded the place. Those who couldn't stand were laid on the tables until the tables were gone. Others had been stretched out on the bar. Still more on the floor.

"In here," one man yelled from a doorway leading to an attached restaurant.

Wounded began to funnel into the area.

Bill found a small lounge behind the main reception desk. "This will do for now." He turned to his crewmen. "We'll stow our gear here."

The three shed their pressure suits, into which they'd begun to sweat.

As for the residents and visitors of Deep West, the dead and wounded, the ailing base systems and the absent—the seemingly nonexistent, or perhaps dead—medical staff: these people, as disorganized as they were, would have to tend to those. Or they would have to wait. Bill's immediate mission priority was to establish a secure base of operation for the approaching military convoy. For that, he needed eyes and ears topside. And, if he could get it, the support of the base director.

Bill motioned his crew closer. "We've got no communication with the convoys or the CATS, and none with Base Administration." To Townsend, he said, "Set up a comm relay at the base of the lift and another one on the surface. As soon as they're up and running, contact Colonel Davis. Tell him he can order the ships in. Recommend that they land in the flat stretch just south of the base. In the meantime, I'll see if I can get to the Base Administration complex. Carter—"

"I know." She flumped down onto the sofa, in a lounge now filled with pressure suits, tool belts, and duffle bags. "I'll watch our stuff."

As for Simeon, Bill had no concern about the likes of him. He approached Ana, who stood beside a man lying on a roulette table, using a cushion torn from the seat of a restaurant booth as a pillow. The man's shirt had been removed. Pieces of two of his ribs jutted through his chest. His breathing was shallow. Ana touched his shoulder in a familiar manner as she reassured him softly.

"Miss?"

Ana looked up.

"Can I have a word?" Bill motioned for her to follow him outside the casino and along the boardwalk far enough to be out of the way of the mayhem. "We're going to need sleeping quarters for three hundred soldiers and airmen, warehousing for our supplies and equipment, and a command center for our operations. Any suggestions?"

"Normally, Deep West would have plenty of accommodations for your men and supplies. You know that or you wouldn't have come. But so far, we don't know anything. If the whole base looks like this—" she swept her hand in a gesture encompassing the crumbled Plaza, then shrugged. The Sharp Shooter was the only building left that could house three hundred men. At the moment, the wounded needed it more than Bill did.

"There's a base map just down the street," Ana continued. "That'll help you get your bearings. Zeke Shepherd, our facilities manager, has gone to try to restore power. When he gets back, he'll probably be able to tell you which parts of the base are accessible. The deputy who went to fetch the doctors hasn't returned yet. I take that as a bad sign."

"Thank you. You've been very helpful." He left Ana and started down the boardwalk at a brisk, bounding pace toward the directory kiosk.

It displayed two separate maps, each encased behind durapane on either side of an upright signpost. One side displayed the various businesses on the Plaza, the other showed the base as a whole, a labyrinth of tunnels and passageways. Based on the map, the Deep West Administration complex was near the main hangar. There probably wouldn't be any survivors there.

Just then, two large men, part Asian, or perhaps Hawaiian or Polynesian, broke away from the crowd and came at Bill. These men, shaped like beer kegs, must have each weighed twice as much as he. They began to crowd him. One had a goatee. The other was bald except for two braids that hung where his side burns should have been. Both were dressed as impeccably as Simeon.

Bill took a step toward the building behind him, then immediately regretted it. Suddenly his only way out was through these men. "Can I help you?" His hand hovered near his sidearm without, he hoped, being conspicuous about it.

The man with the goatee stepped forward. "Why are you here?" His black hair seemed to stick to his head. His suit coat stretched across his massive chest. His fat hands hung at the end of arms that resembled battering rams.

"I needed to see the map." Bill gestured to the kiosk.

The man crowded him further, his sweating face too close to Bill's own.

"Some say Deep West just got hit by a quake or something. Only there aren't no quakes on Mercury. An asteroid then, but someone would have seen it coming."

"Back off," Bill told him.

The man didn't budge. "Then, all of the sudden, you show up." He gestured toward Bill with contempt. "With your soldiers—"

"Airmen."

"—and your illegal guns. That ain't no coincidence. You know what happened here."

Bill locked eyes with the man. "I said, back off."

The man put his hand on Bill's chest and pressed him into the wall behind him. He was taller even than Bill, by three or four centimeters, his eyes jet black. A Lancaster pistol had appeared from somewhere into his hand.

The people here did need to know what had happened. It would help them to better respond to the crisis and help the wounded. It might also give them an incentive to support him and the rest of the military when they arrived—which couldn't happen soon enough, as far as Bill was concerned. He wanted—no, needed—to see Dana. He grabbed the handle of his own gun. "I'll tell you what I can...after you back off."

The man stared at him for a moment longer. Finally, he took a step backwards and waited. A crowd, dozens of men, had gathered behind him.

"Yeah, I know what happened to this base, " Bill began. "More important, I know what's going to happen next." He glanced past the behemoth's shoulder and scanned the buildings down the street toward the Sharp Shooter. "Where's a good place for me to make a public announcement?"

⇜❨ O ❩⇝

Simeon returned to the Sharp Shooter with the sheriff and one of the Plaza's deputies in tow, about the time the air force major, Ryan, was climbing the steps to the hotel's second-floor fire escape. Simeon's own Polynesian bouncers, Kamo and Manu, waited at the base of the stairs.

When Ryan reached the top, he began waving his arms and yelling, "People! People! People!"

Person-by-person the crowd began to quiet, if only grudgingly.

"Hey! Who wants to know what happened here?"

Suddenly the cavern fell silent, save for the moans of the wounded and the cries of mourning that continued to filter from the casino.

The major leaned forward on the railing and stared at the hushed crowd below. "Twenty-four days ago, Chinese military forces seized space station *Venus Rain* and the entire Venus system, taking more than two thousand hostages and seizing control of the Terraforming Project."

"Tell us something we don't know," someone shouted from the street. Everything Ryan had said so far had been on the newsblips for weeks.

The crowd erupted into chaos, most yelling agreement, others calling for silence so the major could continue.

Ryan didn't yell or wave his hands. He simply stood and waited, like he couldn't care less whether he got to make his announcement or not.

Finally the crowd settled down.

The major continued. "Without an orbital launch window from Earth to Venus, the Unites States and Europe can't get troops or supplies to Venus at this time. Even if we could, we couldn't do it without putting the hostages there in jeopardy."

"So you come here?" The voice from the crowd sounded like the same heckler as before.

Simeon motioned the sheriff and deputy forward, then followed them to the bottom of the stairs to join Kamo and Manu.

Low murmurs, rather than raucous shouts, rose from the people this time.

A woman yelled, "What happened *here*?"

"I'm getting to that," Major Ryan said.

"Get to it now," the heckler shouted.

Again the crowd erupted, more angry this time. The front rows were pushed forward by the people behind. Kamo and Manu shoved some of them back.

Ryan, somewhere in his mid thirties, combed his fingers through his brown bangs and once again waited for silence before continuing.

"Just make the damned announcement," Simeon muttered.

Ryan glanced at him but looked as if he didn't consider Simeon a threat, or as if he just didn't care.

Simeon scanned the crowd. Neither of Ryan's crew members appeared to be nearby, nor any other soldiers.

Meanwhile, Ryan said nothing, to Simeon or to the crowd.

The guy had balls. Simeon had to give him that. "Be ready when he comes down," he told Kamo and Manu.

When the crowd finally settled, Ryan continued. "Presidents Powers and Hunt have combined US and EU forces to establish an economic blockade of Venus, in an effort to bring Li Muyou to the negotiating table. That's why we're here."

More murmurs.

"Russia, for whatever reason, has allied itself with China." Ryan paused. "What rocked your base, destroyed your buildings, and killed or wounded your loved ones?"

Absolute silence from the crowd.

"Russia dropped an atom bomb down Deep West's landing elevator and detonated it in your hangar bay."

The crowd fell into a stunned state. Even Simeon's mind refused him a rational response. The destruction around him was devastating, but even his worst nightmares wouldn't have conjured "nuclear war."

CHAPTER 6

After Bill had made his announcement, he climbed cautiously down the steep flight of stairs, a clumsy task in the unfamiliar gravity. Though the Polynesian thugs waited at the bottom, Bill kept his gun holstered. Two of the local police had shown up. The thugs would likely leave him alone with the cops nearby. Besides, he'd just given them what they wanted.

Nevertheless, Bill approached the lawmen. As he did, they drew their weapons—non-lethal Lancaster pulse guns, probably because Bill himself was armed. They would see that as the violation of international law that it was...if they were under the illusion that the weapons ban in the Third Outer Space Treaty was still in effect, given that all four major powers were currently violating it. Either way, with the war now having come to Mercury, allowances would have to be made.

Just before he reached them, the sheriff glanced over Bill's shoulder. The gesture was subtle, almost nonexistent, but it was enough.

Bill spun, drawing his sidearm in the same fluid movement. When he was halfway around, Simeon clubbed him in the temple with the butt of a Lancaster pistol. Then even the red emergency lights went out.

❧❈❖❈❧

Lindsey Carter hovered in the doorway of the lounge behind the reception desk, watching the commotion in the casino proper, torn between her personal convictions and the order Bill had given her. These people needed help. Not just the wounded. The dying needed help too. She had enough morphine in her emergency kit to ease the passing of at least a few of them.

Even the able-bodied needed her help. Lindsey was as fit as anyone on the base. Regardless of her own slight build, she could probably out-lift most of them. Her combat first-aid training could relieve the uncertainty in those toiling, without medical guidance, to save as many people as they could.

Yet to do so, she would have to leave the crew's gear unattended. If someone stole or damaged even one of the EVA suits, that would be bad enough—the suits were the only way the crew could return to the *Black Panther*—but there were weapons and ammunition as well. If those got into the wrong hands—Simeon's, for example—it could be disastrous for all of them.

Lindsey fidgeted in the doorway and assessed the condition of each patient as well as she could from a distance. She knew what to do. Everyone around her floundered. Only one among them seemed to have any sense of poise—the peculiar miniature woman they called Ana, who moved from patient to patient, speaking softly to each. Lindsey couldn't make out her words, but each time the woman spoke, the face of the patient—whether man, woman, or child—relaxed perceptibly.

By contrast, Ana occasionally stopped an uninjured person to say something, or maybe to request something from them. Invariably, they scoffed at her and moved on.

Unable to watch the spectacle or to violate her orders, Lindsey stepped back into the lounge and sat with her back to the wall beside the door, her fists and jaw clenched. Though this put the wounded out of sight, she could still hear the ruckus in the casino. That was almost worse. Because she couldn't see, her mind created its own images of the scene. Finally, she decided it was better to watch after all.

As she rounded the door jamb, she nearly stepped on a man who'd been lain on the floor just outside the lounge. His chest was bleeding from a puncture wound. Left unattended, he would die quickly, but with the right care...

Lindsey rushed to her duffel, stripped it of its medical supplies, and returned to the dying man. She knelt beside him, close enough to the door so that nobody could enter the lounge without her knowledge. "What's your name?"

The man's eyes fluttered, but remained closed.

She pried one open with her thumb and forefinger. "Sir? Can you hear me?"

After a moment, the eye seemed to focus. He opened the other one and smiled weakly.

"Do you know your name?"

He nodded.

"What is it?"

The man gurgled a reply, then began to cough.

Lindsey turned his head to one side. The spittle that ran from the corner of his mouth contained very little blood. That told her what she needed to know. The man's lung was intact.

"I'm going to bandage your wound," she said once his coughing stopped. "It's going to be tight, but I have to stop the bleeding."

He nodded again.

Lindsey had to venture several patients from the door before reaching a man with girth sufficient for his belt to stretch all the way around her own patient's chest. She took it, unpacked a wad of sterile gauze from her kit, and covered the wound, even stuffing a bit of it into the puncture. She rolled the man just enough to slip his wallet from his back pocket, which he seemed not to notice, and placed it on top of the gauze. Its stiff bulk would help keep the belt's pressure firm on the wound.

Another man, who was laid out on a blackjack table, screamed. Two men were trying to set his leg for splinting, but the patient's tibia protruded three centimeters from his shin. One man was holding the patient down while another manhandled the broken leg. They'd lain a couple of pieces of broken stairway railing and some strips of torn fabric beside him. But the way the manhandler was twisting the foot, he was only causing more damage.

Lindsey glanced back at the lounge door before rushing to save this latest patient's leg. "Not like that," she told the manhandler. "Here." She nudged him out of her way. "Hold his shoulders."

In one deft motion, Lindsey snapped the leg back into place. The man screamed once, then sighed. His body relaxed. Lindsey ran her thumb and forefinger gently down the length of the shin to verify the bone's alignment.

The patient moaned as she adjusted the foot position and checked the bone again.

"Try to splint it without moving the foot," she told the men.

Then she stepped to the next patient. The small woman, Ana, watched Lindsey for a few minutes with admiration and gratitude in her eyes.

Within ten minutes, the Deep West medical staff flooded through the front casino doors.

The woman lying before Lindsey at that moment was hopeless, moaning in a half-conscious stupor and drowning slowly in her own blood. Lindsey had been about to administer a lethal dose of morphine. Instead, she stepped away. That was a decision for the doctors, now that they were here.

When she returned to the lounge, a huge, braided Polynesian man stood in the middle of the room with a Lancaster pistol in his hand. Before she could even flinch, he pulled the trigger.

A flood of microwaves swept over her, scrambling the signals at every synapse in her nervous system. For a moment, pain burned through her torso and upper arms. With her eyes open, her mind conscious of everything, yet no longer able to communicate with her muscles, Lindsey toppled forward onto the coffee table, snapping it in two.

∞《○》∞

"That'll teach those Americans to mess with me and mine," Simeon told the sheriff a few minutes after he'd locked the female flier—Carter, according to the patch on her chest—into one of two jail cells that had survived Deep West's destruction. His sheriff had confiscated all of the American military gear as illegal contraband, outlawed anywhere beyond Earth by the Third Outer Space Treaty.

The young black woman groaned as she began to recover from the Lancaster pulse. Her chin, right cheek, and the chest of her flight suit were caked with blood that had been flowing freely from her nose ever since her fall in the Sharp Shooter.

"I suppose I could have waited until she came to a stop before I fired." Manu's face showed the slight twist of a smirk. "Her legs would have simply given out and she would likely have fallen without injuring herself."

Simeon shook his head. "She had it coming, just for associating herself with that major." He stroked his chin slowly, as if his pristine beard needed smoothing. Carter wasn't the one who had embarrassed him, however. Major Ryan had done that all by himself—and on behalf of that whore Ana, of all people. Simeon couldn't afford to lose face, or the control of his hotel. The disaster that had befallen everybody else had thrown an unprecedented opportunity right into his lap.

Decades ago, when the base had expanded from the original solar science outpost to become the International Transportation Interchange, it had taken on a distinct frontier feel—not in looks, per se, but in lifestyle, with little law enforcement, supply hardships, and a single thriving industry: lodging for people and cargo destined for Earth, Venus, Mars, or Jupiter.

Simeon had recognized the frontier-like lifestyle and had started a trend in the architecture of Deep West's Plaza toward the Old West ambience that visitors now enjoyed. With that in mind, he'd built the Sharp Shooter out of old, Wild West-style materials, mostly wood imported from Earth. When copycats began to arrive, they built their establishments out of cheaper, featherweight materials that, as it turned out, couldn't withstand the kind of tremor that had recently shaken the base.

As a result, the thousands of people who were now stranded on Mercury—at least until transports arrived to take them to wherever they were ultimately headed—found themselves without accommodations. Supply and demand had just shifted in Simeon's favor. He could bid out his rooms and make a fortune.

He had things to do first, however. "Speaking of Ryan, he has one more crew member who possesses illegal weapons." Simeon motioned to the sheriff and two deputies who constituted the entire police force on the Plaza. "Follow me, gentlemen."

Together, the four of them headed out toward the Plaza's only lift to the surface.

CHAPTER 7

Zeke rounded a corner and found his way blocked, floor to ceiling, by yet another avalanche of stone. He turned back without hesitation. "This way."

"There's a breeze here." Tanner dipped his scrawny forefinger into his mouth and held it in the air. "It's blowing toward the rubble."

Zeke couldn't feel it through his pressure suit, but he didn't doubt the claim. When the two had backtracked to the nearest pressure door, Zeke pulled it from its magnetic latch, swung it closed, and spun the ship's-wheel handle to seal it.

On this base, there were about a half a dozen routes to just about any-where. Ultimately, he and Tanner tried every passage. The older section—the ship hangars, the loading docks, warehouses, the Administration com-plex, and the bulk of the fuel reserves—was inaccessible, blocked behind a series of collapsed tunnels. For all he could tell, the entire northern section of the base was completely buried by a kilometer of collapsed stone.

The two generator rooms on the heavily populated side of the base, the side that contained the Plaza and the bulk of resident housing, were intact. He and Tanner had gotten them running within a few minutes—that got the air flowing again—but since the warehoused fuel reserves were buried, they had only enough to run the generators for somewhere in the neighborhood of sixteen to twenty hours. Though the oxygen supply was sufficient to last for months, the air-circulation pumps would quit as soon as the generators ran out of fuel, unless they could restore normal power. After that, they'd need to evacuate. Somehow they'd have to transport hundreds of residents, and God only knew how many visitors, a hundred kilometers across the solar-radiation-flooded Mercury wasteland to either Shenming or Gagarin.

Only some of the food stores were accessible.

"Just the thought of food turns my stomach," Tanner said. "It makes my whole body queasy, if you can figure that."

His face, framed by his dust-clotted hair, was at once pale and splotchy. How much of that was the lighting from Zeke's headlamp and how much was real, Zeke couldn't really tell. But the man's eyes were bloodshot and haunted.

"Were you drinking before all this started?" Zeke asked. As far as he knew, the boy never touched any form of intoxicant.

When Tanner shook his head, his twiglike body swayed to one side.

Zeke grabbed his arm. "You okay? You don't look well."

Tanner braced himself against the stone wall for a minute, then nodded. "It's passed. I feel better now."

Zeke helped him down the corridor. "Come on. The hospital is on our way back."

By the time they arrived, Tanner was complaining only of a general sense of uneasiness in his stomach. The hospital was packed beyond capacity. Most of the patients stood around the perimeter or sat in a line down the hall, nursing broken limbs or pressing bandages to cuts and scrapes. The meager medical staff that remained could attend only the seriously injured.

A nurse and an orderly headed toward the Plaza with a cooler labeled BIOHAZARD and BLOOD. Zeke and Tanner followed.

∽◖◗≁

The pit of Dana's stomach felt like a rock, hard and heavy, weighing her down even in the zero-g cockpit of her CATS.

As their trajectory brought them over Deep West while en route to their target satellite, Dana trained her long-range imager onto what was left of the base. A large crater consumed the northwest quadrant of the base's five-kilometer-square footprint, which she could vaguely identify by a sparse scattering of concrete bunkers that housed the emergency exits. Bill was down there somewhere, amid that devastation and radioactivity.

51

Yet even that couldn't take Dana's mind off what she was about to do.

As the base passed from sight, she turned the imager onto the locations where several US satellites should have been orbiting. They were gone, all right—nothing but drifting debris, ripped apart, no doubt, by the explosive tips of Mingyun rocket rounds.

Twice, her comm came to life with encoded reports from the other CATS. The *Jaguar* and the *Cheetah* were already in position, awaiting orders that Dana couldn't give until she reached her target as well.

When she did, the weight in her stomach grew larger and heavier. This scenario was all too reminiscent of her first CATS mission, during the China Dominion Affair, when she'd destroyed a similar Chinese satellite, *Mingyun-81*. Hers had been the first shot in a battle that had killed four of her friends.

And no matter how hard Dana tried, she couldn't convince herself that this conflict, way the hell out here at Mercury, hadn't somehow been sparked by that shot.

She'd spent hours in the Lunar Alpha Base infirmary after that, waiting to see if Bill would survive having been shot down by another Mingyun satellite, one in lunar orbit, on the way back from that mission. Dana had nearly lost him before she finally decided to tell him that she loved him.

She tried to convince herself now that this was different. This time the first shots had not been fired by her. China and Russia had both done their share of shooting already.

China was still shooting. As the *Snow Leopard* approached, Dana's Mingyun target seemed oblivious to her presence, but it was far from dormant. Every few seconds, it fired a barrage of rockets at some target in space, shifted orientation, and fired again. Dana reached for the comm to order evasive maneuvers for all ships, but stopped herself. Those missiles would take hours to reach their target. Evasive maneuvers could wait. Instead, she said, "*Snow Leopard* to CATS. We're in position. You may fire when ready." She clicked off the comm and swallowed hard. "You too, Allistair."

"With pleasure."

A low hum cut through the ship as her gunner opened the starboard bay door. With a thump, a single missile shot from the ship. Seconds later the Mingyun satellite exploded.

"*Snow Leopard* to Colonel Davis. Target destroyed," Dana reported over the comm. "All ships alter orbit. This thing was busy when we arrived, and we've no way to determine who its target was." That said, the convoy was the most visible, and therefore the most likely, possibility.

∘⊰⟨ O ⟩⊱∘

One of the blips disappeared from General Chou's radar display of the incoming US and EU convoys. Another veered away from the rest, apparently out of control. Several peeled off, on a series of vectors that only small fighting ships could have managed. The rest seemed to lumber their way onto a new heading. Chou's smile was grim.

"First blood," Lieutenant Wu said from the Mingyun satellite control station.

"No. Comrade Batkin has already drawn first blood." This was not nearly first blood. Nor was it sufficient blood. The enemy now knew they were under fire. And they probably knew from where. They would change course frequently.

"Blanket as much of that sector as you can. Empty the Mingyun satellites if you have to."

"Yes, sir." Wu bent over his Mingyun operators. "You heard the general. Bring those ships down."

Rockets poured from the satellites, a volley every few seconds for several minutes. The radar, at its current resolution, couldn't pick up the Mingyun rounds. Nevertheless, Chou's computer knew exactly where each round was, its trajectory having been established the moment it left the satellite. Modeling software showed each round streaming toward the enemy in a spotty barrage that would continue until—

The streams stopped. The ammunition count still showed positive for every satellite. Yet no rounds spewed forth. "Lieutenant?"

When the radar scan swept the sector of each Mingyun, it became clear why they had stopped. Instead of a single blip, each satellite appeared as a spreading cloud. Mere debris.

"We just lost the satellites, sir," Wu said needlessly.

"Very good, Lieutenant." Chou turned slowly toward the man, his words overly polite, his tone icy—a practiced response he used to control the anger that raged inside him. "Kindly tell me how that happened."

Wu's career would depend on his next actions. He swallowed hard. "Yes, sir."

Chou keyed his Marauder wing commander. "I'm sending the current vectors for the enemy convoys. As soon as they're in range, launch the squadron to intercept."

"Your orders, sir?"

"Destroy the convoys. I don't want a single ship to reach this planet."

⋘○⋙

The battle to escape Earth had been a nasty piece of reality. Though the operating range of the Chinese Marauders was short, they had proven to be far more maneuverable than the CATS Trainers, the non-stealth versions of the Covert Armed Tactical Spacecraft. In fact, Tony Polaco's ship, the *Siamese*, had been the only non-stealth US fighter to make it out of Earth's orbit. Two of the CATS Trainers had been destroyed in the battle. The fourth, having been damaged too badly to attempt re-entry, was forced to dock at *Protocorp Medlab*, one of the commercial stations orbiting Earth.

Several of the European Raptors had survived to protect the EU convoy, but for Colonel Davis and the Americans, the *Siamese* was it.

Sure, the real CATS were out there somewhere, clearing the way as best they could. And they'd engaged the Mingyun satellites, but they were several hours out in front. If Marauders launched from Shenming Base, the *Siamese* might have to fight alone.

Polaco programmed his radar tracking system to continuously scan the narrow region of space between the convoy and Mercury, at high resolution and at relatively short range—a hundred thousand kilometers. The Mingyun shells he was scanning for were metallic, but no more than a few cubic centimeters in size.

"Ready missiles," he told his gunner, Lieutenant Ramona Johnson.

"Missiles ready."

He fed a copy of his display to Johnson's board. "Shoot anything that appears on the scan. Manual targeting and detonation."

The missile bay doors opened and Johnson's finger hovered over the launch button.

Within minutes, a blurred series of streaks appeared, several Mingyun rounds from the look of them. Too close. "Fire."

With a muffled thump, a missile raced forward.

"Evasive," Polaco said calmly as he gripped his g-seat.

The *Siamese* rolled away. Polaco's eyes never left his display. As the missile reached the incoming rounds, it exploded, scattering or detonating the Mingyun projectiles. A piece of debris whacked the belly of the *Siamese* as they passed.

At this distance, the rounds had to have been fired before the convoy had last altered course. That meant the Mingyun satellites had lain down an array of rockets in anticipation of evasive maneuvers by the convoy—and had likely fired shots since. They'd all have to change course again.

⇜❲○❳⇝

Eventually the convoy left the missiles of the dead Mingyun satellites behind and Colonel Davis was able to focus his efforts and remaining fuel on the business of landing. The problem was, he couldn't contact the base or the stealth ships that were supposed to have paved the way for him to land. "USS *Virgil Grissom* to Deep West. Do you read? Over." His throat was raw from repeating his hail time and again for the past hour.

Finally, a voice came over the speaker in Davis's helmet. "Status report, Colonel." It was Private Mendez, the marine he'd sent on EVA to check *Gus*'s comm gear.

"Go ahead."

"The comm dish took a hit. It's out of alignment and has a hole in it that I can stick my fist through. I'll try to realign it manually. We may still be able to get a signal out."

Davis watched the mission chronometer and waited. Everybody but Mendez remained strapped into his g-seat in preparation for the de-orbit burn. Fortunately, the fuel tank hadn't been hit and there was probably enough air in the remaining O_2 reserves to last until *Gus* was on the ground.

"Try it now, Colonel," Mendez said after an interminable four minutes.

Davis keyed the comm. "USS *Virgil Grissom* to the *Black Panther*. Do you read? Major Ryan, do you read? Over."

Nothing for several seconds. He'd tried to get a status report back to Earth but had again received no reply.

Then, "Colonel, this is the *Snow Leopard*."

Thank God somebody was still out there. "Go ahead."

"The *Black Panther* landed three hours ago to reconnoiter the base." Major McCaughey swallowed hard through the comm. "We haven't heard from them since." She paused, and an encrypted data stream came in. "I'm sending orbit parameters."

Gus's pilot spoke up now. "Major, we've taken a hit from a Mingyun rocket round. It's pretty bad. Our navigation sensors have been knocked out. Can you get a radar fix on us? I'm afraid the hit may have knocked us off course."

"Stand by."

Another long pause. It would take one reading to get a fix on *Gus*'s position, and several more to determine her speed and trajectory.

"Affirmative, *Virgil Grissom*. We've got you on radar and have calculated your vector. We're sending course-correction burn parameters. In the meantime, we'll scout the base for a safe landing site and transmit coordinates."

"Roger that, *Snow Leopard*."

Major McCaughey would have assumed *Gus*'s mass hadn't changed since they'd left Earth, so Davis's navigator adjusted the calculation by the mass of thirty-two men. Even if Davis had been able to contact any of those who'd been swept into space during the initial attack, he had no means to retrieve them.

He glanced at the gaping hole in the rear quarter of the ship. With its structure so badly compromised, *Gus* might not be able to handle the thrust that descent and landing would require.

CHAPTER 8

President Powers settled into her seat, laid her cane across her lap, and stared down the enormous oak table in the White House Situation Room, where her staff, an intelligence contingent, and a delegation from the European Union waited for her to begin.

This same group had assembled here a little under a month ago when Chinese troops had hijacked *Venus Rain*, jammed communications within the Venus system, thrown up a chaff screen to mask the location of the station, and threatened to destroy any incoming ships. In short, their president, Li Muyou, had seized control of the planet itself and every station and satellite in Venus space.

Muyou's ultimate goal in the hijacking, by his own admission, was to complete the Terraforming Project over the next several decades and then claim the planet for China and its allies. That meant Muyou had no intention of ever relinquishing its hold on *Venus Rain*, no matter what the rest of the worlds decided to do.

So the question became how to hinder or devalue the terraforming project, preferably stalling it indefinitely, in order to bring Muyou to the negotiating table.

The only way to do that was to stop the shipments of the one external resource the Project needed: hydrogen—specifically hydrogen harvested from the outer atmosphere of Jupiter, the only source abundant enough to supply the needs of the Project.

Powers had therefore expected trouble when the military convoy reached Mercury. Hell, she'd even expected trouble from Russia, who'd been supportive of China. But she'd never expected this. "A nuclear attack?"

Tom O'Leary, head of the CIA's Office of Asian Pacific Analysis, slammed his palm on the long, narrow table. "I knew it!" The Irish brogue he'd grown up with was nearly gone, after forty years in the States.

"You expected this?" Powers asked him.

O'Leary snapped his mouth shut, then spoke carefully. "N—No, ma'am. Of course not. We would have informed you immediately. But we've suspected for years that Russia was manufacturing atomic bombs somewhere. Damned if we've been able to prove it, though."

This was no secret from the White House. In fact, it had been the topic of many intelligence meetings over the years. But the suspicion had always been based upon hunch and a general knowledge of the disposition of the Russian government, rather than upon any real evidence.

All of Russia's nukes had been accounted for and dismantled when the Global Nuclear Disarmament Treaty was ratified some fifty years before, and any effort to manufacture, purify, or use a sufficient quantity of nuclear material to begin building warheads would have been detected. At least it would have if it had taken place on Earth. Elsewhere, then. But where?

That was a question for another meeting.

"What is the status of Deep West?" Powers asked her Secretary of Defense, Dan Norton.

"Unknown." Norton stood at his chair, a subtle power play to usurp the attention from those in the room who outranked him. His artificially youthful features had begun to look plastic from too many dermal regeneration treatments. His intense eyes focused on President Powers. "Shortly after the detonation, the CATS wing commander, Major Bill Ryan, landed to investigate. He never reported back. The rest of the convoy is on approach, except for the *Aries*, which has been destroyed by Mingyun satellite rounds. Our troop ship, the *Virgil Grissom*, has been damaged and may be unable to achieve orbit, let alone land. They're assessing options.

"Major Dana McCaughey, second-in-command of the CATS wing, has reported the elimination of China's Mingyun satellites. Unfortunately, we didn't get to them before they destroyed every US and European satellite in Mercury orbit."

President Powers took in a sharp breath. "All of them?"

O'Leary nodded. "Shot down just before our fleet arrived. So even if some of Deep West has survived, they can't talk to us unless we have a ship overhead to serve as a comm relay."

"Or unless the transmitter at the pole is still alive," Norton added. "So far, it's been silent."

Powers tapped her ring on her cane for maybe half a minute before responding. "Any activity from China or Russia here on Earth?"

"None," O'Leary said. "Both Muyou and Petrov seem content to let the conflict play itself out on Mercury, rather than starting World War Three here."

Secretary of State Tony Mariano had been chewing his upper lip for the duration of the meeting. "That, at least, will keep the casualties from climbing into the millions."

"Until someone gets desperate." Powers frowned. "What is the current status of our Earth-bound forces?"

"All branches of the military remain on full alert," Norton said, still standing. "Reserves activated and deployed. The early warning and anti-missile defense systems at one hundred percent. Satellites are monitoring activity at every Russian and Chinese military base in the world. If they so much as flinch, we'll know it. Navy and Air Force strike teams are on standby, just in case they do."

"Until then, we wait." Powers looked at O'Leary, hoping he would suggest some way to glean additional information.

"It appears so," he said.

Powers sighed. "I'm not good at waiting."

Finally, Norton took his seat. He folded his hands on the table in front of him. "I have confidence in our troops. And so do you. If you didn't, you wouldn't have sent them."

"So far, we can't even get our men on the ground." Powers couldn't help herself. If Norton got overconfident, he'd be of no use to her.

"Ours will be there shortly," said Peter Yates, the European Secretary of State. "We've received only a brief update. No news from the ground, but our troop ship is undamaged and on approach."

"Good for them," Norton spat.

"Easy, Dan," Powers said. Then she addressed the whole committee. "In the meantime, we to need work on that bastard Petrov. If he uses any more nukes…"

She turned to O'Leary. "Find out where he's making them."

⁓❨ ◯ ❩⁓

Minutes after the meeting, President Powers pulled O'Leary aside. "What's the status of Operation Venus Flytrap?"

O'Leary scanned the hallway in both directions. The operation was about as top secret as it got, and this was not a place to discuss sensitive matters, but Powers couldn't help that. If she sequestered herself and her intelligence people in a classified conference room while the *Venus Rain* and Deep West crises were in full bloom, Yates and his European entourage would get wind of it. They'd want to know what the discussion was about. Powers could throw up some smoke screen about "other important matters," but that didn't seem likely to fly with Yates.

And she didn't want anybody, even her European allies, learning of this operation. Its objective was just too touchy.

"Give me the unclassified version," Powers said.

"Well…" O'Leary scratched his red beard. He seemed uncertain of how to begin. "Of course we're still in the planning stages."

Of course? Powers had initiated the project three weeks ago.

Before she could interject her concern, O'Leary pressed on. "We're looking at logistics and feasibility of materials."

"I understand there are some challenges—"

"We're talking about—" O'Leary stopped himself just short of a security breach. He made an exasperated gesture toward his clothing.

He couldn't say "stealth pressure suits" in the hallway, but Powers got his meaning.

"Given our next window from Mercury to Venus, we need to launch from Earth in sixty-six days." She gave him a hard look and pointed the crook of her cane toward his chest. "Be ready by then."

"Yes, Madam President."

"I'm counting on it."

❧(O)❧

Dana adjusted orbit to bring the *Snow Leopard* in a low pass over Deep West. The primary landing pad was gone. The subterranean hangar beneath it had collapsed upon itself, leaving a giant hole in the planet's surface. And the auxiliary landing pad, not far from the edge of the crater, had been blown outward by the explosive pressure from inside. "Hold here," she said.

Miller brought the ship to a hover over the base.

A single figure wearing an Air Force pressure suit was installing an auxiliary comm antenna atop a small concrete bunker about a kilometer south of the crater. The figure stopped and waved to the *Snow Leopard*, then placed a hand near the collar of his pressure suit. "Townsend to *Snow Leopard*."

"*Snow Leopard*. We read you."

"Base integrity compromised, but southern sections are habitable. What is your status?"

"Primary targets destroyed. US and EU comm-satellites gone. Convoy on approach. Await instructions. Over."

"Major Ryan's orders are to land the convoy south of the base, as close to my location as possible."

"Roger that. *Snow Leopard* out." She wanted to ask if Bill was okay, but Townsend would have said something if he wasn't. And Dana would be on the ground in a few minutes. After twenty-two days without him, she could wait *that* much longer, at least.

As Townsend went back to work, Dana began to survey the surrounding landscape. It didn't take long for her to locate a flat stretch to which she could direct the convoy, but security would be a problem. Nevertheless, that's what they had to work with. She relayed the coordinates and a descent vector to Davis through the *Cheetah*, who had maintained orbit to serve as a comm relay to pass instructions to convoy ships beyond the horizon.

As Dana circled Deep West—a standard recon of the area before landing in potentially hostile territory—she saw movement on the ground, a mass slowly approaching from the southwest. It looked like the shadow of a cloud, but Mercury had no atmosphere.

She zoomed in her long-range imager on a hoard of multi-legged robots scurrying toward Deep West. "Take us out over that black mass," she told her pilot.

Without a word, Miller reoriented the thrusters and the *Snow Leopard* eased out over the little scurrying bots. Further out, nearly on the horizon in the direction from which the little mechanical creatures had come, sat Shenming, China's Mercury base.

"Fire a missile into that clump over there." Dana pointed.

Allistair set the targeting laser and released one missile.

Where it hit the ground, a dozen robots vanished in an explosion much larger than the missile alone could account for. The rest crawled inexorably forward.

"That's not good. Shoot one with the guns." Dana clicked on her comm. "Townsend, you'd better warn the others, you've got incoming. It looks like a crawling swarm of spiderlike robots."

"A swarm of *what*?"

Allistair's guns fired a barrage into the mass. One round hit. The little bot exploded in a brief ball of flame, which quickly starved for oxygen in the void.

"Make that a swarm of *exploding* spider robots," Dana told Townsend. "If these things get inside, they can probably take out whatever's left of Deep West. We'll do what we can before they reach the base, but there are too many of them. You've got to warn Bill."

"I'm on it."

Dana keyed off the link. "Let's take them out."

The *Snow Leopard* made a pass through the cloud of bots. Allistair launched a missile at each of several small clumps. Secondary explosions took out a few more, but most were spaced far enough from one another that they had to be destroyed individually, hundreds of them. Maybe thousands.

The ship hovered at the leading edge, backing slowly as the spiders crawled forward.

They climbed down the sheer face of a lobate scarp not more than two kilometers from the base. Dana flipped her controls, took over one of the guns, and began shooting as well. One by one, the spiders exploded. It was like a virtual reality sim-game. It might have been fun if the stakes hadn't been so high.

Eventually she and Allistair destroyed most of them, but some got through. Those that did clambered through the damaged auxiliary landing pad into Deep West.

∞《○》∞

Townsend left the comm relay unfinished and descended on the emergency lift to Deep West's Plaza. When he cycled out at the bottom, the local sheriff and two deputies were facing him, Lancasters drawn. They were backed up by the casino owner, Simeon.

"Guys—" Townsend began, his hands extended in a placating gesture.

A microwave pulse blasted the thought from his mind and sent any semblance of muscle control spiraling beyond his capability. Helpless, he crumpled to the floor. His mind screamed to them the danger the whole base was facing. Tunnel warfare robots designed to infiltrate fortified enemy entrenchment were notoriously indiscriminate in their killing. Scream though he might in the confines of his mind, Townsend's vocal system failed to respond. The lawmen stripped him of his pressure suit, comm link, and weapons, and then dragged him to a jailhouse.

CHAPTER 9

When Zeke entered the Sharp Shooter with his bubble helmet clipped to his waist, it took him only a moment to locate Ana in the bustling casino. Her grace stood out among the grunting efforts of the others. In her own small way, she had a greater presence than any of them.

Gently, he laid his big hand on her shoulder.

For a moment, she just stared into his eyes, perhaps trying to read something there. Then she threw her arms around him.

He stood, lifting her clear from the ground, one arm wrapped around her waist and one around her thighs.

"How's the base?" she asked when he set her down.

Zeke shook his head. "Just about everything north of resident housing is gone. Buried in rubble."

He expected…not hysteria or panic, not from Ana. But he expected something—disappointment, at least, or anger. She exhibited none of these. Just a resolute determination to face whatever came at her.

Ana's skin looked ashen in the light of the battery-powered lamps the medical staff had set up throughout the casino. "That's more than half the base."

Zeke nodded.

"It's the…" Ana faltered.

"It's what?"

An orderly wheeled a covered body past them on a stretcher. Ana glanced at it and swallowed hard. "The Russians dropped a nuclear bomb down the landing-pad elevator shaft."

Zeke's mind froze.

"Where'd you hear that?" Tanner asked.

"A fighter crew from the US Air Force came in a little while ago. Their commanding officer told us what happened."

"I'd better sit down." Tanner looked ill once more, his eyes sunken in his narrow face.

Finally Zeke began to put it together. "Son of a bitch."

"What?" Ana said.

"President Powers."

"What about her?"

"She and President Hunt launched a pair of military convoys toward the end of last month. She never said where they were going. I assumed they were on a long trajectory to Venus, despite the fact that they'd missed any reasonable launch window. I figured she was trying to surprise the hijackers."

Ana shook her head. "They're here. That Air Force crew is just reconnaissance, to make sure the base is still habitable before they land the convoys."

A triage nurse began to examine Tanner, but Zeke paid no attention to her while Ana filled him in on the details of Major Ryan's announcement.

A moment later, the nurse addressed Zeke. "Do you have any symptoms?"

"Symptoms of what?"

"Symptoms of any kind? Injuries? Internal pain? Dizziness? Nausea?"

"No. I mean my ears buzzed for a while after the blast, but I don't think I'm injured, if that's what you're asking."

"Then you need to lend a hand or clear out. We need all the room we can get for the patients."

"He was in the tunnels with me," Tanner told her.

The nurse looked at Zeke for confirmation. He nodded.

"Then you'd better take one of these too." She extracted a bottle from a pocket of her scrubs and dispensed a pale blue capsule into his hand.

Zeke examined it as though it might suddenly grow legs and try to bite him. "What is it?"

"Granulocyte. It counters bone marrow damage and boosts white blood cell count. We're prescribing them for everyone with symptoms of radiation sickness or who have been in areas where there's potential for exposure."

"We've already sent several people to look for Geiger scanners and to make radiation warning signs," Ana said.

"Facilities has Geiger scanners." They were used to monitor daily fluctuations in surface radiation due to changes in solar activity.

Ana nodded. "I told them."

Zeke swallowed the pill and turned to Tanner. "You okay?"

"God willing, I'll make it." He stood. "Let's do this."

"What is it we're going to do?" Ana asked.

We. With Ana, it was always "we." She didn't want to know what *he* was going to do, perhaps about the electricity, or air, or communications, or whatever else. She wanted to know what she was going to help him do.

"*We*—" Zeke pointed to himself and Tanner, leaving Ana out of his next action—"are going topside to see if the solar array is still intact. And if so, to run a power feed from it to—" To where? The base's primary battery bank was buried or destroyed. Where exactly was he going to dump the power from the array, assuming there was an array to dump power from? "To the base," he said finally. "To life support." Wherever he could find a viable hookup. One thing at a time. First he would see if the array was even still there.

Around them, the doctors and nurses continued to sort the wounded from the healthy, the dead from the dying, and the helpful from the hysterical.

"Excuse me." A nurse nudged her way past Ana to a man and woman on the floor behind her. The nurse touched the man's shoulder. "Sir?"

He looked up. "Help her." There was pain and pleading in his voice, but no hope.

"Step aside, sir, so I can examine her."

The man, squatting beside the pale, bleeding woman, scooted perhaps two centimeters.

The nurse looked him squarely in the face. "I need you to move."

Zeke began to step around Ana to move the man out of the nurse's way, forcibly if necessary.

Ana put a hand on his arm. "I'll get him. You two go." Without waiting to see if he did, she squatted next to the distraught man, putting one hand around his shoulders and the other on his knee. "What's her name?"

The man didn't take his eyes off the patient. "Sonya."

"Sonya's going to be fine," Ana said.

He shook his head. "She's dying."

Ana took his face between her small palms and turned it toward her own. "The doctors will take care of Sonya."

His eyes began to focus.

"Let's get them some hot water."

He nodded, and she led him to the bar.

When Ana glanced back, the nurse mouthed, "Thank you."

Zeke couldn't help smiling at the way Ana connected with people, always on a personal level, always deducing whatever it was they needed most—in this man's case, the need to help his wife without knowing how.

He tapped Tanner's arm with the back of his hand. "Let's go find you a pressure suit."

Dana and her crew entered Deep West through the same elevator shaft upon which Townsend had rigged his partially completed comm station.

As she stepped from the lift, a guard, one of the local deputies, jumped with a start and pointed his Lancaster. "Hold it."

Dana's pistol was already in her hand, ready for the spider bots from the moment the door slid open. She leveled it at the deputy.

Miller and Allistair ducked behind the edges of the lift door, out of the field of the deputy's Lancaster. Both men had their weapons drawn.

"I need to confiscate your weapons," the deputy said. "International law prohibits them here."

It took a forced effort for Dana to keep from rolling her eyes. She touched the external microphone switch at her collar. "This base has been invaded."

The deputy leveled the Lancaster at Dana's head, where the flexsteel in her pressure suit wouldn't protect her from the gun's microwave pulse. "Your weapons."

Dana sighed, thick and heavy in the confines of her helmet. "All right." She holstered the pistol, unclipped her belt, and held it out to him.

He reached to grab it, eyeing the rifle slung over Dana's shoulder. "All your weapons."

As his hand clasped the belt, Dana balled her free hand into the best fist her bulky EVA gloves would allow, and jabbed it into his face. The Lancaster, had it gone off, would likely have caught her in its blast, but Miller and Allistair could then have overpowered the deputy before it could recharge. The gun, however, remained quiescent and the deputy staggered backward.

Dana clasped her hands together and, as if swinging a baseball bat, clubbed the startled man in the face with her combined fists.

The Lancaster and Dana's own holstered gun flew from the stunned man's grip, and he landed on his ass.

Dana took a moment to pop the fishbowl helmet from her head, not just to conserve her tank's oxygen, but to talk to the deputy more directly.

He tried to stand, so she sat on him, her pressure suit, O_2 tank, and gear adding twenty kilograms to her mass, and pressed his head to the floor with a hand on his chest. His nose bled freely, but his eyes remained focused and alert.

"Now then," she said. "The enemies of the United States and those of the European Union have sent an army of tunnel-delving robot bombs to bring down what's left of this base from the inside out. We killed as many as we could on the surface, but a lot of them got through. They've infiltrated the tunnels and they're coming here. When they arrive, they'll kill everybody. You understand? Everybody."

He nodded uncertainly. Miller and Allistair stood beside her, looking down at the helpless guard, sidearms still in their hands.

"They came in through the damaged eastern landing pad. I need to know the quickest way to get there."

This time he shook his head. "I don't know which tunnels are still open. Try the Sharp Shooter Hotel." He pointed. "Ask for Ana Davenport."

Dana nudged with her head in the direction of the stone building, where the survivors seemed to have massed. Her crewmen took off at a dead run.

"Am I going to have a problem with you?" she asked the deputy. "Because in a couple of hours, this base will be swarming with military, who will put it under martial law. If I need to, I'll arrest you now."

"No," he said. "No trouble."

Dana climbed off his chest. She gathered her weapons and the Lancaster pistol, then sprinted after her crew. She caught up to them outside the only intact building in sight, talking to an impossibly small woman with an exquisite face and long black hair. "You Ana?"

The woman studied Dana's face for a moment. "Yes."

Briefly Dana told her about the robots.

"Exploding what?" Ana asked.

"Spiders," Dana said. "Infiltration robots Small, but with a big bang."

"Where?"

"They came in through the auxiliary landing platform." Dana paused. "Do you have a map of the base?"

Ana nodded. "This way."

"Wait." Dana looked past her into a casino-turned-trauma-center. "You know Bill Ryan? Air Force major. He and his crew came in here dressed like us a couple of hours ago."

Ana nodded. "He was here, but I haven't seen him in a while. Come on." She led them to an information kiosk farther down the Plaza's main street. She stood on her tiptoes and drew a line with her finger in the layer of dust that coated the sign. "Our facilities manager made a survey of the tunnels. He said everything north of about here is buried."

Dana pulled her thinpad from the thigh pocket of her flight suit. The device, this one a little larger than her hand and barely thicker than a data card, served as a computer, backup comm link, and as she needed now, a vid scanner. First she snapped a still image of the entire base layout, which probably excluded the "employees only" sections of the base, and then took a close-up vid scan, sweeping the most direct route from the You ARE HERE sign to the secondary landing pad.

"Thank you. You've been very helpful." Dana led her crew toward the Deep West warrens. Ana would have to tend to the problems on the Plaza while Dana, Miller, and Allistair did the fighting.

Fighting, Dana thought. Scurrying around like rats in a hole. Neither she nor her crew were foot soldiers. But they would do what they must until the marines arrived.

"Close these," she told Miller as they passed through the pressure door that would seal off the Plaza from the rest of the base.

While he did, Dana tried to reach Bill on the comm. *Where was he?* She should have seen him in the Plaza's main street or someplace near the lift, now the base's only entrance, clearing room for Davis's command center. They hadn't even seen Townsend, who couldn't have come down more than ten minutes ahead of them. She tried Colonel Davis, but couldn't reach him either.

Within minutes, Dana arrived at the base trauma center. "Wait."

Thirty or so patients were strewn about the place, laying on beds or sitting on the floor. Most had splints, bandages, or rents in their skin that had been sealed with dermaplast. A few showed radiation burns. Two bodies lay covered in the corner. A doctor and two nurses scurried among the wounded.

One looked up from his patient. "May I help you?"

"You need to evacuate to the Plaza."

The man started to say something.

"This place is going to be a combat zone in about ten minutes. You've got to get these people out."

"Most of our equipment is here," the doctor said.

"Take what you need with you. If we can keep this place from getting a breach into space, you can come back for more later. But right now, this is the most dangerous place these people can be."

He looked down at the automatic rifle in Dana's hand, then at the Air Force patch on her sleeve. He nodded and turned to his staff. "Let's get them out of here."

Instantly, they began to gather supplies. The patients who lined the walls started to stand if they could.

Dana hurried back into the hall. "Helmets on. Let's go." She threw hers onto her head as she ran, snapped the collar clamps into place, and hailed her crew. "You guys, on."

"Yes," Allistair replied.

"I hear you," Miller said.

From that moment on, Dana told every soul they met to clear out of the corridors—to go to the Plaza.

The main tunnel had been carved from the rough Mercury bedrock, then smoothed to an almost polished sheen. Lighting panels, now dark, hung from the ceiling, strung together with visible wiring. At intervals, Dana and her crew clattered over steel grates that spanned deep black pits bored into the floor, possibly leading to former nickel veins from the base's mining days. The whole place seemed to have been jury-rigged together.

Dana and her crew closed every pressure door they passed in an effort to protect as much of the base as possible, for as long as they could.

Dana rounded one corner, then another.

Where could Bill be?

A report rumbled down the corridor with a shock wave that blew Dana backwards. The pressure dropped suddenly and a draw of air pulled her down the tunnel like some giant vacuum cleaner.

The draw lasted less than a minute. Then the air was gone.

Sometime during that interval, the light—even the crimson emergency lighting—went out.

Dana scrambled to her feet, flipped on the spotlight attached to her helmet, and charged ahead, knowing the spiders were now inside.

Two more corners. Another grate. Dana rounded the next bend and stopped. Small things, maybe the size of squirrels, moved at the edge of the light. She darted back behind the corner, expecting a spray of small-caliber rounds. But none came.

"Back." She waved.

Miller and Allistair shuffled backward, over one of the yawning pits, this one so deep that Dana's spotlight failed to reach the bottom.

She bent down and lifted the edge of the grate over the lip of the inset that held it in place. She clipped the lifeline from her belt to it and then backed off with the others.

Just as the robots reached the pit, Dana heaved on the lifeline and began to pull the grate toward her. Two or three of the spiders tumbled down the hole. As soon as she could reach the grate, Dana unclipped her line and waited. For a moment, the robots stopped at the pit's edge. Then they began to crawl up the walls to skirt the opening. *Damn.* If the things could climb the walls, they could climb out of the pit.

She yanked a hand grenade from her belt and skipped it down the tunnel, where it dropped into the hole. Four seconds later, it blew, bigger and hotter than any grenade she'd ever seen.

The ground trembled and a ball of flame shot from the pit. Rocks and boulders shook loose from the ceiling and dropped into the hole. Others littered the corridor on both sides. Two more robots tumbled into the pit and became buried in the rubble.

More began skirting the hole and navigating the rubble. Dana tossed another grenade down the hall, this one only halfway to the pit, hoping to provoke gunfire if the things could, in fact, shoot. None did. The grenade exploded and shrapnel flew for a dozen meters in each direction.

Still the things came.

Cautiously, Dana stepped around the corner into full view.

"Careful," Allistair said.

Dana waved him back.

A dozen or more spiders skittered into the beam of Dana's headlamp. She aimed her rifle, but held her fire. She was more interested in the machines' reaction than in whether or not she could hit one, which at this range was too dangerous to do.

The things made no response. They just kept coming.

Pattern recognition, barrier detection, sophisticated terrain-navigation algorithms, Dana concluded, but apparently no threat-detection capabilities. The robots weren't designed to kill individuals. They were here to bring down the tunnels.

Dana strode forward.

"Major?" Allistair said as soon as she stepped from view.

"Hang on." Dana marched up to the lead robot.

Still no response.

Each carried a brick of C-4 military explosive on its back. Dana's heart was pounding. A single one of the things definitely contained enough energy to bring down the ceiling. Her palms sweated in her suit. The question was, how to stop them?

Several moved near enough so that if one exploded, the others would blow as well.

"Fall back!" Dana rushed around the corner at a dead run—frequently pushing off the wall—trying to regain some distance between herself and the robots in these low-g tunnels.

The spiders, as though they'd just detected her, picked up pace and scurried after, scrambling over the loose rock that now littered the cavern.

Dana, Miller, and Allistair barreled down the passage.

A few corners later, they came to the last pressure door they'd closed. Because it was designed to open toward the populated areas of the base, the pressure in the tunnel beyond forced the door closed against the vacuum seal. Even if they had time to twist the handle to release the clamps, the three of them could never push the door open against the pressure from the other side—about fifteen metric tons against a door this size.

Miller and Allistair tried anyway.

Out of options, Dana spun toward the spiders and flooded the corridor with bullets.

The lead robot and several of its nearby friends exploded. A wave of heat engulfed the tunnel. The ground shook.

And the ceiling collapsed.

CHAPTER 10

Colonel Davis received the approach vector and prayed that his broken ship would be able to make the landing, which on any other planet would be impossible. A ship with far less damage would never survive an atmospheric reentry.

"All ships, begin descent," Davis ordered. "You too," he told his pilot. "Gently." He twisted in his g-seat to keep an eye on the damaged aft quarter as the reverse thrusters fired.

A distinct bow flexed the waist of the ship. Half the marines on board gripped their seats. Some whipped their heads around toward the hole. Many did both.

A tear ripped downward from the ragged edge, past the floorboard.

"Easy!" Davis yelled.

The pilot let up on the controls. "Any easier and we'll miss our window for Deep West."

"Then we'll miss it. A load of good it'll do us if *Gus* comes apart before we get there."

"Aye, sir." The pilot nudged the controls ever so slightly. A barely perceptible drag tugged on the ship.

Davis's display showed the convoy as it braked and began to descend. A sudden flash erupted from one of the leading cargo ships.

"Mayday. Mayday," the freighter captain called over the encrypted comm channel. "This is the *Taurus*." A flame shot sideways from the ass end of the ship. "We're going down. Repeat. We are going down."

Davis centered the *Taurus* on his visual scanner. She was dropping in a flat spin, not as steep a vector as those making the prescribed descent, but there was no doubt about it: she was definitely going down, and taking with her the command and control equipment for all of the American robotic infantry, which made up a solid fifty percent of Davis's fighting force.

Davis keyed the comm. "*Taurus*, can you stabilize?"

Though the jet of flame had died away, the *Taurus* continued to spew something out the side of the ship. The trail of vapor sparkled in the Mercury sun.

"Negative. We're still venting. The spin is getting worse." Strain became evident in the captain's voice. "Hard to talk." A pause. "Spin worse…vision going…*aaughhh!*"

The comm went silent.

"*Taurus*," Davis called. "Come in, *Taurus*."

Nothing. The entire crew must have blacked out from the g-forces caused by the spin.

"Track her trajectory," Davis told his navigator. "We're going to need any cargo that survives."

A shudder shook Davis's own ship. Seats, control panels, men, and gear trembled wildly as the vibration increased. Just as Davis was about to order a stop-thrust, it began to subside.

He peered nervously back at the hole. Only the front of the ship had settled. The rear continued to quiver. He shook his head. They weren't going to make it, none of them were.

"Colonel Davis to fleet. Proceed with landing per assigned vector. *Siamese*, you're with me for as long as we can hold this ship together. Our thrust is limited. We're going to be…" He tapped the original vector into the navigation computer and programmed their current thrust as the maximum available. Within seconds the computer displayed an alternative vector for the same landing site. "We're going to need at least three additional orbits before we'll have slowed enough for landing." He didn't say *safe* landing. There was nothing safe about their situation, and the landing would be the most perilous step of all.

The *Siamese* dropped back to look over *Gus*'s shoulder, letting the transport define their approach speed and vector.

All of the European ships showed on radar...except for one of the Raptors, which must have been lost to Mingyun fire. The rest were descending on target. If they'd taken damage, it didn't seem to be affecting their flight controls. They'd had more fighters to fend off incoming Mingyun rocket rounds.

If Major McCaughey was right, the CATS had destroyed the missile satellites. Davis wouldn't need fighters for the remainder of the approach. Unless...

"Radar contact," the pilot said. "Four ships rising out of Shenming Base. All Marauders."

⋖⋘○⋙⋗

The tremor from the spider-bot explosion threw Dana to the ground. Flames washed over her, hot enough to feel through the thermal insulation her pressure suit provided. Brief though it was, she feared it would sear through the layers of flexsteel and neoprene...or simply melt her faceplate.

By the time the firestorm subsided, soot and dust covered everything. She wiped her visor with her hand and peered ahead.

The tunnel was so clogged with dust that her headlamp couldn't penetrate more than a meter. Her breathing sounded harsh in her own ears, as did the breathing of the others. Someone moaned through the speaker.

"Sound off," Dana said.

"Miller. I'm okay."

"Allistair. All green."

Dana resisted the temptation to wave her arms to clear the dust. Though it settled slowly in the low gravity, it had no air to suspend it. Within minutes, it cleared enough for her headlamp to illuminate an avalanche, not more than a meter and a half in front of them.

"Think we stopped them?" Allistair asked.

"They stopped us." Dana stepped forward and tested the wall before them with her hands. A few of the smaller rocks came loose, but there were so many boulders lodged in it that they had no hope of budging the barrier. "Let's try the hatch again."

Dana made sure to spin the wheel all the way open, and the three put their shoulders to the door. Nothing.

They took a half-step back against the fallen-rock barrier.

"On three," Dana said. "One. Two…"

They lunged at the door together, shoulder-first, and with a collective grunt, landed in a heap.

"Ow," Miller muttered as they climbed to their feet.

The door hadn't budged.

Dana activated her comm, hoping against hope she could get through to somebody. "This is Major Dana McCaughey. Can anybody read me?" She shook her head. All the base systems were down, and there was a kilometer of rock between her and anybody on the surface.

She continued to try anyway.

Meanwhile, Miller began to bang on the door with the butt of his rifle: three rapid taps, three bangs, three rapid taps—S.O.S. in Morse code.

After several minutes, Dana stopped hailing and put a hand on Miller's arm. "We chased everyone out of this section of the base and sealed all the pressure doors. There's nobody there to hear us." Her foremost thought was that she'd never see Bill again.

◈《○》◈

The Chinese Marauders had two advantages over the American CATS: speed and maneuverability. Captain Etre's mission specs had provided everything American and European intelligence had gathered about the Chinese fighters. In this case, though, *spec* was short for *speculation*, rather than *specification*. The CATS had never been pitted against the Marauders in real combat.

According to the data feed from the non-stealth training ship, the *Siamese*, Etre was close enough to intercept the Marauders before they reached the damaged American troop transport. None of the other CATS, however, were near enough to help.

"Catch them," Etre told his pilot.

Instantly, g buried him in his seat as the *Jaguar* fought to get there in time. But the Marauders were deceptively far away. The *Jaguar*, racing at nearly 50,000 kilometers per hour, seemed to gain at a sluggish pace. All the while, Etre had plenty of time to estimate the odds one CATS had against four Marauders, having battled the lens-shaped fighters dozens, if not hundreds, of times in the simulators. Even with a stealth advantage, the odds looked terrible.

But he had no choice. The *Jaguar* and the *Siamese* were the only ships standing between the enemy and more than a hundred men on board the crippled *Virgil Grissom*.

Etre's vector brought the *Jaguar* in from the Marauders' starboard side. A thousand kilometers from the transport, the *Jaguar*'s guns roared to life. Moments later, the right-rear Marauder exploded. The Marauder next to it spun away, but too late. Thirteen-millimeter rounds raked the ship. Bits of hull flew off and atmosphere spewed into the void. One of its oxygen tanks ruptured and it cartwheeled away.

The remaining Marauders peeled off at disparate angles. Etre's pilot, Lieutenant Jim Holt, chose one and pursued. The machines were every bit as agile in real life as they'd been in the simulator, perhaps more so. Holt struggled just to keep up. Never once did the Marauder pass through the *Jaguar*'s firing arc.

Etre let his crew do what they could. He clicked on the active radar— might as well now that the enemy had them on visual—and watched the blips of the other two Marauders.

How many times in the simulator had a wounded enemy ship circled around to take them from behind? The lesson had been drilled into him over and over. This time though, the wounded ship continued to tumble ever deeper into space.

The remaining undamaged Marauder was more of a concern. It began a gradual loop to intercept the *Jaguar*.

⋘(○)⋙

Colonel Davis watched the blips of the Marauders on his radar display. The CATS themselves were invisible. It was eerie to see the Marauders respond to the ghost ships as if they were fighting some hallucination. It might have been comical if it hadn't been so serious.

The more he observed the enemies' behavior, however, the more he realized there was only one CATS among them, and that CATS was in trouble.

78

"Break formation," he told Captain Polaco of the *Siamese*. "Engage the Marauders."

Instantly, the CATS trainer, his only escort, left him. *Gus the Bus* was alone in space, paralyzed by its wound. A single shot from a Marauder, even from a distance, could send them all into oblivion, if Davis didn't see it coming early enough.

He turned up the gain on the radar and slowed down the sweep to improve the resolution. His eyes never left the display until Mercury itself came between *Gus* and the enemy.

"Scan the surface," Davis told his navigator. "The *Taurus* went down somewhere along this vector. We need to find her."

He watched the sky for bogies while the pilot tried to keep their vector true, the navigator searched the planet, and a hundred-eighteen marines muttered into their pressure suits, praying their ship would hold together.

CHAPTER 11

Zeke donned an extra layer of radiation protection—a tinfoil-like jumpsuit beneath his 2XL pressure suit—and swapped his O$_2$ bottle for a fresh one from the rack. A few minutes later, Tanner pulled up in a battery-powered luggage cart, the trailer loaded down with half a dozen meter-diameter spools of power-grade electrical cable.

In a sprawling base like this one, where all the utilities had to be routed through existing tunnels, there was no such thing as a short run of cable. Nevertheless, Zeke eyed the load skeptically. "That all we got?"

"There are a few smaller spools—scraps really—that we can splice together if we need to, but I'd hate to do that with power cable."

"I hear you, but sometimes you've got to do what you've got to do." He paused. "How much is there?"

Tanner pointed to the markings on one of the spools. "Six kilometers, maybe a little less. God willing, it'll be enough."

"Okay. Let's load up." They unhitched the trailer and pushed it into the airlocked lift—the cart and trailer would never have fit into it together.

"Go ahead and suit up." Zeke retrieved both their toolboxes from their lockers and set them on the cart's front passenger seat. He clipped on his tool belt over his pressure suit and added a Geiger scanner to their gear.

At the top of the lift, he manhandled the trailer into the deep Mercury regolith, the layer of fine dust that covered the surface from eons of meteor bombardment, and the lift door closed behind him. It reopened a few minutes later, with Tanner squeezed into the driver's seat of the cart, which wasn't designed to accommodate a pressure suit. Tanner muttered a quick prayer and drove out of the lift.

Zeke helped him hook up the trailer, then set out across the blazing surface. The Geiger scanner in his hand monitored the space before him. When he'd walked scarcely a hundred meters, he waved back to Tanner, who levered the cart's accelerator.

The tiny wheels spun for a moment before finding some measure of traction and yanking the load forward. The base had had all-terrain cycles and rovers, but that was before the bomb. Those vehicles had been housed in the underground hanger, which was now an enormous crater that looked more like a meteor strike than it did anything else.

As the radiation count climbed higher, Zeke turned to his left and began a long trek around the crater, leaving it to Tanner to find a navigable track of land for the cart. Close to the base, it didn't seem to be a problem. Halfway around the western side of the crater, however, the cart became stuck in a spit of sand.

Zeke trudged back. He offloaded the pair of toolboxes, which would have weighed more than fifty kilograms on Earth, while Tanner dumped half the coils of power cable. The two hefted the cart out of the holes the wheels had dug, then reloaded the cargo. Now that Zeke had a good idea where the safe-radiation boundary was, he clipped the Geiger scanner to his belt, still active, and put his muscles to work pushing the cart through the rough spots.

He was sweating freely in his pressure suit despite the over-taxed cooling system, and before long, he began to smell it on his body. "I hate working outside. Especially here."

"I like it," Tanner said. "I've been EVA so few times, it's all still new to me."

"A far cry from restaurant work, huh?"

"I'll say."

"What gets me," Tanner said after a moment, "is the sun shining on the ground while the stars fill a black sky. That kind of beauty doesn't exist on Earth."

"Yeah. I think it's the vastness of it all that causes some people to have space sickness." Zeke grunted as he shoved the cart through another mound of regolith, which clung to the legs of his EVA suit. "It makes me feel small, insignificant."

"That's not necessarily a bad thing. It keeps us humble. You want me to take a turn pushing?"

"No. I got it."

By midday, they had made it past the rest of the radiation zone and back onto the road that led to Mercury's northern pole and the base's two-kilometer-diameter field of solar collection panels—if it was still there. The hundred-meter-high research tower at its center, which always stood in sunlight, had been responsible for more learning about the sun than had all of mankind's earlier research projects combined.

Today, Zeke cared only about the power array itself, and whether enough of it was still hooked up to Deep West's backup battery system to keep what was left of the base alive.

To get there, they had to ascend a narrow road that had been blasted out of the cliff face of one of the lobate scarps. It climbed at nearly thirty degrees, an angle that would have proven impossible for most vehicles in any substantial gravity. Even at one-third g, the luggage cart labored to reach the top.

As Zeke rounded the lip, he let out a long sigh. The frameworks that held the panels were still standing, at any rate. He couldn't inspect the panels themselves until he got closer, but most of the solar array appeared to be intact. "Looks okay so far," he called back to Tanner.

"Hang on a second." Tanner's attention was on the cart, still navigating the last switchback on the cliff, the cart's wheels slipping all the way. A few minutes later, he too topped the rise.

"Looks intact," Zeke repeated.

"Praise God. Hop on."

Zeke stepped onto the bumper, grabbed the upright pole at one of the back corners of the cart, and let Tanner drive him the rest of the way to the array. The lobate scarp had shielded the area from the worst of the intense heat, and the planet had no atmosphere to support a shock wave. The only damage appeared to be a fine layer of dust that had settled over everything. The dust would reduce the panels' efficiency, and someone would have to come up here to clean them all off, thousands of them, one by one. Yet the coating didn't appear thick enough to prevent the panels from producing sufficient electricity for the time being, especially since many of Deep West's power-consuming systems were now buried under rubble.

Both men turned toward a dome-shaped bunker that sat near the closest edge of the array. It had once housed the original solar research center but had later been converted to a power substation when nickel mining began. When the base became an interplanetary interchange and outgrew the substation, the battery bank was designated for emergency backup use only.

"Let's check it out," Zeke said.

Tanner steered the cart in that direction.

When they got there, the place looked unchanged since Zeke had inspected it the previous year. He produced a key that looked like it belonged in a time two centuries past—oversized, as was the padlock, so he could easily manipulate it with EVA gloves.

He undid the lock, spun the door's handle, and pulled. Once they cycled through the airlock, Zeke found a switch just inside the door and levered it into the ON position. Bright white lights from three solid-state ceiling panels lit the room. These were not the emergency lights he expected. This building had power.

After verifying the bunker's environmental integrity, he swapped his EVA gear and tinfoil pajamas for some cotton coveralls and a pair of insulated gloves. He'd be damned if he was going to risk getting battery acid on his pressure suit.

Tanner did the same. Together, they inspected the massive battery bank, a cube-shaped structure that now dominated the room. Each face consisted of a ten-by-ten array of high-voltage batteries.

"You start with those." Zeke pointed to one face of the battery cube. "I'll work my way around this direction."

He extracted a wire brush from his toolbox. "You know what we're looking for?"

"Cracks? Corrosion?"

"Mainly. Brush off the contacts. If the connection looks solid, leave it. If not, bypass that cell." He pointed out the bypass switch in the upper right corner of each battery. "Don't take anything offline that you don't need to. Every cell we bypass means less power for the base."

"Got it."

Zeke began his inspection, scrubbing flecks of green, corroded metal from the terminals.

For most of the batteries, the charge read FULL, despite the fact that nobody had used them since the power distribution system had been upgraded, back when the Plaza was brought online nearly twenty years before. Well, Zeke would put them to good use today.

Whenever he found leaking fluid, he wiped it up and inspected any surface the acid had leaked onto. They couldn't afford to lose these cells to a chemical fire, not with Deep West counting on them.

It took maybe an hour to inspect all four hundred cells.

"That's it," Zeke said finally.

"You suppose the cable is intact from here to the base?"

Zeke shook his head. "This backup system would've kicked on. We wouldn't have lost air circulation."

"Is there any way to verify that? I'd hate to run an extra cable all the way down if we don't have to."

"That's what we came out here to do. Isn't it?"

Tanner paused. "Yes, sir, but—"

"No buts. We've got to run it. Problem is, we would normally dump the charge from this entire bank before splicing into the power feed. Today we can't. It would take too long for the array to recharge it." He popped a panel open and used a Gauss driver to trip the magnetic latches hidden beneath the corners of the cover. "We'll use the main disconnect here."

The electrical contacts looked good, at least visually, but the disconnect switch showed signs of rust. If the switch opened partway and then stuck, or if flakes of rusted metal shorted the switch to ground, it could create an arc blast, a flash of superheated air and molten metal caused by a high-voltage arc.

Zeke would normally disconnect it anyway—it was a simple matter of donning the protective gear hanging in a cabinet on the far wall. The real issue was that an arc blast would destroy the whole power distribution box and possibly ignite any residual acid remaining on the outside of the battery bank. On behalf of the base, he couldn't take that chance. He was going to have to do it hot.

As soon as they had cycled back through the airlock, Tanner stopped. He stared into the black, star-strewn sky. "Hey, Zeke. You got to see this."

Twenty or more assorted ships were coming from over the pole. Low to the ground. Slowing.

For nearly ten minutes, they streamed past in a slow procession of ones, twos, and occasional threes.

Several of the designs were from commercial freight companies—Soaring Aerospace, Europa Company, and Freight Enterprises—but these were not commercial ships. A tanker cleared the horizon, bearing a prominent USAF logo on the side. These were military ships, some with European insignia, others American.

Two ships in particular caught Zeke's eye. Small, almost like corporate intercontinental shuttles, but Zeke had only seen those used on Earth. Though similar in size, these had significant differences. The roughly cylindrical craft had no wings to speak of and thruster ports almost as large as those on the tankers. With thrusters like that, they had to be the fastest ships in the convoy. Smaller ports—gun ports?—protruded from the front of each. They had to be fighting ships, European by the gold-stars-on-a-blue-field insignia. Last to land was a Soaring 1067 passenger transport, also sporting an EU logo.

"Ever seen anything like this?" Tanner asked.

Stunned mute, Zeke simply shook his head.

"Let's go see." Tanner squeezed onto the luggage cart.

There was way too much work to do for a break to be prudent, but Zeke simply couldn't let a spectacle of this magnitude pass unobserved.

Tanner drove them back to the top of the bluff, which gave them a spectacular view of Deep West and the gaping wound that had been ripped into the base's vital organs. A plateau just beyond the base became a makeshift landing field. With his thinpad, Zeke captured a vid-scan of the military fleet. Whatever game the political powers were playing, it was on now.

◅⦗ ○ ⦘▻

Bill regained consciousness in a small stone-block chamber with his hands manacled to the wall just above his head. His skull felt like it had one of those old-fashioned railroad spikes—a rusty one—driven into it.

Simeon stood some six meters in front of him, speaking to his Polynesian thugs. When a groan slipped past Bill's mouth, Simeon glanced over, then continued his conversation in a lower voice.

The chain that held Bill's hands appeared to have been hammered into the wall recently. The pin that anchored it looked new compared to the worn, rust-tinged bands that encircled his wrists. His weapons and other gear had been stripped from him. His feet, however, remained free. If either of Simeon's hit men, or Simeon himself, came near enough…

Bill would worry about that when the time came. For now, he turned his attention to what the men were saying. They weren't far away. He ought to be able to make out the words, but he couldn't coax his throbbing brain to focus.

Finally, he said, "Look, Simeon. In a couple of hours—"

Simeon gestured toward Bill with a disinterested flap of his hand. "Shut him up, will you?"

Yes, Bill thought. *Come closer.*

But they didn't. One of the big Polynesians, the one with the ridiculous braids down the sides of his face, withdrew a Lancaster pulse gun from his voluminous pocket and leveled it at Bill.

"Listen, you f—" Pain burned through Bill's wrists as microwaves heated the metal cuffs. Yet his scream made no sound. His eyes peered unsteadily at the floor some two meters in front of him. He could see Simeon's polished black cowboy boots stepping closer, but instructions from his brain didn't make it past his overloaded synapses. He couldn't lift his head to look the scoundrel in the eye. The dead weight of his body hung from the searing shackles, the burns swamping out the pain he barely remembered having felt in his head moments before.

Simeon took Bill's chin, almost tenderly, between his thumb and forefinger, and raised Bill's head. He peered into Bill's eyes as if seeking a sign of consciousness.

Listen, you fuck, Bill raged in his mind, determined to complete his statement, if only to himself. *This base will soon be swarming with US military. And when it is, your cowardly ass is going down.* Try as he might, Bill could not make his mouth form the words.

"Look around you." Simeon twisted Bill's head so his eyes took in most of the room, albeit in an unfocused, bobbing wave.

The throb at the back of Bill's skull returned.

"I hope you like the accommodations," Simeon continued. "When my guys are through with you, I'm going to bury you in here."

He dropped Bill's head so his chin thumped against his own chest. Then Simeon donned a pressure suit and left the room, the steel portal clanging shut with an ominous finality.

But that sound merely signaled the beginning of the nightmare. Moments later, a giant fist slammed into Bill's jaw. He felt the blow but couldn't cry out in pain—not that he'd have given these thugs the satisfaction. Fortunately, the men pounded his head and face only occasionally, choosing to spend the bulk of their time softening his gut and kicking his shins. Once, Braidface kneed him in the groin.

Finally, the Lancaster pulse began to wear off. He could lift his head and glare at his captors. "Why..." His tongue was thick, the word slurred.

The fat Polynesian with the goatee grabbed a fistful of hair and yanked Bill's head to the side. "You have to ask?"

"You crossed Simeon," Braidface said. "Nobody does that."

CHAPTER 12

One of the Marauders circled to come around behind the *Jaguar.* The other proved to be too maneuverable to catch.

"Let them go." Captain Etre switched off his radar so the enemy couldn't trace its signal. "It's time to lose ourselves."

"Hold on to something." Jim Holt, the *Jaguar's* pilot, slammed his joystick hard to the right.

The edges of Etre's vision began to blacken with the hard g. Then Holt burned for deep space. Thirty seconds later, he rolled the ship and broke into another hard turn.

Etre sent out one radar sweep, not enough to trace, but enough to give him a fix on the Marauders. Neither was following. The *Jaguar* had slipped into the dark. Both Marauders had turned toward the *Siamese*, which had no stealth properties and little chance against the nimble enemy ships.

"Come at them again," Etre ordered.

The *Jaguar* came back around to an intercept heading. Unfortunately, the Marauders had launched from Mercury. They hadn't spent the fuel they'd have needed to escape Earth's gravity. They would have more stamina here than the ones who'd attacked the convoy as it left Earth. "Lamont, launch two non-stealth missiles."

Etre's gunner glanced at him. "They'll see them coming."

"I'm counting on it."

The look Lamont gave him seemed to say, "If you say so," but he launched them.

Just before the missiles arrived, both Marauders peeled off to escape them.

"As soon as the ships settle back on course," Etre said, "Launch two more."

Lamont smiled, apparently catching on to Etre's game: forcing enemy maneuvers, burning Marauder fuel, and slowing their advance on the *Siamese*.

All the while, the *Jaguar* edged closer.

⊹《○》⊹

The *Jaguar*'s missiles bought Polaco and the rest of the *Siamese* crew some time, but only minutes. Then the pair of Marauders were on him, playing a form of erratic chicken. Green flashes along their front told Polaco the enemy lasers were firing, though he couldn't see the beams themselves in the void. The bark of Ramona Johnson's guns blasted back in rough spurts. All three ships twisted, bobbed, and rolled to avoid being hit.

Then it happened. A high-energy laser cut through the windshield. It seared a hole through Polaco's leg and out through the floor. He wrapped his hands around his thigh in an effort to keep the air from escaping his pressure suit, and gritted his teeth against the pain.

Johnson kept shooting. Sparks lit up the front of the lead Marauder, bits of metal and instrumentation flew off, and it veered away.

The other Marauder came straight on.

"Missiles." Polaco could barely speak the word, the pain in his leg was so great, but he didn't dare take his eyes off the enemy to see how quickly he would bleed to death or suffocate. "Hard over!"

Four missiles flew from beneath the wings as the *Siamese* peeled up and to the right.

Air was streaming from the cabin and leaking from Polaco's suit. The oxygen in his helmet had grown thin and the valve from his O_2 tank had opened wide in an attempt to compensate. That might keep him alive for a few more seconds.

"Again," Polaco said.

Four more missiles flew. The Marauder had moved beneath Polaco's field of view, so he relied on his radar display to keep track of it.

When it pulled up to avoid the missiles, Johnson detonated them manually. In an instant, shrapnel filled the radar screen. By the time the display cleared, both enemy ships had taken full flight, back toward Mercury.

Then Polaco looked down at his leg. A hole the size of a checkers piece had been drilled clean through it and his seat. There was no blood—the laser had cauterized the wound—but his air was escaping. "Help," he gasped.

His pilot glanced down. "Oh, shit." He clicked on the autopilot and scrambled for the vacuum tape, a pliable but sturdy patch that could seal nearly any vacuum system if the breach wasn't too large.

In the meantime, Johnson leapt from her seat and wrapped her hands, along with Polaco's, around his leg to help slow the escape of air.

Polaco didn't fixate on his wound. Beyond his initial assessment, he didn't look at it at all. He stared instead at the radar display. At that moment, his entire crew was incapacitated, and the enemy was still out there.

⁓(O)⁓

Dana and her crew sat in the confined space of the collapsed tunnel.

"What if we set one of the O_2 tanks up, aim it at the door, and sheer off the valve?" Allistair said after an intolerable silence that had probably lasted only a few minutes.

Miller tapped Alistair's tank. "You really want one of these rocketing around in here?" He gestured at their tiny space.

"Probably not," Allistair admitted.

"Maybe we don't have to." Dana consulted the gauge inside her helmet. "How much air do you guys have?"

Each of her crew reported a pressure similar to hers.

She pulled out her knife and began to scratch figures into the door. Numbers. Mathematical equations. *Pressure times volume is proportional to the amount of gas in the tanks.*

The others stood to observe her computation.

"What are you doing?" Miller asked finally.

Dana continued her calculations. "If we release the air from our tanks into this chamber, which is—" she estimated the dimensions of the space by the number of arm lengths it took to span its depth, width, and height—"about fifteen cubic meters."

Scale the pressure by the ratio of the volume of the tanks to the volume of the chamber... She scratched more numbers. Paused. "I think we can raise the pressure in here to something close to the pressure on the other side of the door."

Miller began to catch on. "Then how much force will we need to push the door open?"

Dana scratched some more. "If this is right, maybe half a metric ton."

"Five hundred kilograms," Miller mused.

"I don't know," Allistair said. "That's pretty tight."

"Won't hurt to try," Dana said. "At that pressure we should be able to breathe without our suits. As long as the air doesn't seep out through the rocks, we can still use it."

"That's a big if," Miller said.

"Do we have a choice?"

Silence.

"All right then." Dana turned her O_2 tank toward Allistair.

He reached up and popped Dana's release valve. Dana did the same for him and for Miller. Within minutes all three tanks were empty. They had no way to verify Dana's calculations, no way to know whether the actual pressure in the space had even risen to a safe level. The billow of their EVA suits suggested it was still well below the pressure the tanks had maintained in their suits. Dana, for one, was going to keep hers sealed until she'd consumed the oxygen trapped inside it.

They lined up against the wall of fallen rock and braced themselves to lunge. "Ready?" Dana asked.

"Ready," the others said in unison.

"One...two..." On "three," they threw themselves against the pressure door.

As one, they tumbled to the ground, the door unmoved.

∽《○》∾

"Two Marauders returning, sir. Both damaged."

"Tell me something I don't know, Lieutenant," Chou said in that dangerously polite tone. "Perhaps you'd like to mention any enemy casualties."

"One cargo ship destroyed. Minor damage to the American fighter."

"How nice."

The lieutenant spoke his next words a little too quickly. *Coward.* "Maneuvers of the American troop ship are sluggish. Suspect major damage." The man looked up at Chou. "It might not be able to land, sir."

"You are relieved, Lieutenant."

The man's eyes grew wide and fear-stricken.

"Have a nice day."

The lieutenant swallowed hard, stood, and walked stiffly toward the door.

Before he reached it, Chou drew his pistol and shot the man in the back of the head. He motioned for another to take the lieutenant's station. "Kindly tell me if the American troop ship can land. I suggest you refrain from using the words *might* and *suspect.*"

One by one, he gestured to individuals within his command center. "You, get a damage report from each of those Marauders. I want any parts and equipment needed for repairs laid out on the hanger floor before they arrive, and crews working on them before they so much as come to a complete stop. Notify me as soon as you know how long the repairs will take." He selected another man. "Give me the location and damage estimate for every American and European craft in the Mercury system, on the ground or in space. And—" he chose another—"you, get rid of that." He pointed to the lieutenant's body. "There's not enough room in here for incompetents."

On his own thinpad, he displayed a list of his military assets. He didn't have enough, by far. Fortunately, his superiors had provided him an ally. "Corporal, get me Comrade Batkin on the comm."

❧⟨O⟩❧

Before long, the Plaza fell into a sort of hurried routine. The doctors and nurses had taken over treatment of the wounded. The air force crews had disappeared, presumably to do whatever they had come here to do, which was just as well. God help them all if Russia decided to drop another nuke on the base. Zeke had gone outside to see if he could restore some portion of the base's power before the generator fuel ran out and made the whole endeavor a waste of time.

Finally, Ana planted herself at the bar, out of the way, exhausted. How long had it been since the blast? Hours, obviously, but how many? Six? Twelve? She scanned the wall for a chronometer and found one. Noon. Almost straight up. As she watched it, it seemed to be keeping the time, but it still didn't answer her question. It was the first time she'd looked at a clock since the previous evening.

Simeon stepped behind the bar with two steaming porcelain mugs in his hand. "Coffee?" He laid one on the counter in front of her.

She eyed it, and then him, suspiciously.

"How much?" She could imagine how high the price had risen since all of Simeon's competition had crumbled to the pavement.

"Oh, come now—" Simeon began.

"You don't do anything for free. How much are you charging?" Ana tried not to melt at the aroma streaming from the mug. The more she wanted it, the higher the price would climb.

Simeon just smiled and gestured for her to take the coffee.

Finally, she decided it didn't matter what he was planning to charge. She would drink the coffee and pay him nothing. She lifted the cup and drank deeply of the smell before taking a sip. For the first time, it seemed, the coffee actually tasted as good as it smelled. "How did you brew it without power?"

He pointed to a small gel-powered cooking stove on the counter behind him. It had a large pot of coffee heating above it and a small Air Force Space Command logo on the side. Military issue.

Her eyes narrowed. "Where did you—"

"You should know by now, Ana. The Sharp Shooter has all the best accommodations."

Ana's face hardened. She put down the cup as though she suddenly realized the contents could burn her. "If you're trying to recruit me again—"

"No. That shuttle left years ago. You decided to work for yourself. Now this—" he raised his cup at the casino—"is what it finally comes down to. You're out of business, along with everybody else. Including that space jockey who came to your rescue earlier."

"As if I needed rescuing from you."

Simeon stared at her for a moment, then waved to several of his casino staff who had apparently been offered enough money to return to work. Each wore the Sharp Shooter uniform, clean and unwrinkled—free from the dust that seemed to coat everything else. "Get the names of everyone here," he told them. "I'll bill them for the use of my building."

Every employee but one moved out onto the casino floor, among the doctors and patients. Only the bartender remained.

"Start running tabs for the coffee," Simeon told him. "Ten credits a cup. Twice that for whiskey, whether for medicinal use or not."

"This cup—" he motioned toward Ana's—"is on the house."

Something in his look suggested it would be the last one she'd ever get.

"If you'll excuse me," he told Ana. "I have business to attend."

"Sure." Ana left her coffee on the bar and walked, as nonchalantly as she could, from the Sharp Shooter. She talked to several people milling in the Plaza until someone told her that Major Ryan had been arrested immediately after his announcement. She should have known.

She ran as fast as her little legs would take her down to the far end of the Plaza, where the jailhouse sat, mostly intact. One of the deputies, Todd Kravitz, a regular customer of Ana's, sat at a desk just inside. A battery-powered lantern rested by his elbow, casting odd shadows throughout the room. She stepped into the light.

"Ana," Todd whispered. "I told you never to come here."

"I hear you've got some prisoners."

"That's right. Possession of illegal weapons."

"You could have just confiscated the weapons. It's not the first time—"

Todd stood. "But Simeon—I'm sorry. It's police business."

"Since when is Simeon the police?"

"Ana, don't do this. You know what he can do."

"I'd like to see the prisoners."

When he began to shake his head, Ana spread her arms at her sides, as if to display the whole of her diminutive body. "What am I going to do? Besides, I just want to talk to them."

Todd's shoulders relaxed visibly. "All right."

He led her through an iron door and into the cellblock. A total of three cages, separated by iron bars, backed up to the stone wall of the Plaza's immense natural cavern. The outer wall of the third cell was cracked, the cage unusable. The center cell contained two air force prisoners: the young black woman who had helped treat the wounded in Simeon's casino and a tall, dark-haired man whose name Ana hadn't caught. They sat on cots against the walls, each wearing a flight suit, their hands shackled behind their backs.

The male prisoner, identified by a patch on his chest as TOWNSEND, stood when Ana approached.

"Is it true?" she asked. "Russia dropped a nuclear bomb on the base?"

Townsend nodded. "They're going to do a lot worse if we don't stop them."

Todd snorted. "What could be worse than a nuclear bomb?" His voice held a subtle, shrieking hysteria beneath a cracked façade of authority.

Townsend met his eyes evenly. "They've only just begun. But they're not nearly the threat China is."

Todd straightened. "Yeah, and you brought them here. We could hand you over to them and declare neutrality. Maybe then they'd leave us alone."

"Don't be a child," Ana told him. "You really think all this is about a few soldiers?"

"Airmen," the black girl behind Townsend shot back.

"One of two things is going to happen," Townsend continued. "Either this base is going to fill with American and European troops who will use it as a base of operations, or it will be overrun by the enemy. It just depends on who gets here first."

CHAPTER 13

"Here," Dana said. "Give me your air tank."

Allistair turned his back to Miller, who unclipped the oxygen bottle from Alistair's back, and handed it to Dana.

"Yours too," she told Miller.

"Why? There's nothing in them."

"We're going to use them as battering rams."

Miller let Allistair unhook his bottle, which weighed about two kilograms empty, less in Mercury's gravity.

Dana laid Miller's bottle on the ground, held it in place with one foot, and pounded the valve tip with Alistair's bottle until the connection sheared off. She did the same with Alistair's. "Fill them with dirt. Make them as heavy as you can."

When they finished, each man took his bottle and stood to either side of the doorway.

Dana drew her combat knife and crouched on the floor between them, near the lower threshold of the pressure door. "Ready? On three."

As she counted, the men swung their makeshift rams forward and back, in rhythm.

On "three," both men slammed the butt end of the bottles into the door, near the handle. The plate popped slightly ajar, opening a fraction of a centimeter before the air pressure on the other side slammed it shut again. In that split second, Dana slipped the blade of her combat knife into the opening, preventing the door from resealing. A crack remained, and air whistled through into the small chamber.

"That's it," Miller exclaimed. "We got it."

It took a few minutes for the air pressure to equalize. When it did, the door swung open easily. They stepped through and sealed it behind them, just in case the avalanche wasn't quite airtight.

Miller pulled off his helmet. "That's one disaster averted, anyway."

Dana removed her helmet as well. The air in her suit had already begun to grow stale. "For the moment, but I've seen combat robots in action. Their programming won't let them quit. They'll be back."

◦❧⟨ O ⟩❧◦

As soon as Dana returned to the Sharp Shooter, the little woman, Ana, intercepted her. "Did you find Major Ryan?"

"No." Dana searched the woman's face. "You know where he is?"

"He and his crew were arrested for possession of illegal weapons. Two of them are in the jailhouse down the street, but Major Ryan isn't with them." She briefly described the previous altercation between Bill and Simeon.

When Dana marched from the Sharp Shooter a few minutes later, she passed her crew, who were waiting near the door. "Come on."

They followed her to the jailhouse. Inside the front room, a deputy—not the one she'd assaulted on her way into the base—looked up from a thinpad. He stood and came around the desk. "May I help you?"

Dana handed her air force security badge to the guard.

He examined it, then her, then her numerous weapons and other gear. She was still wearing her pressure suit with her helmet fastened to her waist, along with her sidearm, a brace of hand grenades, smoke bombs, a flashbang concussion grenade, and a combat knife. Her rifle was in her hand, pointed at the ceiling.

The deputy waved at Dana's badge. "What's this?"

"A get-out-of-jail-free card."

He snorted and handed it back. "You have no authority here."

She took a step closer, encroaching on the man's personal space. "I have the authority of the United States government—" she made a show of reading his badge—"Deputy Kravitz. My orders came from President Powers herself."

97

Kravitz stepped back. "Even she has no authority here. It's not American soil. By treaty, this is an international base."

Dana advanced as though she intended to bull-rush him. "Now you listen to me!" Her rifle waved, seemingly carelessly, in the air.

Kravitz backpedaled.

Dana grabbed a heavy ring of keys hanging from the cracked back wall and tossed them to Miller. "Go let them out."

"Hey!" Kravitz yelled as Miller and Allistair opened the door to the cell-block. "That's a felony."

Dana raised her eyebrows, calm now that her outburst had served its purpose. "A felony in what country?"

Kravitz stammered. "Umm…uh. All countries."

A moment later, her crew returned with Carter and Townsend.

"Where's Bill?" Dana asked.

Townsend shook his head. "Not here."

"Simeon's men took him away," Kravitz said.

Dana spun back to the deputy. This time she pointed the rifle at his chest. "Where is he?"

"I don't know."

"Where's our gear?" Townsend asked.

Kravitz glanced briefly at him, then back at Dana. "Simeon's men took that too."

Dana grabbed a fistful of his uniform. "Where would Simeon have taken Major Ryan?"

"Simeon didn't take him. His bouncers did."

"Where would *they* have taken him?"

"I don't know."

"Come on. Deep West isn't that big a base to begin with. Now half of it's buried in rubble. Simeon must have a place he uses for this kind of thing."

"I'm sure he does. I just don't know where it is."

"Stop protecting him," Carter said.

"I can't." There was a pleading look in the deputy's eyes. "Someday you're all going to leave, and Simeon will still be here."

"Simeon will be in prison for kidnapping, or worse, by the time we're done," Carter said.

Kravitz shook his head. "No, he won't. You'll never pin anything on him. You may get his flunkies, but not him. Not ever."

"I've heard enough." Dana snatched the Lancaster pulse gun from the deputy's belt and shoved him at Allistair. "Lock him up."

"On what charge?" Kravitz pleaded.

"Does it matter?" Carter asked.

"Obstruction of justice," Dana said. "Or better yet, interfering with our mission. This is the second time these so-called deputies have cost us time."

Allistair marched the man through the back door and returned alone. He tossed the keys to Dana.

She handed them back. "You stay here. If anybody gives you trouble, lock them up too. In the meantime, see if you can find our supplies."

Allistair shifted uncomfortably, but said, "Yes, sir."

"Did you get a chance to complete that comm relay on the surface?" she asked Townsend.

"Not yet."

"Miller." Dana shoved her thumb in the rough direction of the lift to the surface.

"I'm on it."

"There are some O_2 tanks on an emergency supply rack near the evacuation exit."

"I saw them." He hustled out of the jailhouse, snapping his helmet on as he went.

"Townsend. I want your eyes on the main entrance to the Plaza. Check in every five minutes. If you see Simeon, his cronies, or worse—more of those damn spider bots—holler. We'll come running.

"Carter, you're with me. We're going back to the Sharp Shooter to get some answers."

⊰❨◯❩⊱

Lieutenant Colonel Brannon, commander of the European troops, approached the concrete-encased hatch at the top of the lift that, according to his specs, led to the area of Deep West known as the Plaza. One of Brannon's sergeants walked in front of him, monitoring the background radiation with a Geiger scanner.

"Report," Brannon ordered.

"Trace levels of radioactive compounds, above normal background levels, but safe."

Brannon eyed the crater, whose edge wasn't more than a kilometer from the lift. With no atmosphere and with the walls of the landing elevator to channel the explosion, most of the radioactive matter from the blast might have been blown clear into space or would have been buried when the majority of the rock between the underground hangar and the surface had fallen back into the hole. Nevertheless, he pondered the fine powder, the regolith, that clung to the legs of every pressure suit. "I don't want anybody to track contaminants inside. Get a blower and clear the regolith from around the entrance. Blow off everybody's suits and scan them for contamination before they board the lift." He paused. "And set up a decon station at the bottom."

If the base still had power, he would have begun bringing equipment down, but since he'd heard from nobody—including the two CATS teams he knew had already landed—he had to assume the power was out. The panel on the emergency lift, however, remained lit. The base was likely running on emergency backup: batteries, generators, or both. In the meantime, he had no way to know how limited the base's power supply actually was, or how much the lift would consume. Better to conserve.

Brannon ordered his captain, Mike Kamieniechi, to organize the infantry and to assign a detail to guard the ships until power could be restored and the freight could be moved underground. He selected his aide, two additional officers, and twenty grunt infantry to accompany him down. Half of those filled the elevator. As soon as he stepped into the crimson-bathed Plaza, he popped off his helmet to conserve his suit's oxygen supply.

It appeared little had been done since the blast, though some ad-hoc rescue efforts seemed to be underway.

He stopped one of the American fliers, a Lieutenant Miller, who was waiting to board the lift. "Report."

"Just heading up to complete the comm relay on the surface, sir."

"What's taking so long?"

"Sorry, sir." He motioned at the bustling Plaza. "Lot going on down here. Major McCaughey can fill you in. She should be in the Sharp Shooter—big building down the street."

Brannon nodded. "Carry on." To his own men, he said, "Get this place cleaned up. I want a clear corridor down the length of the Plaza." He could see the wounded in the street farther down. "Move everyone and anything out of the main road."

"All right," his lieutenant yelled. "We have orders. My team, listen up."

Brannon waited for his second load of men to descend the lift and remove their helmets. "You men, follow me." He marched down the street to the only building still standing, which had obviously become the hub of post-blast activity. When he got there, he found two of the American crewmen in the lobby.

One woman, a major from the US Air Force, had her handgun pressed to the temple of a slender civilian in clean business wear. "Where is he?"

The businessman seemed unconcerned, though he was careful not to move his hands or head suddenly. "I'm sure I have no idea."

"Bullshit. I *will* shoot you."

Two local police officers stood behind her. Wounded littered the floor around them all.

One officer, whose badge identified him as the local sheriff, glanced at Brannon and the squad of uniformed soldiers that had come in behind him. He suddenly looked very nervous. "I wouldn't do that if I were you," the sheriff said to the woman with the gun.

She glanced at Brannon, then turned toward the sheriff. "This man kidnapped one of our men, and you know it."

The sheriff fidgeted with the Lancaster in his holster. "You have enough military here. I can't possibly enforce the weapons ban, but if you shoot Mister Tuck, whether he's guilty or not, I *will* arrest you."

"What's going on here, Major?" Brannon asked.

"Our commanding officer is missing. He was last seen being abducted by this man's bouncers."

"And your Major McCaughey is obstructing justice," the sheriff said, now addressing Brannon. "She freed two prisoners from our jailhouse and is now holding one of my deputies there. Nothing has been proven against

Mister Tuck, but Major McCaughey has broken several laws." He gestured to the gun she had pointed at the businessman's head. "Including assault with a deadly weapon."

"I think you'd better stand down, Major," Brannon ordered, "or I may be forced to arrest you myself. Mister Tuck isn't going anywhere. As of this moment, I'm putting Deep West under martial law. All military peace-keeping and law-enforcement protocols apply." He turned to the sheriff. "Escort Mister Tuck to the jailhouse until we can spare someone to question him."

"Now wait just a minute—" Tuck began, but Brannon motioned the sheriff to move out.

As soon as Tuck and the lawman were gone, Dana rounded on Brannon. "Can you spare search parties?"

"For your commander?"

She nodded. "Major Bill Ryan."

"Of course."

"Have them wear pressure suits and send a Geiger scanner with each party," Dana said. "Some areas of the base are flooded with radiation, others have lost vacuum integrity."

Brannon assigned one of his men, a sergeant, the task of organizing search parties. The sergeant nodded and began rounding up his men.

"There's a station map down the street." Dana pointed.

Suddenly the comm came to life in Brannon's ear. "Lieutenant Miller of the USS *Snow Leopard* to Lieutenant Colonel Brannon."

"Brannon. Go ahead."

"One of our ships, the *Cheetah*, reports incoming. An infantry force, both men and robotic units, from Shenming Base. A lot of them. Details follow."

"Sorry," Brannon told McCaughey. "Looks like the search parties will have to wait."

He sprinted down the main street toward the lift, nearly pitching himself off balance in the unfamiliar gravity, to where a corporal and a pair of privates were setting up his temporary command console. "You got that thing up and running yet?"

"Yes, sir." The corporal flipped a switch, and the display, which had been black except for a fine green grid, blinked into life, along with a comm uplink to the transmitter on the surface and a dynamic list of resources and deployments. "Only just."

Brannon punched in the CATS comm frecuency and activated the encryption algorithm he and Colonel Davis had agreed upon. "Lieutenant Colonel Brannon to the *Cheetah*."

"This is *Cheetah*."

"I've got a whole lot of chaos and very few men down here. I need to know exactly what's coming and how long we've got until they get here."

"Yes, sir. It looks like a couple hundred robotic infantry with a variety of hardware onboard: machine guns, high-caliber cannons, rocket launchers, you name it. Several special-application bots. I can't discern the purpose of all of them, but some look like high-explosive roving mines—metal-encased shrapnel-throwers—probably with proximity triggers. I wouldn't get close to one with a pressure suit on."

"What else?"

"A pair of armored assault vehicles. I can't tell if anyone's in these things or if they're automated, but they're packed with armaments."

"Any live troops?"

"Yes, sir. Several dozen. I'm sending a video feed now."

"That all?"

"So far, sir."

"Very good. I need your eyes and ears up there. Keep me posted."

"No can do, sir. I've burned just about the last of my fuel holding position this long. I've got to come in right now or we're not going to make it."

"Acknowledged." Brannon silenced the microphone and surveyed the mayhem around him. There was too much to do. Too many people to save. The incoming troops outnumbered his own. He had the solar array and convoy ships to protect, civilians to control, the base to clean up, survivors to locate, and the dead to dispose of. "Looks like we got here just in time," he muttered.

"Sir?" the corporal asked.

"Just in time to get our balls lynched."

CHAPTER 14

Sheriff Ted Cromwell escorted Simeon to the jailhouse as the European military commander—what was his name? Brannon?—had ordered. Just before they entered, however, Simeon gave Cromwell that you-really-don't-want-to-do-this look. He was right. Cromwell didn't want to do it. In fact, he knew at that moment that he *couldn't* do it.

Sooner or later, the military crisis would subside. Brannon and his soldiers would leave, and Cromwell would have to answer to Simeon for whatever he did right then.

If he defied Colonel Brannon, there was only so much Brannon could do. He would probably round up Cromwell and his deputies and lock them up for the same obstruction of justice charge of which Cromwell had accused Major McCaughey. Less likely, he could take Cromwell back to Earth and try him there. Cromwell would spend a few months, or maybe years, in jail. Worst case, with martial law and all, Brannon could probably have him executed for treason. Somehow, Cromwell couldn't see it going that far.

Simeon continued to stare at him.

"Just for a little while," Cromwell pleaded.

Simeon raised an eyebrow.

"Colonel Brannon will spare someone to question you soon. Then I can let you go."

Simeon waited, his eyebrow still raised.

Cromwell sighed heavily. "Can you at least stay out of sight for a while? Maybe Brannon will forget he ordered me to take you into custody?"

"You don't take orders from Brannon." Simeon's voice was like dry ice—hard and cold. "You take orders from me."

Cromwell stepped aside and let Simeon back into the Plaza, resigned to suffer the consequences of whatever trouble Simeon might cause. If Cromwell decided to detain him, Simeon would employ none of the consequences Colonel Brannon had at his disposal. Simeon would do much worse. He would probably do, for example, whatever he was doing to Major Ryan at that very moment.

⋅⋙《○》⋘⋅

Blood had run freely from Bill's mouth, nose, and lacerations across his cheeks, but had since dried to a crust that pulled his skin every time he moved his face. His testicles ached, dull and hollow, from kicks he'd received. His stomach had hurt once, but it seemed it could no longer remember the beatings.

What consumed Bill's consciousness now was the pain in his wrists, blistered and raw from metal shackles that had been heated to a red glow by repeated microwave bursts from Braidface's Lancaster. That and the fact that Simeon's thugs would soon return to dole out even greater punishment.

In the total blackness that filled the room, Bill imagined a faint glow still emanating from the shackles—probably just his mind playing tricks. It had been long enough since his last beating that the metal should have cooled. Hadn't it been long enough? He could no longer tell.

Carter and Townsend would have told Dana by now that Simeon's men had taken him. She would have had the CATS crews initiate a search as soon as they arrived. Hell, the whole convoy, with over three hundred US and European marines, might have already landed. Still, they probably wouldn't find him.

Simeon's men, when they came, always arrived in pressure suits. Wherever they were keeping Bill, he was beyond some damaged portion of the base, separated from any search parties by at least an evacuated corridor. Somewhere out there was a pressure door that search parties couldn't, or wouldn't, pass.

Bill was on his own.

The only good news was that his dungeon didn't seem to be vacuum-tight. Slowly, the air was thinning. Again, it might have been his imagination, or it might have been his pummeled diaphragm having to work harder to pull air into his lungs, but Bill didn't think so. The air felt thinner. Sooner or later, there wouldn't be enough left to keep him conscious. How blissful it would be when that time came.

He just wished he could have seen Dana at least once since their trip. The past twenty-two days had been agony without her. He would continue to fight, for her sake, until his air gave out or Simeon's men finally murdered him.

His hands remained chained to an eyebolt driven into the stone wall. He gritted his teeth against the coming pain and yanked his fists forward. The chain snapped taut. His raw wrists seared. Lightning flashes of pain lit the backs of his eyelids, and his mind cried out for oblivion. Relentless, Bill yanked the chain again. And again. And again.

He stopped when he heard a sharp click, the squeak of the ship's-wheel door handle, and a soft hiss of air. Simeon's thugs stepped in carrying a propane lantern, probably Bill's own.

Bill blinked against the sudden light and groaned. He wasn't sure which hurt more, the beatings or the self-inflicted pain he endured trying to yank the eyebolt from the wall. At least the latter served a purpose, albeit a futile one.

The two Polynesian behemoths began to shed their pressure suits. Braidface, as always, had a Lancaster pulse gun on his belt.

Once they'd stripped their gear, he pointed the weapon at Bill's head and fired. Instantly, the pulse short-circuited Bill's synapses, and his body went limp. His mind, though alert and able to feel the pain, could no longer speak to his muscles. He just hung by his fried wrists from metal cuffs that once again burned red-hot.

The pummeling began again.

✥⟪ ◯ ⟫✥

An extraordinarily small woman approached Colonel Brannon. "Excuse me, sir."

"Not now," he told her.

"But, sir. We—"

Brannon turned to his corporal. "Get her out of here."

"Yes, sir." The corporal motioned to two privates, who grabbed the woman by her arms and carried her bodily from Brannon's presence.

"Set up a perimeter around this console," Brannon told the corporal. "Every civilian in here's probably got a need I can't begin to meet. And I got problems of my own right now. Don't let anyone approach unless I ask for them. Understand?"

The man hustled off to comply. Beyond that, Brannon didn't give it another thought. He'd compiled a list of ships that had survived the battle to escape Earth, the battle the Western newsblips had begun calling "the Freedom Flight." It took him mere seconds to turn that list into an inventory of resources, excluding whatever survived of the American convoy. Of those that had survived, Davis's own troop ship and two of the American freighters hadn't checked in since they'd been ambushed by Mingyun rocket rounds during their approach to Mercury.

In that light, Brannon wasn't counting on *any* American resources until he had a definite inventory and the access codes he'd need to use them.

In the meantime, his priorities were clear. Establish reliable communications and visual surveillance capability over and around Deep West; turn back the assault force now approaching from Shenming; watch for any further activity from Gagarin Base; assess the damage to Deep West and establish an estimate of how safe the base was, from both structural and radiation standpoints; provide protection for the solar array and for the convoy ships that sat, naked, on the plain outside; determine the whereabouts and status of the missing American troop ship; locate Major Ryan; and finally, if he had anything left to do so, assist these poor disaster-stricken civilians that so clearly needed his help.

How to allocate his meager list of resources to those monumental priorities was not so clear. "Squad leaders," he said over the encrypted EU channel, "I need all available hardware configured for immediate deployment."

Then he called to the leader of his Raptor squadron. "Brannon to Captain Stratman. Come in."

"Stratman."

"What is the status of your command?"

"I have six ships and crews. Minor injuries to three crew members and damage to two ships. All can fly, but only four are fit for combat. We're refueling now."

"I need all six in the air, ASAP. Establish a polar orbit with one ship every sixty degrees. You'll be my eyes and ears over Shenming, Gagarin, and Deep West. Do not engage the enemy unless you're attacked directly."

"Got it."

"Notify me, and send orbit parameters, every time you launch a ship. I need to see what's happening."

Brannon scanned his screen. At the moment, his men were the most important of those resources, and the most taxed— they would deploy and operate every piece of equipment in his arsenal. He had one company—a hundred and seventy-three men—organized into three platoons of three squads each.

"Captain Kamieniechi," Brannon called.

"Kamieniechi."

Brannon repeated the list of enemy forces the *Cheetah* had relayed. "Here're your deployments. Ready?"

"Yes, sir."

"Send one squad with all six defense pylons to the northern pole. The solar array is their priority."

"Got it."

"About two clicks west of here, there's a rise—a sheer cliff that, according to my topo map, is about forty meters high with a road cut into its face. I don't know if the enemy is planning to come down that road or skirt around the escarpment. Either way, I want them stopped before they reach it. You've got thirty minutes to get two platoons and all your automated troops into place on top of that ridge. Allocate your men as necessary to get that done. Use everybody else to guard the fleet and garrison the entrance to this base. Understood?"

"Yes, sir. I'm on it."

Before Brannon could even consider his next action, Stratman's frequency lit up the comm. "First Raptor's in flight, Colonel."

"Good. Get me eyes on those Chinese troops."

From somewhere deep within the bowels of the base came a long, low rumble.

◦◦《 ○ 》◦◦

Ana left the European commander to his duties. Why should he so much as give her the time of day when nobody else did? He hadn't even glanced at her. Probably thought he was talking to a child. No matter. He clearly had his own responsibilities to attend, though none could be more important than these civilians—not just the wounded and dying in the Plaza, but those who must be trapped in stale air pockets throughout Deep West. Only the commander and his troops had the manpower, muscle, and equipment they would need to move the tons of rock that undoubtedly lay between the living and the dying.

Ana could begin that task, at least. She sprinted up the stairs to the same balcony Major Ryan had spoken from earlier, her tiny legs taking the steps two at a time. At the top, she let loose a piercing whistle, trying to quiet the crowd that milled like cattle below. She whistled again, a long shrill noise that could not be ignored. When the air in her lungs gave out and the keen faded, everyone except Colonel Brannon's troops, several blocks down, seemed to have their eyes on Ana. *That's better.*

"Listen, everybody!" Her voice could be surprisingly loud when she needed it to be. "You." Out of the crowd, she picked a man standing near the entrance to the Sharp Shooter, deliberately selecting someone whom she didn't know personally.

The man looked around as if trying to determine who Ana might be pointing at. He was nicely dressed, though his fancy clothes had been just as ravaged by the disaster as everybody else's.

"You. In the maroon shirt…" She waited as he looked down at himself. "Yes, you. Go inside. Bring out everybody who's not doing anything. If they're sitting around and they're not injured, get them off their asses and out here. We *all* have work to do."

For once in Ana's life, everybody was listening, looking literally up to her. They were lost and confused. Nobody else was leading. Why shouldn't she?

"Look around you," she hollered to them, sweeping her hand in an all-encompassing gesture. Many—but not nearly enough—of the able men were searching the rubble for survivors. "People need our help. Not just here in the Plaza, but elsewhere in the base."

The man in the maroon shirt emerged from the casino with ten or twelve grumbling civilians. Some of them she knew. All looked reluctantly up as though they had no interest in her words. None of Simeon's uniformed staff were with them. Two of the men who knew her turned and went back inside.

Ana brought her hand down in an axe-like motion that split the crowd roughly in half. "Everybody from here over—" she swept her arm toward the right—"start at this end." She indicated the end farthest from Colonel Brannon and his men. No need to get in his way yet. "Search every building in the Plaza. Clear as much debris as necessary to make sure nobody's buried in the rubble. Then go on to the next building."

The crowd grumbled, but many people nodded as though they'd been more than willing to work, if only somebody had told them what to do.

"Take breaks individually, if you have to," Ana continued. "But don't stop the collective effort until you've found everybody. Dead or alive."

"Everybody else." She swept her hand over the left half of the crowd. "Search the base. If you know how to use a Geiger scanner—" surely in a crowd this size, somebody did—"grab one from an emergency station. Use materials from the buildings around here and shore up any unstable tunnels. Scour every business corridor, residence, warehouse, and facilities tunnel. Find everyone. If you know how to operate excavation equipment, stay put. If we find any intact and accessible, you'll have your work cut out for you." Zeke, when he made it back to the Plaza, would know where to look for such equipment, if the search parties didn't find it first.

Ana's audience was rapt. Was this leadership really coming out of the little-girl hooker from the Sundown? Why not? She'd always been capable of more than anyone ever gave her credit for, if they'd only given her a chance.

"Let's save some lives!"

110

Michael Kamieniechi—or Kamikaze Mike, as his men called him—split first platoon into squads. He assigned squad one to defend the solar array.

Mike and most of his troops had seen action before, on peacekeeping missions in those few corners of the world whose leaders had steadfastly resisted any form of civilized government but who weren't above requesting aid to maintain order. None of them, however, including Kamikaze, had any idea how to fight a war in low g and with no atmosphere.

"All right, men," Mike said on the encrypted EU channel. "Listen while you work. You all heard what we've got coming. The American forces have apparently been delayed or destroyed. We alone stand in the gap between every weapon China and Russia have deployed on Mercury and complete communist control of the solar system." He paused to let the gravity—and truth—of that statement sink in. "No pressure."

A few of his men released uneasy chuckles.

Mike allowed himself a grim smile. If the dipshit Americans were worth the fabric their uniforms were made out of, they'd be here right now, and Mike and his men wouldn't have to face the Chinese alone. *Assholes.* "It's likely to all go to shit before this is over, but that's the mission, and we'll get it done."

He took a deep breath. "Ready the mobile defense pylons first." They were the slowest fighting machines in the European arsenal.

In this case, the squads were way ahead of him. Immediately, the six pylons, each four meters tall and a meter square at the base, laden with sensor arrays and armed with machine guns, cannons, and mortars, lumbered northward on steel treads. Their operators drove them by short-range, infrared remote control, in a wide arc around the bomb crater. The rest of the twenty-man squad ran, in bounding strides, ahead to reconnoiter the array and to provide advance warning if the enemy arrived earlier than expected.

That was the extent of the attention Mike gave them. His job, first and foremost, was to lead the second and third platoons, over a hundred men, into battle.

Those men now unpacked their support troops, the combat-ready infantry robots for which, due to the elimination of the orbiting EU comm-sats, the men would have limited command and control capability. Nevertheless, Mike was counting on them to thin the first wave, and if possible, to take out the two armor units reported to be spearheading the enemy attack.

With the inventory in front of him, he directed the assignment of every piece of gear. To his right, two men hoisted an automated gunnery robot from its pallet, a job that would have required at least four soldiers on Earth. One man loaded a belt of 13mm ammunition into the magazine. Another inserted an umbilical for programming and manual control into the robot's data port. He drove it, on its fat, all-terrain wheels, to the tail end of a line of similar machines.

Two ships over, a team of infantry assembled the first of two surveillance and strike hover drones.

"Get that thing off the ground as soon as possible," Mike ordered the men. "I need to know how long we've got."

"Not long enough," somebody said through the comm.

Kamikaze didn't recognize the voice. "Pipe down."

Whoever had made the comment said nothing more, and within ten minutes, the drone was in flight and the entire column was moving out.

Behind them, a refueled Raptor, the second of six European space fighters, took flight.

⊰⟨○⟩⊱

Dana marched up to Colonel Brannon. His men had tried to stop her at the perimeter of his command post, but she outranked them all. It didn't really matter that her rank was in the US military and theirs European. In a joint mission, rank was rank. She had it. They didn't.

They let her pass.

"Colonel." She came to attention beside Brannon.

He didn't look up from the screens on his mobile command board. "What is it, Major?"

"Request permission to speak freely."

He turned to her, his face a mask of practiced calm. "Make it quick."

Dana relaxed her shoulders and met his gaze. "You haven't sent out search parties for Major Ryan."

"No. I haven't."

"Why?"

"I can't spare them."

Dana's heart tightened in her chest. She could actually feel her blood pressure climbing. "With all due respect, sir—" her voice was stiff with her effort to control it—"Major Ryan is the commander of our squadron."

"I'm aware of that."

"You need resources. Bill Ryan is one *hell* of a resource. Nobody can command the CATS wing like he can."

"Then I guess you'll have to do your best."

Dana studied his face. "Sir?"

"In Ryan's absence, you're the ranking CATS officer, are you not?"

"Yes, sir."

"That makes you the interim squadron commander. Do I need to remind you that until Colonel Davis arrives, this mission is mine?"

"No, sir. You don't."

"Good. Now, look at this." He pointed to one of the screens on his board, which showed a mass of human and robotic units advancing across Mercury's surface. "Our first surveillance drone just arrived at the enemy column, about halfway between here and Shenming. My men are forming up to stop them. But they're not enough. I need you and your crew engaged in that battle."

On the monitor, one of the men in the image shouldered a rocket launcher. A round streaked from it toward the drone. An instant later the screen went black.

"Gather your crew, Major. Refuel your ship. And get out there."

Dana stared at the screen and imagined bits of plastic and metal settling to the ground where the drone had been.

"That's an order," Brannon finished.

Dana snapped to attention. "Yes, sir." She spun on her heels, strode a few steps, and then turned back. "Colonel, you find Bill Ryan, you'll have one more CATS to support your troops." She hurried away, hailing her crew on the comm link in her ear.

Both responded immediately.

"Fuel up the *Snow Leopard*. We're being deployed."

"Deployed?" Miller said. "I didn't think Colonel Davis had landed yet—"

"He hasn't."

"Then with Major Ryan still missing—"

"Lieutenant Colonel Brannon is running the show. His men are forming up to oppose a ground force advancing from Shenming Base. Our orders are to provide air support for his troops."

"Where are his Raptors? Why doesn't he send out his own ships?"

"It wasn't my place to ask. Now get moving. I want the *Snow Leopard* refueled, resupplied, and ready to fly in thirty minutes." She sprinted in a sort of loping bob toward her gear and her crew.

When she and Miller stepped off the lift into the blazing sun, Allistair was already supervising a handful of men from a European support crew as they loaded crates of ammunition into the *Snow Leopard*'s hold. Miller climbed on board and began his preflight checklist.

The *Cheetah* stood nearby with a fuel umbilical attached to her hull.

"McCaughey to Duval. What's your status?"

"We came down pretty hard," the captain of the *Cheetah* replied. "Minor damage to the landing struts—nothing that'll keep us out of the fight. Refueling now. Estimate ready to launch in twenty minutes."

"Good. Have you heard from the *Jaguar* or the *Siamese*?"

"The *Jaguar* managed to achieve a stable orbit, but now she's coasting. Out of fuel. The *Siamese* has been wounded. She's lost vacuum integrity. By Davis's order, they're escorting his damaged troop ship the rest of the way in."

"Okay." Brannon had ordered Dana to support his men, but he had acknowledged her authority to command the CATS squadron. That left her some leeway, which she intended to use. "As soon as you're launch-ready, rendezvous with the *Jaguar*, perform an in-flight fuel transfer, and bring them down."

"Where will you be?" Duval was looking at her through the *Cheetah*'s windshield.

Dana pointed a little south of west, toward the road that led to Shenming Base. "Out there, flying cover for the European infantry—" Colonel Brannon had been right about one thing. His men would never defeat the advancing hoard without air support. The vision of the surveillance drone being destroyed by a single rocket round remained vivid in Dana's mind. "—For as long as we last."

Chapter 15

With Townsend a short step behind her, Carter moved toward the EU command station. She approached a private in Brannon's perimeter guard and pointed to his handgun. "Give me that." The private had a rifle slung over his shoulder. He wouldn't need both.

After his eyes flicked to her lieutenant's bar, he looked over his shoulder toward Colonel Brannon.

"Come on," Carter said. "I haven't got all day."

With a sigh, the private removed his sidearm and handed it to her.

"Thank you." Carter tucked the gun into her belt at the small of her back and led Townsend to the Sharp Shooter, where two triage nurses were assessing the mob of patients.

The diminutive hooker, Ana, stood in the doorway as if she alone could allow or deny entry. "How are we doing?" Carter asked her.

Ana glanced nervously at the emergency lighting. Carter had become so accustomed to their glow she'd forgotten they turned everything to blood until Ana drew her attention to them.

"I don't know how much longer the generators are going to last," Ana said.

"What about Simeon?" Townsend thrust his chin toward the open casino door. "He giving you any trouble?"

Ana chuckled aloud. "He thinks he is, and that suits me fine."

"What's he doing?" Carter asked.

"What he always does. Cheating people. I sent ten of the biggest men I could find to clear out every room in the hotel so the doctors could use them for the patients who've stabilized enough to move but need rest to recover." Ana glanced inside, as if to make sure Simeon was out of earshot. "Simeon's taking names and running tabs. He's thinks he'll be charging a whole night's rent for every hour of occupancy."

"Can he do that?" Townsend asked.

"Sure. It's his hotel. But I don't think he'll be able to collect the money. If it makes the man feel good…well…" She shrugged. "That's what I do best."

Carter looked over her head into the casino. "And his bouncers?"

"They're not here. Unfortunately, they're probably with your missing major."

"Yeah," Carter said. "Speaking of that, we need to have a chat with Simeon." She slipped past Ana, and Townsend followed her in.

They found Simeon behind the bar. He looked surprised for a moment before schooling his features into a pleasant smile. "What can I get you?"

"You mean besides our stolen supplies?" Carter spat the words at him.

"I'm sorry." He recoiled in mock indignation. "I feel badly that they were stolen from my hotel, but you had no permission to use the premises. Therefore, I can't possibly be held liable." He raised a bottle of rum and a margarita mixer. "If you'd like something from the—"

"We're not here to drink," Townsend said coldly.

Simeon looked from one airman to the other. "A room then? I still have a few on the—"

"Look, you son of a bitch—" Carter began. She stopped, not because of Simeon's raised hand, but because Townsend laid a restraining palm on her shoulder.

He stepped in front of her. "Where's Major Ryan? We know you're holding him."

"Me?"

"Your goons took him from outside the casino this morning."

"Kamo and Manu? If that's true, I had no idea. I haven't seen either of them for hours."

Ana strode over from the doorway. "Come on, Simeon. Everybody knows they don't do anything without your say-so."

"Look around you." Simeon spread his arms. "Half my staff quit when they found out what I'm charging for my rooms. But, hey, a guy's got to take advantage of the market."

"It's extortion," Ana said.

Simeon shrugged. "In any case, Kamo and Manu haven't shown up for work. How am I to know where they are? I have half a mind to fire them. When you find them, though, I hope you find your stolen belongings and your missing captain."

"He's a major," Carter said.

Simeon dismissed the distinction with a flap of his hand. "If you're not drinking and you're not checking into a room…the Sharp Shooter is for pay-ing customers only." He ran his fingers under the bar as if seeking a panic button.

Townsend's hand whipped out, grabbed Simeon by the collar—by his pressed bow tie—and hauled him bodily over the bar. The small man couldn't have weighed more than twenty-five kilograms in Mercury's grav-ity. He landed with a *whump*, flat on his back.

Carter snatched the pistol from her belt and pressed the barrel to Sime-on's beaklike nose.

He stared, eyes wide and frightened.

"You have one chance," Carter told him. "I'll go to prison for murder before I'll let you keep Bill Ryan."

⊸≼❨O❩≽⊹

There were three electrical junction boxes on the surface. Zeke would use the one in the old solar bunker to connect the north end of the cable to the old backup battery bank. The primary feed to base facilities, near the main landing pad, had been vaporized by the Russian attack. The auxil-iary feed, farther south, was still intact but sat dangerously near the edge of the crater.

The Geiger scan readings rose steadily as Zeke and Tanner crept toward this southern junction, and reached redline a hundred meters short of the box, with indications that radiation levels would continue to climb the clos-er they got. "Crap."

"Not going to make it?" Tanner asked.

"Not by a long shot." Zeke backed the cart away.

"Hold on," Tanner said. "Let me look up the specs on these pressure suits." He poked the stylus at the keys on his thinpad.

Zeke surveyed the terrain, which was fairly flat as far as the box. Beyond, deep within the radiation zone, the ground seemed to be littered with debris that was too uniform in size and shape to be shrapnel from the nuclear blast. In fact, each piece, no larger than an American football, looked like a stalled robot.

Tanner leaned over, read the display on Zeke's Geiger scanner, and poked some more. "With our EVA gear, we've got half an hour at this distance. Less the closer we get to that crater. How long we'll have at the junction depends on the radiation reading there."

"That include the radiation suits underneath?"

"Unfortunately, yes." He thought for a moment. "We can use readings out here, taken at various distances, to calculate the radiation level at the junction, assuming the center of the crater is ground zero. It should be accurate enough to tell us if it's worth making the attempt." As if they had a choice.

They'd need several readings to determine the shape of the radiation fall-off curve, but given enough data, they should be able to make a reasonable estimate. "We'll need a laser range-finder."

Tanner climbed out, pulled the range-finder from his toolbox, and handed it to Zeke.

Zeke tossed a coil of bright red wire onto the ground as a marker. Then he fastened the range-finder to the hood of the cart by its magnetic mount, aimed directly at the junction box. He had his thinpad but couldn't hope to be able to press the right buttons with his fat-fingered pressure gloves, so he dug a screwdriver from his tool belt to use as a stylus.

"Forget those," Tanner said. "You drive. Read off the distance every ten meters. I'll type it in, along with the radiation reading."

Zeke did, though it took precious time. He wasn't about to sacrifice himself in order to get base power turned back on. At least not until he knew there was no other way.

"Okay. That's good," Tanner said. "Plotting."

Zeke backed away farther, just to be sure, and then stopped the cart.

119

"Well?"

"Hang on. I'm trying extrapolation curves to see what kind of distribution gives me the best fit…oh, my."

"What is it?"

"Once you get to the junction box, you'll have four and a half minutes, give or take, depending on your overall health and susceptibility."

"To a lethal dose?"

"I used the median dose for acute population illness. I figure if you become incapacitated by radiation sickness in this crisis, the base has had it." Tanner paused. "For that matter, maybe I ought to do it. I can make an electrical connection just as well as the next guy, but I don't know the entirety of the base's systems as well as you do. If somebody's going to take this risk, it ought to be me."

"I don't know if it can be done in four and a half minutes."

"How about four minutes each? I'll get started, then haul out in four minutes, whether I'm done or not. You can finish."

"Sorry. These systems are my responsibility, as are you. I'm not going to let anybody else take this risk."

Tanner stared at him for a long time. For a moment, Zeke thought Tanner might actually try to stop him physically, despite the man's significantly slighter build. Finally, Tanner stepped from the cart. "You're the boss."

"Okay then." Zeke walked around to the toolboxes, unloaded and laid out everything he'd need, and checked the charge on the power tools. He pulled the trigger on his battery-powered screwdriver and watched it whir to life, ostensibly to make sure it was working but more to stall for time and to build up the nerve he needed to get started. Not only could the job take him five or six minutes, but Zeke wasn't as young and healthy as he used to be. He probably didn't have the whole four and a half minutes Tanner had figured as a population average.

And if he died out here, Ana would never forgive him.

⋙(O)⋘

Tanner stripped the ends of the cables to get them ready for connection and prayed silently that Zeke would have speed, dexterity, and skill—and that they would both survive the next few minutes. Then Zeke backed up slowly, giving himself room to build up as much speed as possible before hitting the radiation zone.

Tanner walked alongside. "I should go with you. I can hand you tools and watch the clock." As soon as Zeke stopped, Tanner wrapped his hand around a luggage tie-down loop and rested one foot on the cart's rear bumper.

"Watch the clock from back here," Zeke said. "Holler out my time every thirty seconds. I'm not willing to risk us both." He thumbed the cart into forward and floored the throttle.

Nothing doing. Zeke was going to need help. Tanner shifted his weight to the cart just as it started to move. God willing, Zeke would find out he was there after it was too late to argue.

The cart, designed for indoor use, didn't have any shock absorbers to speak of, and the clearance from the ground to the floorboards was minimal. It bumped and bounced with every pebble and rut it hit. A pair of pliers leapt from the seat and onto the ground. Tanner left them. He had a spare in his tool belt.

He started a stopwatch on his thinpad as they passed the coil of red wire Zeke had left to mark the radiation boundary.

When they reached the junction box, Zeke slammed down the brake and the cart skidded to a stop. "What the—"

By the time Zeke realized he was there, Tanner had the power screwdriver in his hand, extending it to Zeke. "Better get to work." *Lord, don't let him argue now.*

Without a word but with huffiness in his movements, Zeke snatched the tool and fitted it to one of the screws holding on the box's front cover. When he pulled the trigger, the screw spun loose and disappeared with a puff into the thick layer of radiation-contaminated dust at Zeke's feet. He ignored it and started on the next screw.

Tanner ran the procedure through his head, anticipating what Zeke would need next. "You've got three and a half minutes."

Zeke was fast. He removed all four screws and the front cover in the time it took Tanner to locate the Gauss driver. They traded tools and Zeke dove back into his work. He had to pull a second cover off, this one an interior panel that would expose the lugs he needed to tie power into.

Tanner readied the voltmeter so Zeke could verify that the lugs were indeed power-free, and therefore safe to work on.

The inner panel fell away.

"Three minutes."

"Not that." Zeke reached past Tanner to a wrench that had clattered to the floorboard during the short, mad drive to the box.

"Wait—" Tanner began. Just because the Plaza didn't have power didn't mean this box was dead. If it wasn't, Zeke's pressure suit wouldn't provide enough insulation to protect him from the voltage this junction would carry.

Apparently Zeke was willing to take the risk. He slammed the end of the wrench onto the first lug and began the arduous task of twisting it off, one third of a turn at a time. The position of the lugs didn't provide enough room to get a powered nut driver, or even a ratchet, onto it. It had to be done the hard way.

Zeke didn't jump and shudder when he touched the lug, so it must have been dead. Either that or he'd decided to attach the ground connection first.

"Two and a half minutes." If Tanner could have started on the second lug, it would have cut their time in half, but there wasn't room for both of them to work simultaneously. Instead, he climbed into the cart and turned it around so they could use the forward gear, rather than the slower reverse gear, to escape the radiation zone.

"Two minutes."

Had Zeke started on the second lug? Tanner couldn't tell. Zeke's body blocked the view. But it didn't matter. Tanner's next step was the same either way. He grabbed the end of the cable and his own pliers to replace the ones that had fallen from the cart.

"Ninety seconds."

Still, Tanner waited.

"Sixty."

Finally, Zeke reached back for the pliers and cable. He twisted the stripped ends onto the lugs and crimped them into place with the pliers. That would hold them long enough to tighten the nuts, which he must do if they expected the connection to carry the kind of current necessary to power Deep West. But it had taken too long.

If Zeke could get his fingers into the tight confines of the box to tighten the nuts, that would have been quicker, but there just wasn't room.

"Thirty seconds." What was keeping him?

"Hand me that." Zeke pointed to a shred of stripped wire lying on the passenger's floorboard of the cart.

"This?" It was too thin to handle any substantial current, just a scrap someone had left there.

Zeke made a frantic beckoning gesture and Tanner gave him the wire.

"Fifteen."

Within seconds, Zeke had wrapped it around his index finger, cinching the pressure suit tightly around the digit—which was now thin enough to reach the nuts. He shoved his finger in and spun each of the nuts until they rested against the newly connected cables.

Tanner's clock said four minutes. "We have to go."

Zeke gave each nut a final quarter turn with the wrench to snug it up against its contact, then dove into the passenger's seat.

Tanner floored the cart and they cleared the safe-zone marker at four minutes and thirty-eight seconds. "You suppose we ought to go down for a checkup?"

"No. The power first."

As they traded seats so Zeke could drive, Tanner had to stop and grab hold of the cart. He stood for a long three seconds, his insides churning. *Oh, Lord, not now.* His legs weakened and he collapsed to his knees.

CHAPTER 16

Kamikaze Mike pulled onto the top of the ridge some two clicks from Deep West on his command vehicle, an all-terrain four wheeler with a comm station and tactical display on the dash and an auxiliary tank of breathing air behind the seat. At the moment, the display was nothing but a field of white noise, and he wasn't willing to send up his only remaining surveillance drone until he'd neutralized the enemy rocket launchers.

The crater-ridden landscape that extended from there toward Shenming Base looked much like the plateau that stretched from the bottom of the cliff to Deep West—defensible, in its own way, but with numerous routes with the potential for enemy approach. Regardless, Mike had no intention of letting them anywhere near the ridge. Once there, they could throw anything and everything they had at the exposed convoy below.

Behind Mike, his company, such as it was, lumbered single-file up the steep, one-lane road that had been blasted out of the cliff face. It would take another twenty minutes, he guessed, to get the entire company to the top. *To hell with that.* He didn't have that kind of time.

As soon as the first squad had formed up—twenty men and nearly as many robotic troops, including a few with mounted machine guns, a rocket launcher, and a pair of high-explosive bomb bots for those bigger jobs that hand-thrown grenades couldn't handle—he put a lieutenant in charge of the remaining five squads and moved out with his twenty men to stop the hundreds that advanced against them.

It was suicide, but it had to be done. Besides, they didn't call him Kamikaze for nothing.

Mike drove his command cycle ahead, darting from crater rim to crater rim. At each crest, he stopped just short of the lip, climbed off the bike, and crawled to the top. With only the tip of his bubble-helmet exposed, gray in Mercury's washed-out landscape, he spied the region ahead for some sign of the approaching enemy.

Whenever his own men caught up, he returned to his bike and zipped ahead to the lip of the next crater.

By the third time he repeated the process, his tactical station had begun receiving a live feed from one of the Raptors in orbit. He keyed the comm in his helmet and synced it to the transmitter on the bike. "Kamikaze to Raptors. Pan out far enough for me to see both Shenming and Deep West."

He didn't receive a verbal response, but the display changed in compliance with his request. Once he had the two bases as landmarks, he overlaid a topographical map of Mercury from a database stored on a chip in his tactical board. That gave him the complete picture. "Now zoom back in so I can see the troops."

Again the display complied without so much as a "yes sir" from the asshole on the other end of the comm.

"Hold it there." Now he could pan and zoom within the image, using the functions on his own board. He did so in order to get a detailed look at the forces coming at him.

An array of light robotic infantry with a variety of weaponry led the way, with the two tanks behind them. Mike studied the deployment for a long time. He didn't see a human operator paired up with each of the RIs, as Mike's own men were. Therefore, the Chinese commander was using a remote station and satellite control, which the European Union had intended to do until China had wiped out every EU satellite in orbit. If the Chinese controllers had state-of-the-art equipment—and Mike had to assume they did—then they were transmitting the instructions via orbital laser, difficult to intercept and impossible to jam. And, with no cloud cover to disrupt the beam, the technology was ideal for use on Mercury.

Kamikaze and his men had no such luxury. They had to rely on line-of-sight infrared programming from the ground or standard radio broadcasting, which would almost certainly be jammed as soon as the two armies collided.

His breathing heavy in his ears, Mike studied the display until his squad caught up again. By then, the enemy was close. "Line the machine guns and rocket launcher along that ridge." He pointed toward a berm at the edge of the long, shallow crater in front of them. "Except Carstairs and McNair. You two to my right."

The machine gun infantry bots were little more than a set of six tires with a mounted gun, vid-scanner, sensors, and sophisticated pattern recognition and data analysis software, all packaged into a unit the size of an end table. He parked them among the rocks and on the lee side of the crater rim, so only their vid-scanner and gun barrels were exposed. The men operating them stayed out of the line of fire, using the robots' video feed to target them.

When the enemy's robots rolled into the open, Mike and his men opened fire.

⸙⟨◯⟩⸙

Bill Ryan yanked again on the eyebolt that anchored his cuffed wrists to the wall. The frequent bombardment of microwaves from the Lancaster would eventually take its toll on the metal. *Sooner or later it'll make it—*

The metal snapped.

—brittle.

Bill stumbled forward in the darkness, his wrists still chained together. From their weight, the eyebolt wasn't dangling from them. The little S-shaped piece that connected the chain to the eyebolt must have finally given up.

Now what? He'd hoped the cuffs themselves, or the chain between them, would break. As it was, even if he could somehow overpower Simeon's thugs in his weakened state, he couldn't don a pressure suit with his hands cuffed together. His only hope was that he could overpower them *and* that they would bring a key to the cuffs with them, which seemed unlikely. Simeon was no idiot. He wouldn't let his cronies walk around with the key.

What else could Bill do? He felt his way to the door and sat down in the darkness beside it.

He had no idea what time it was, or how long it had been since his last drink of water. Or since his last beating, for that matter. He *did* know it had been at least twenty-two days since he'd seen Dana. He was determined to see her again, one way or another. So, with her image set firmly in his mind, he waited.

And waited.

And waited.

Finally, he heard the creak of metal as someone spun the ship's-wheel door handle, and he hopped to his feet. When the door opened, light from a stolen air force lantern blazed into the room, blinding Bill's unadjusted eyes until he could discern nothing more than the bulk of a man shining in the doorway.

He balled one fist into the opposite hand and swung his hands at the man's faceplate, as if they were a club. *Crack.* The cuffs carved into his charred wrists and he had to bite his lip to avoid blacking out from the pain.

The shape in the doorway fell backwards. The man—unconscious, if Bill was lucky—was shoved forward from behind and two more figures entered the room. So much for luck. This time Simeon was with them. Come to gloat one more time before his thugs finished Bill off.

Sure enough, the smallest figure of the three, Simeon, held a pistol. Apparently he was through messing around with the Lancaster.

Bill rushed him before he could bring the gun to bear. Fortunately, the small man was light and unprepared. He went down under Bill's weight, and the gun clattered to the stone floor.

Rather than attack, the third man reached up and snapped off his fishbowl helmet. "Bill! It's okay."

The voice was familiar. Pinning Simeon to the ground with one elbow, Bill looked up. As his eyes began to adjust, he recognized Lieutenant Townsend, his own gunner, collecting the dropped pistol.

"You okay?" Townsend asked.

Bill looked down at Simeon. He couldn't see through the faceplate, but the name patch on the pressure suit read CARTER. The insignia of the Air Force Space Command adorned one sleeve. The CATS patch adorned the other.

"Lindsey?" Bill looked at Townsend for confirmation. If Carter was in the suit, she couldn't communicate without activating her external microphone, and Bill had no intention of giving her that kind of freedom until he knew for sure.

"Yeah. That's her."

Bill let her up. "Who's that, then?" he asked Townsend.

Townsend had the pistol trained on the figure he'd shoved into the room, who now stood against the far wall, where Bill had been chained for God knew how long. "Take your helmet off," he told the man.

Slowly, Simeon did as he was told.

As soon as Bill saw his face, a guttural rage boiled beyond his control. A primal scream rose from his parched throat, and he threw himself at the man.

Townsend snatched his arm. In Bill's weakened state, it took little to restrain him.

He spun on Townsend, his heart pounding in his temples. His jaw clenched so tightly it ached. "Let! Go!"

Townsend shook his head.

"That's an order!"

Again, Townsend shook his head.

Bill took a deep breath. Townsend had left him with only two choices. Either allow insubordination within his ranks, which he couldn't do—it would undermine his ability to lead—or set his friend up for execution. "Insubordination is a court martial offense."

Townsend's voice was calm, sure. "Not this time."

Bill's eyes narrowed as he studied his friend's face.

"The order is unlawful," Townsend said.

Carter climbed to her feet and removed her own helmet. "The air's thin in here."

Bill ignored her, his focus entirely on Townsend. "How is letting go of me unlawful?"

"You're ordering me to let you commit a crime."

Bill said nothing.

"You do intend to kill him. Do you not?"

Bill nodded.

"I can't let you do that. But I have an idea I think you'll like just as much."

CHAPTER 17

Two dozen Chinese robotic infantry crawled across the crater floor toward Mike's position. The small-caliber machine gun robots along Mike's defense opened fire, but most of the rounds bounced off armor plates that protected the working parts of the incoming machines.

Mike keyed his comm. "Anders, see what you can do with those bots in the valley."

Anders, who controlled the single high-caliber cannon in Mike's advance squad, crawled his robot to the top of the crater rim. Huge flashes exploded silently from the RI's muzzle. In half-second intervals, showers of purple sparks flew from one of the advancing bots. Three hits, four, five. Finally, the machine stopped. Black smoke gathered like fog around it.

One down, but the rest had already closed half the distance. Mike continued to pour down rifle fire, glancing up periodically to make sure a second wave hadn't descended the rim behind the first.

Suddenly, a dust cloud erupted a few meters from Mike's head. Dirt and rocks pelted his helmet. A cannon round. *Shit!* The RI that had launched it almost had him pegged.

He ducked behind the berm, rolled along the hillside to his right, and scrambled back to the top. By then, Anders had knocked out two more of the enemy. Three or four of the RIs in Mike's company appeared to be dead as well. His men had taken up their rifles and fought alongside the robotic units they commanded.

"Use hand grenades," Mike yelled. He'd hoped to save them for use against human troops—shrapnel would be particularly deadly against men in pressure suits—but the advancing robots left him no choice.

Most of his men initially misjudged the gravity. Mike's first grenade overshot his target by a good twenty meters. Two of the advancing bots, however, succumbed to a second wave of grenades.

"I'm hit!" a voice called over the comm.

Anders yelled, "Man down!"

Smoke and light, but no heat, no sound, and no blast waves from the explosions. The whole thing was surreal. The void made it feel like a three-D sim game with the sound turned off.

"Heads down!" Mike yelled, just as machine gun fire raked the hill in a wave from his left. He dove, headfirst, for cover, flinging his arms up to protect his faceplate as he hit the ground and tumbled down the hill. The impact blew the air from his chest. When he stopped, his eyes sought the vacuum integrity light inside his helmet. It remained green.

Cries of, "Medic!" rang out through his comm, but there was nothing a medic could do for a man in a pressure suit. Several of his men were down. Others scrambled to apply vacuum tape to those whose suits had been compromised, though the wounded would likely bleed to death before they made it back to Deep West for aid.

Above them, his RIs continued to rake the enemy, following the last command they'd received.

Mike scrambled to his tactical display and scanned it for evidence of an enemy flanking maneuver. None. In truth, there seemed no need for any. Because China still had satellites in orbit, their information would be more reliable than Mike's own. It also meant the Chinese had a tactical overhead display. With only twenty men and a few robots to face, the enemy had every reason to believe they could simply plow through Mike's squad. And they probably could.

When he crawled back to the ridge, advancing infantry, maybe ten robots, were climbing the last few meters to the top of the EU-defended rise.

Mike froze. Robotic infantry usually couldn't pick out a target from the landscape unless it moved. And then, whether the moving object was recognized as an enemy—as opposed to a friend or civilian—depended on the parameters programmed into its threat-detection algorithm.

Yet that didn't rule out the possibility of a Chinese soldier spotting him in a real-time satellite image and targeting a bot manually. Either way, Mike was hardest to see if he remained motionless. The men of his squad, all trained in combat tactics against automated troops, did the same.

His own infantry robots stopped shooting at the nearest Chinese machines. According to their targeting parameters, anything closer than twenty meters and anything behind them they left for human troops or for the next wave of RIs to identify and destroy. That was the surest way to keep the European robots from shooting at European soldiers. Instead, they targeted the next wave of the enemy advance, which had begun to crawl its way across the crater floor.

"Second squad, what's your position?" Mike whispered into the comm. He needn't have lowered his voice in the vacuum, but old training habits took hold.

"Two clicks behind you."

Mike made a quick count of the robots that had slipped past his line. "Automated infantry headed your way. Nine units. Can I trust you with them?"

"No worries. We'll be ready."

"In that case, we'll hold tight and hit the second wave."

◄◊《 ○ 》◊►

By the time Bill reached the Plaza, his crew had filled him in on what they knew of Deep West's military status. And with the comm relay now up and running, it took only a moment for him to contact the *Cheetah* and learn what the CATS were up to. He could not, however, reach Colonel Davis or anyone else in the troop ship.

He marched up to Lieutenant Colonel Brannon, snapped to attention, and saluted. "Major Ryan reporting for duty, sir." The effort was more painful than he'd expected, especially in his gut, where the muscles had taken much of Kamo and Manu's beatings. His wrists, their blackened skin flaking off and the surrounding tissue blistered and seeping, still burned, but that particular hurt had been with him so constantly that it now seemed natural.

Brannon examined his battered face, his scorched and bleeding wrists, and finally his disheveled flight suit before returning the salute. "Report to the Sharp Shooter and have your wounds dressed."

"I understand the CATS have been deployed into combat."

"That's correct."

"With all due respect, sir, the *Black Panther* should be with them."

"That's my decision. And you're in no shape to fly. Now get those wounds taken care of so you'll be ready to launch when I do need you."

"But—"

Brannon's expression hardened. "That's an order."

"Yes, sir." Bill spun on his heal, a move that made his face throb and his head swim.

"You two," Brannon told Carter and Townsend, "refuel your ship and get her ready to fly. Major Ryan's right. I'm going to need her in the fight."

A smile touched Bill's face when he overheard the order. He had no intention of sitting this one out when any of his crews, especially Dana's, were in the line of fire.

"I've been ordered to report for medical care," he said, walking up to Ana, who stood in the doorway to the Sharp Shooter, the same place she'd been when he first met her. Only now, she was facing outward. She'd become the gatekeeper for Simeon's hotel. Bill almost wished Simeon was here to see it.

Ana's face darkened with concern. "Look what he's done to you."

"I'll be okay."

"Where is he?"

"Simeon?"

Ana nodded.

Bill's crew had removed the shackles with Simeon's key and used them to cuff his own hands together. They'd dismantled the compressed O_2 apparatus that Kamo and Manu had rigged up in a short section of compromised corridor to serve as a makeshift airlock. That way Simeon's thugs couldn't get back in to free their boss.

"He's holed up in the same dungeon he was using for me."

Ana looked into his eyes and then examined the whole of his face. She took his hands in hers and turned them over, inspecting the charred and split skin on his wrists.

"I'll be right back." She returned a few minutes later with a triage nurse.

Apparently Bill was worse off than he felt. The nurse bumped him to the front of the line.

"Surely there are people here with more urgent needs than mine," Bill began. "If Ana asked—"

"Wait here. The doctor will see you shortly." She began to walk away.

Bill grabbed her arm. "I'm serious. If Ana asked you to let me go first..." Something in the nurse's eyes stopped him.

"Have a seat." She motioned to one of the restaurant chairs that had been lined up in front of the hotel for waiting patients, then crouched beside him. "Some of those burns are third degree."

"Yeah, but—"

"Burns are particularly prone to infection, especially since you've managed to tear most of the skin off yours." She lowered her voice. "We don't have nearly enough antibiotics to handle this scale of crisis, so we need to prevent infection where we can. If those burns turn gangrenous, you'll lose your hands."

Bill said nothing. He couldn't speak. He felt as though his pummeled diaphragm had caught in his throat.

Just then, a doctor appeared at the door and ushered him into the casino.

It didn't take long for the man to clean his wrists. The medical staff seemed to be using whiskey to clean most of the wounds, but for Bill they broke out the good stuff—genuine isopropyl alcohol. When he poured it over the burns, Bill screamed with a pain sharper and deeper than he'd experienced from the glowing metal that had made them. He nearly passed out. Then the doctor began to scrub them with sterile gauze. The pain grew worse as he worked, but with the initial shock of the alcohol behind him, Bill was able to limit his reaction to clamping his teeth and grunting at each touch. After several eternal minutes, the doctor slathered his burns with a pain-killing ointment, wrapped the wounds, and treated the cuts on his face with dermaplast. "You need dermal regeneration. Come back in a couple of hours, once this line goes down." He asked Ana to take him to the bar to get him some clean water to drink.

Bill staggered through the doorway and took an empty seat at the counter. In the mirror, he saw his own face for the first time since he'd been abducted. His skin was stretched taut over purple bruises, giving his flesh the translucent blue color of raw shrimp. It was amazing, the kind of pain the human brain could ignore when more serious hurts demanded its attention.

◈《〇》◈

When Zeke pulled onto the plateau near the solar array, a pylon, maybe twice as tall as a man, stood in the road. It whipped around, bringing to bear weaponry that ranged from a machine gun, to a high-caliber cannon, to what looked like a rocket-propelled grenade launcher, all trained on Zeke's harmless little luggage cart.

Zeke yanked his foot off the throttle and threw his hands into the air, where they could be seen by the scanner peering down at him from atop the pylon. The lens twisted this way and that, as if trying to focus, or to zoom in, on Zeke.

He sat, eyes wide, and stared at the thing, waiting to see what it would do.

"Good gracious." Tanner was draped listlessly beside him, not really having recovered from his bout with radiation sickness. "Where did that thing come from?"

Zeke didn't reply, afraid to move or speak.

"State your business," a voice said over the comm.

"I'm Zeke Shepherd. I'm the facilities manager for Deep West. I need to get to the old solar science bunker so I can restore power to the base."

The voice didn't respond. The scanner swung slightly to the right, examining the back set of seats. The trailer and spools of cable were gone. Zeke and Tanner had left them down by the base, where they'd more likely be needed, but whoever was on the other end of the scanner would be able to see their toolboxes.

Several seconds later, the weaponry spun away. The scanner remained trained on the cart.

"Proceed," the voice said.

Zeke drove cautiously as he approached the bunker.

A soldier guarding the open doorway raised his rifle. "That's far enough."

Zeke came to a stop.

"Step away from the cart."

Carefully, Zeke and Tanner climbed out, keeping their hands in sight at all times, and backed twenty meters away. Tanner stumbled but managed to keep his feet.

The guard inspected the toolboxes and floorboard before finally giving them permission to enter.

Once inside, Zeke moved to the aged disconnect panel and the raw electrical leads he'd tied to the piping nearby. Tanner walked all the way around the battery bank, as though seeking something.

"What are you looking for?" Zeke asked him.

"A shepherd's hook, or something else insulated that I can use if you... you know. God forbid."

"Don't bother. There's enough voltage in this circuit that if I get hung up on it, I'll be crisp before you can blink. It'll probably short the battery bank as well. Hell, as old as it is, the whole thing could explode."

Tanner eyed the switch for a long time.

"I want you outside this time," Zeke said. "No chances. The base can't afford to lose both of us."

Tanner hesitated. "You sure about this? That's a touchy connection."

Zeke shook his head. He wasn't sure of anything, except that Deep West needed power or everyone in the base would suffocate as soon as the generator ran out of fuel. Fortunately, the polarization of his visor would prevent Tanner from seeing the doubt on his face. "I mean it. You stay out this time."

Again, Tanner didn't answer right away. "All right."

"Promise?"

"Okay. I deserved that."

"Swear to God."

"The Bible says, 'Above all, my brothers and sisters, do not swear—not by heaven or by Earth or by anything else.' But my promise is good."

Zeke knew the man well enough to know that was the best he was going to get. But he also knew Tanner's word was good. "Out, then."

As soon as he was alone, Zeke turned to the massive bulk of the antique battery bank that hunched in the middle of the bunker, looking too much like an adversary, daring Zeke to press it back into service after a decades-long sabbatical.

"Come on, old lady. Let's do this and be done with it."

⋘◯⋙

Just as the remnants of the first wave of Chinese infantry reached a crater rim about a half a kilometer behind Kamikaze Mike, the majority of the EU infantry topped the ridge and wiped them out.

"Get up here!" Mike hollered to them.

Three squads, nearly sixty soldiers and their robotic infantry support, made a loping sprint forward. They were none too soon. Mike and the few men he had left, maybe half a dozen, with about as many RIs, fired a steady rain of bullets at the far crater rim, trying to hold at least fifty Chinese troops—nearly all of them robots—at bay.

Then the enemy artillery started. "Cover!" Mike yelled. Others echoed the call as everyone dove behind whatever hummock they could find.

At first the barrage was nothing more than a series of silent explosions behind Mike's line, until three of his advancing men disappeared in a single blast, their pressure suits shredded by shrapnel, their RIs silent and still, awaiting instructions from men who no longer lived.

Mike had no time to check the tactical board on his command cycle. He scrambled to a comrade, snatched the thinpad from his dead hand, and examined the display. It showed the view from a scanner mounted on a machine-gun-equipped RI, which was still targeting muzzle flares from the opposing line.

Two of his own men began to back down the rise.

"Hold your position," Mike yelled. "Mortar teams, take out that next ridge."

The machine gun Mike had been operating blew up into a shower of sparks and pieces. A ragged scrap of the barrel landed, smoking, in the regolith, three centimeters from his knee. Moments later, an RI farther down the line exploded.

"Come on!" he called to his troops over a din of overlapping oaths, curses, counter-commands from the squad leaders, and the cries of the dying. "Move it! Move it!"

As the last of his own line formed up along the ridge, Mike dared a peek over the top. Several gaps had formed in the opposing line, black stretches of nothing but stars along the horizon where a solid line of muzzle flashes used to be.

That's when the first tank rolled over the hill, the engine and treads shaking the ground as it did. A low rumble worked its way up through Mike's elbows and knees into his suit.

"Shit." Mike scrambled back to a dead RI unit that, when it was working, had launched rocket-propelled grenades. He disconnected the launcher, already loaded, and sprinted over the hill, jumping as high as he could when he cleared the top. The ridge beneath him erupted with spewed regolith as an enemy RI strove to target him with its machine gun.

"Mike!" someone yelled into the comm.

"What's he doing?" another voice asked.

Mike moved as quickly as possible. Each time he touched the ground, he leapt up in a trajectory that he hoped seemed random but that moved him relentlessly toward the enemy line. With each leap, his legs strained for altitude. The automated targeting software of the RIs was likely written for Earth engagements, without having taken into account the height Kamikaze could achieve here. And if his own men had programmed the European RIs properly, they would target objects approaching only *from* the west, not those moving away *toward* the west. Still, he'd have to plant himself somewhere out of the line of fire soon, before one of the Chinese human soldiers took over manual control of one of the robots. If a single bullet so much as grazed his pressure suit, it would all be over, at least for him.

Meanwhile, the tank's path remained perfectly straight. It had been hit with several grenades and high-caliber rounds, but the armor on the front of the thing was made of no lightweight composite and was simply too thick. It must have cost a fortune to transport from Earth. No wonder they'd brought only two of them.

A small hummock just ahead of Mike lay directly in the tank's path. It was within the line of sight of several enemy guns, but if he played this just right...

Behind him, one of the squad commanders ordered a suicide bomb bot over the hill to intercept the tank. Good. It never hurt to have a backup plan, just in case.

137

The next time Mike came down, he tucked his arms in, one across his stomach holding the grenade launcher, the other over his head to protect his faceplate. He threw his legs out to the side and hit the ground with one knee and hip. He took an awkward tumble and came down flopping, he hoped like a dead fish. As he rolled to a stop, flat on his back, he let the grenade launcher slip from his hand to land about a meter away.

Without moving anything but his eyes, he checked the status of his suit and waited for the enemy to rake him with gunfire. His lights shown green, though he'd already spent more than half his air in the battle. The bullets never came. His ruse had apparently worked. The enemy must think him dead.

"Mike's down," someone yelled.

"Then I'm up," his lieutenant replied. "And we're going to hold this line."

Mike peered out the edge of his faceplate and located the demolition bot that had been sent over the hill. It sat smoking, not ten meters from where it had come into enemy view. So much for plan B.

With the battle raging over him, from ridge top to ridge top, Mike waited. Eventually the tank rumbled out of sight, beyond the hummock. The ground's vibrations continued to grow as the beast edged closer. Finally, the gun barrel came into view, followed by the treads.

Mike surged to his knees and snatched up the rocket launcher. The chest of the tank became visible between the treads, followed by the belly of the beast. At nearly point-blank range, Mike pulled the trigger.

The rocket-propelled, armor-piercing round punched through the softer skin of the tank's underside and exploded.

There probably weren't any human troops inside, but that didn't matter. The blast would pulverize any electronics and the heat would slag the wiring. At the top of the hummock, the tank canted forward and settled to a stop.

Its dead hulk provided Mike with cover from the machine guns on the enemy ridge, but he'd brought only the one round. He had nothing left for the second tank, which had just lumbered into view.

CHAPTER 18

The *Snow Leopard* cleared the horizon, and the battle blazed into view below. European infantry huddled behind the rim of a vast, shallow crater. Along the opposite rim, a row of Chinese machine gun RIs peppered the EU troops, covering the RIs that were advancing across the crater floor. The Chinese robotic troops alone outnumbered all of the Europeans by three or four to one.

And right in the middle of it all, a single armored tank lumbered past the burned-out hulk of another, its cannon systematically blowing out large chunks from the berm that was supposed to be protecting the Europeans.

"Take out that tank," Dana ordered, just as its cannon swung toward the *Snow Leopard*.

A pair of missiles streaked from beneath the ship, and the tank exploded before it could bring its cannon to bear.

But there were other dangers down there.

"Pull up!" Dana yelled.

Miller yanked on the stick and the *Snow Leopard* jerked into a steep climb. Dana kept her vid-scanner trained on the battlefield below, selecting their next target.

"That's a hell of a firefight down there," Allistair observed.

"That's why we're here," Dana said. "Bring us around for another pass." This time they wouldn't have the element of surprise. This time they'd likely go the way of the hover drone. Nevertheless, they would do what must be done.

139

The ship leveled out and made a wide loop back to the battle.

"There. Along the ridge." Dana zoomed the display in on the Chinese-held rim of the crater. Attacking the robots there, those covering the advancing RIs, might keep the *Snow Leopard* out of the line of fire while neutralizing a threat the ground troops couldn't reach.

Miller lined up for the pass and Allistair opened up with both guns. Dana could do nothing but hang on to her seat and watch her status board for signs of danger.

When they completed the pass, about a third of the RIs along the rim had gone still. The remaining guns continued to light with a rapid display of muzzle flares.

"Again," Dana said.

This time, halfway through the pass, another wave of Chinese troops topped a ridge farther west. Machine gun fire raked one of the *Snow Leopard*'s wings as Miller banked away. The vacuum integrity light remained green. The crew cabin hadn't been breached, but the ship wobbled.

"Hold her steady," Dana said. They were way too close to the ground to lose control now.

A sharp crack vibrated through the structure and sounded in the cabin. The *Snow Leopard* spun out of control, into a tight corkscrew spiral.

"Steady!" Dana shouted.

"I'm trying," Miller yelled back. But the rotation picked up speed.

Vertigo whipped through Dana's mind like madness. For the first time since she'd entered the CATS program six years before, she had to close her eyes to keep from vomiting in her pressure suit. "Report." She forced the word out through gritted teeth.

"The port thruster's fuel line has been hit." Alistair's voice was calm enough to steady Dana's nerves a little. "We're venting fuel on that side. There's no way to stop it as long as the fuel's still flowing. We need to transfer everything to the starboard tank."

"Do it." Dana's eyes remained closed. "Miller, keep us off the ground."

"Like I said, I'm trying."

Dana opened her eyes. Immediately she understood Miller's problem. The ground whipped around them so fast that the whole scene looked like a uniform gray blur, halfway between the shade of Mercury's surface and the deep black of space. Any adjustment in course would just as likely take them toward the ground as away from it. The best Miller could do was hold a straight line until all the fuel was transferred, and then try to stabilize the spin.

The image in the rear scanner looked a lot like Dana felt—the constant g from the spin had begun to darken the edges of her vision. Similarly, the ground whipped by so quickly that the edges of the scan display were blurred.

Dana blinked slowly and tried to focus on the central, clear part of the image. It seemed to be clouded with smoke. Right in the middle, a rocket-propelled grenade was flying straight up their ass.

With no other choice, Dana triggered the exploding bolts on the cockpit door. The cabin air pressure blew it out, and the stream of atmosphere caused the *Snow Leopard* to lurch to the side. Any direction would do, as long as it wasn't straight down.

As the grenade streaked past the opening, Dana held her breath. They would either hit the ground or they wouldn't. The rest was up to Miller.

"That's it," Allistair said, maybe two minutes—maybe twenty minutes—later.

Miller began to apply a slight counter-rotating thrust from the starboard side, and the spiral began to slow.

Then Dana asked, "Can you even get her onto the ground with only one thruster?"

⊰⟨○⟩⊱

Colonel Brannon watched on the real-time image streaming down in shifts from his six orbiting Raptors as the Chinese forces steamrolled over his own men. Kamieniechi and his men were making a good show of it. They'd eliminated over half of the enemy RIs, but the automated European units were almost gone and the Chinese had cut deep into the human ranks as well. Kamieniechi simply didn't have enough left to stop them.

Static blasted from the comm speaker, drawing Brannon's attention away from the horrifying display. For a loud moment, he stared at the blaring speaker. Then he keyed the comm. "Who's there?"

When he let up on the button, the static had vanished and silence prevailed. He shrugged, turned back to the display, and zoomed in on Kamieniechi. The captain was engaged. There was no way he was trying to report in at that particular moment.

The battle was hopeless. Brannon considered sending in some or all of the orbiting Raptors, but even they wouldn't be enough at this point, and it would cost him his only source of real-time information. He would lose his ability to command beyond that one, final order to the Raptors.

The speaker squealed again. Maybe it was some sort of Chinese jamming signal that still originated from too far away to have more than a momentary impact on Deep West's communications.

Brannon's mind returned to the Raptors. Should he give the order? It was a desperate thing to do, and it would serve no purpose but futility, but he had no other options. And if he was going to do it, he had to do it while there were still men on the ground to support.

As he keyed the link to give the order, the lights in Deep West—the big, blazing, overhead lights—came on. They shone down on the wreckage, giving the Plaza a sudden stark whiteness. A cheer rose from every throat in the giant cavern.

Apparently the comm receiver at the pole had come online as well. The speaker on Brannon's command board blared to life. "Colonel Davis to Deep West Base, come in. Does anybody read me?"

Half stunned, Brannon thumbed the mike. "This is Brannon. It's good to hear from you, Colonel. What's your status?"

"Thank heavens someone's there." Davis' voice was hoarse. "We're approaching Deep West. We should clear the horizon in a few minutes. Ship's damaged beyond repair, but we have a hundred twelve souls on board. All ready to fight."

"Good. We need them. China's coming at us, and we haven't got enough men to stop them. I'm afraid even yours might not be enough. We've got your robotic infantry down here, but without central control..." He paused. "My men have been split between trying to operate their RIs and fighting for themselves. It's just not enough."

"Look," Davis said. "We have an orbital command-and-control system, but the ship carrying it was damaged. It went down on the surface. If we can recover it, we might be able to deploy it with one of the CATS."

"All right. Where's this ship of yours located?"

"Sending coordinates now."

A moment later, another voice broke the silence. "Colonels, this is Major McCaughey on the *Snow Leopard*. We've been knocked out of the ground battle. The ship will barely fly, but as luck would have it, we're headed in the general direction of those coordinates. With your permission, we'll try to locate that comm gear."

"Permission granted with pleasure," Davis replied. "Brannon, we're on approach now. See you in a few minutes."

⊷⟨O⟩⊷

"What's this?" Chou asked when his intelligence officer handed him a thinpad.

"An enemy transmission we intercepted just after they reactivated their comm tower at the pole."

Chou's smile broadened when his cryptography team played back the unscrambled exchange between Davis, McCaughey, and Brannon.

"How long ago?"

"Eighteen minutes."

Chou's gaze shot toward the lieutenant, the corners of his mouth turned up in a begrudging grin. To crack an enemy code in just eighteen minutes... The lieutenant shrugged. "They used an old EU cipher."

Chou nodded. Just as he wouldn't divulge China's latest encryption algorithms to Russia, even to facilitate secure communications, the US and EU weren't using their most recent codes when talking to one another. International communications were tricky that way.

"We got lucky," the lieutenant said. "They used an algorithm we'd already broken."

That alone was worrisome. "They could have used that code deliberately, knowing we'd intercept it."

"Yes, sir. That's possible."

With a nod, Chou studied the written transcript, which detailed the importance and location of a downed American cargo ship. The coordinates were remote. Little would be gained from a false lure to that location, other than temporarily diverting one of Chou's Marauders. He handed the thinpad to the corporal at the satellite control station. "Give me a visual of these coordinates."

Surprisingly, a ship *had* crashed there. And the *Snow Leopard* was on approach to the site. If it was a ruse and the *Snow Leopard* was prepared to fight, a Marauder should be able to handle it.

He thumbed the comm. "Are my Marauders ready to fly?"

"Yes, sir," his wing commander replied. "Both of them. Crews are standing by."

"Excellent." Chou relayed the intercepted transmission. "Launch one to these coordinates. Destroy the American fighter and bring me their communication module. I want it on my desk."

"It's probably as big as your desk, sir."

Chou's smile widened. "So much the better."

CHAPTER 19

"Easy now," Dana said as Miller used the starboard thruster to slow the spin of the *Snow Leopard*. They would get only one shot at this. With the port thruster offline, if the ship began to roll the other direction, there'd be no way to reverse it.

Miller tapped the controls again and the spin came nearly to a stop. It was touchy. The ship went past level and took five minutes to come upright again.

One more nudge, and she settled in.

"Nice," Allistair said.

"Couldn't have done it better myself," Dana agreed.

That's when Colonel Davis's message came over the comm.

Dana checked her navigation display. The *Taurus* wasn't too far off their current trajectory, so she fed the coordinates to Miller's terminal. "Can we make it?"

"I think so."

"I don't want to know what you think. Can we make it or not?"

Miller punched a variety of calculations into his board, analyzing thrust vectors and fuel consumption estimates. "We can make it."

Dana keyed the comm and got permission to locate the *Taurus*. Twelve minutes later, Miller began to decelerate. At this point, altitude control came from a combination of velocity and gravity. The result was a long, shallow, airplane-style landing at an incredible speed. Once the wheels touched down, he coasted to a stop and taxied back to the shattered freighter.

Dana handed Allistair a thinpad that displayed the markings of the crate containing the RI command-and-control module, information she'd just received from Colonel Davis. "You look for that. We'll assess the damage and call for a ride, if necessary."

Miller climbed out the hatch and onto the *Snow Leopard*'s wing, while Dana dug the toolbox out from under Allistair's seat. There wasn't much in it, just the basics: screwdrivers, wrenches, sockets, pliers, wire strippers and cutters, and a battery-powered drill, all clamped onto a tool belt. A drawer beneath the unused passenger seat contained a small variety of clamps, fasteners, nuts, bolts, washers, gaskets, and a generous supply of the all-important vacuum sealing tape, all of which had been provided in the vain hope that if something broke in space, it might actually be possible to fix it in flight.

She leapt from the open hatch to the barren landscape below, a drop much too high to have braved in an Earthlike gravity, and walked around the *Snow Leopard*. Bullet holes perforated the wing and tail. What mattered, though, was whether or not the port thruster's fuel line could be repaired. By the time she reached the far side, Miller was waiting on the wing, nearly six meters above her.

She tossed the tool belt up, then a whole roll of vacuum tape. "You never know."

Miller held up the tape. "If I need this, we're in serious trouble."

Dana gave him time to remove the outer panel before asking, "How's it look?"

"Not too bad. The rip in the line is close to the thruster. I can cut out the damaged portion. With luck, the remainder of the line will be long enough to span the gap. Otherwise, we'll have to find some way to splice the two ends together and pray that it holds long enough to get back to Deep West."

"Do what you can." The last thing Dana wanted to do was leave one of the United States premier fighting ships behind for China to dismantle and study. Besides, the *Snow Leopard* had been with her through so much, she had no intention of abandoning her or initiating the self-destruct that would be necessary if she was forced to leave her. "I'll help Allistair find the RI gear."

"Go ahead. I've got this."

"Good luck."

Based on the freighter's condition and the debris field, the *Taurus* had apparently turned sideways and rolled for over a kilometer. As a result, the lowest hatch stood a full ten meters off the ground.

"Is it there?" she called to Allistair, who had somehow managed to get inside. "Is anybody alive?"

"No. And no," Allistair replied somberly. "The crew is dead. If the comm gear is here, I haven't found it yet." Miller poked his head out of the hatch. "Stand aside."

He tossed down a small crate made of high-impact plastic, which he'd tied to a long stretch of nylon cargo netting. When the netting snapped tight and pulled the crate to a stop, it formed a convenient rope ladder all the way to the hatch.

"All right," Dana said. "I'm coming up." The climb turned out to be relatively easy, despite the bulk of her pressure suit. Inside, however, movement became more awkward. The whole cargo bay sat at an unnatural angle, with the corners of boxes pointing into the air, making it difficult to stand on anything. The low g helped some, but it wasn't like they were in space and could just float from point to point.

"How you doing, Miller?" Dana asked through the comm.

"Progressing. I think she's going to be okay."

"Keep me posted." Dana clicked on her helmet lamp and began scanning the crates, half of which were buried under others that had come loose during impact. All she had to go on was a text marking that was supposed to be on the crate's exterior.

"Davis to *Snow Leopard*."

Dana keyed her comm. "McCaughey."

"Status."

"We're in the *Taurus* now. Her crew didn't make it. About half the cargo is intact, most of that buried under crates we're going to have to move. The rest is in pieces, scattered across a couple square kilometers of the planet surface. We don't know yet which half your gear falls into."

"Well, you've got another problem. Orbital surveillance has picked up two Marauders that just launched from Shenming Base. One of them is headed your way."

"We're in no shape to fight, sir. The *Snow Leopard* has lost a lot of fuel. Miller's repairing the line now. With luck, we'll get her off the ground, but—"

"Then you'd better find the comm gear and get out of there. At the Marauder's current trajectory, you've got about twenty minutes."

"You hear that, guys?" Dana asked her crew.

"Yup," Miller acknowledged.

"I heard it," Allistair said.

"Then let's get this done." She pointed to the front of the cargo bay. "Check every box you can see. If we end up moving and stacking stuff, we'll start at the front end and work our way back."

"You got it."

Almost frantically, Dana began checking labels. There were too many crates. Twenty minutes wasn't nearly enough time.

•≪ (O) ≫•

Ana selected two glasses from the bar, filled them at the tap, and handed one to Bill.

He inspected it. It was real crystal, by the look and feel of it. The water was not only running in the Sharp Shooter, but it actually looked clean. "I can say a lot of things about Simeon, but the man knows how to build a hotel." He held up his glass as if toasting, then downed the water in one gulp.

Ana scrutinized Bill, looking more into his eyes than at his damaged skin. "That seems like a pretty healthy attitude toward someone who's treated you so badly."

"In war, nothing is quite so important as having an accurate assessment of the enemy."

"How are you doing?" Ana asked after a moment.

He held up his hands, displaying his bandaged wrists. "These seem to be the worst of it. The salve they put on has killed the pain for now. So I guess I'm doing pretty well, all things considered."

They were silent for a moment, and then Bill said, "What about you? Zeke's your man, isn't he?"

She nodded. "He would say he's one of them."

148

"Would he be right?"

"Yes. And no. In my line of work, there are others, of course. But Zeke's the only one I don't consider to be a client."

"How does he feel about that?"

Ana frowned. She never talked about her clients to anyone, let alone another man. But as she'd just said, Zeke wasn't a client. Finally, she shrugged. "We've never discussed it. He still tries to pay me, though."

"Tries? You don't accept?"

"No. I don't." She hesitated, considering how best to explain. "It's awkward. Somehow it makes me feel cheap, like a whore. It's funny. I've been in the business for so long, I almost never feel that way anymore. Maybe that's because I make enough money that I can pick and choose my clients." She stared into her empty glass for a long moment. When she continued, she did so without looking up. "I love Zeke. When I'm with him, I want to do it for *him*, not for money. You know?" She refilled their water glasses.

"Does he feel the same about you?" Bill asked.

Ana stared across the room for a moment and then shook her head. "I don't think so."

"What makes you say that?"

"The fact that he tries to pay me. I figure when he falls in love with me, he'll start treating me differently."

"You're a good woman, Ana."

She studied his face, trying to determine if he was just flattering her. Finally, she decided he wasn't. "It's been a long time since anybody's told me that, unless they were referring to my sexual talents."

"I mean it. You've done an extraordinary thing out there." He gestured toward the door that led to the Plaza.

Ana fell silent then. She'd done nothing, really. Those people had needed direction. They'd needed it so badly they'd have followed anybody willing to provide it. They'd even followed her, a hooker. How desperate was that?

Bill had gone quiet too, and the uncomfortable pause stretched between them. Ana finished her drink. She was about to leave, when he spoke again. "Well, I, for one, am honored to have met you." He extended his right hand. "Bill Ryan, by the way."

Ana took his hand gently, careful not to disturb the bandage on his wrist. "Anathea Davenport."

Bill smiled.

"What?"

"Nothing. Sounds aristocratic, that's all."

Ana laughed. "More like hypocritic."

"Why do you say that?"

"Oh, my mother—both parents actually, but mostly my mother." Ana walked around the bar and climbed onto the stool next to Bill's. It was a long story, which she hadn't shared with anyone but Zeke since she'd left Earth eight years before. But it needed telling, for the sake of her own soul, especially since Zeke was causing her to rethink her profession for the first time in nearly a decade. And Bill Ryan was a captive audience for the moment.

"It's my height. I grew up, such as I am, in Mayfair, an upscale part of London. By the time I turned three, it became clear that I wasn't thriving. At first, my mother blamed herself. She figured she wasn't feeding me enough, or wasn't feeding me the right things, or something. I'd always been off-the-charts small, but by then it was obvious something was wrong with me, physically.

"Within a couple of years, I was diagnosed with 'hypopituitary dwarfism.' It's caused by an insufficiency of the pituitary growth hormone somatotropin.

"Mother was relieved by the diagnosis. It meant it wasn't her fault I was small. But as I got older and my stunted growth became more and more apparent, our highfalutin' friends began to whisper. They talked behind our backs. Mother said her so-called friends began to shut her out of the social cliques 'Some friends,' I'd say. 'Who needs them?'"

Ana picked at a dent in the wooden bar top with a chipped, scarlet fingernail. She remembered her mother, looking down at her when Ana was twelve, talking to her as though she was a toddler, still using baby words like "pee-pee" and "boo-boo." Ana rubbed at the dent with her thumb, as if it was just a stain she might scrub away. Finally, she continued.

"Apparently my mother needed them. When I entered my teen years, my body matured—I developed all the right curves in all the right places—but I never really grew. I looked like a six-year old with tits. A freak. Anytime a man looked at me with interest—and by my late teens, plenty did—it creeped my mother out. She began to hide me, if you can believe that. My parents took me out of school and hired a private tutor. Whenever we had company, they confined me to my room."

She raised her eyes and met Bill's. "I'd become an embarrassment to my own family."

"I'm sorry," Bill said. "That must have been hard."

"As soon as I turned eighteen, I asked her for money so I could move out. All too happy to oblige, she said I could have as much as I needed, as long as I never came back home. To this day I don't know if she meant that I just couldn't move back in when the money ran out, or if I was never welcome to enter the house again."

She shrugged. "I'm not sure it mattered. I used the money to get as far away as I could. At the time, the Jupiter system was still pretty rough-and-tumble—not many people there but the Union workers—"

"There still aren't," Bill said.

"Mercury was as far as I could go with reasonable safety. So I came here. The rest, as they say, is history. Not that I'm complaining." Her smile was a bit sad. "I mean, I get to have sex for a living."

Just then, a man came in, a civilian in relatively clean clothes. He appeared to be uninjured and reported to Ana as though the small woman was his superior officer. "More soldiers have arrived—Americans."

Bill's face brightened "Americans?"

The man glanced up with annoyance, but his features softened when he saw Bill's bloody flight uniform and damaged face. He nodded before turning back to Ana. "A contingent of Colonel Brannon's men have taken over local law enforcement. He's already put Simeon's bouncers in jail, along with the sheriff and his deputies. They're looking for Simeon."

Bill and Ana exchanged glances.

"The American commander seems to have taken charge," the man finished.

"That'll be Colonel Davis." Bill pushed himself to his feet. "I've got to go."

Ana gestured toward the hotel desk and the small room behind it, the lounge in which Bill had originally stowed his crew's gear. "Your supplies are back in there, just in case you want to change your uniform before you report for duty."

Bill examined his flight suit in the mirror behind the bar. Much of the top half was stained with blood. "Yeah. I think I'd better. Thanks."

∽❀《 O 》❀∾

Zeke and Tanner descended to the Plaza. An EU soldier in a radiation suit tested them with a Geiger scanner before they stepped off the lift. "You're both contaminated. This way, please." He gestured to Zeke's right.

Contaminated? Soldiers at the top of the lift had blown off all the regolith that had clung to their suits.

Nevertheless, as they moved to a portable decontamination station, three soldiers stepped onto the lift with a pressure sprayer, a suction cleaner, and a bucket full of long-handled, foam-covered sponges, all marked RADIOACTIVE WASTE.

Another man stretched a barricade across the approach to the lift with a sign labeled TEMPORARILY OUT OF SERVICE.

Zeke helped Tanner into a poly tub that resembled a child's wading pool. There, soldiers scrubbed their EVA suits with a foamy, sticky soap, and then went over them with a combination pressure water sprayer and high-powered suction nozzle—like a dental rinse tool on serious steroids. They moved to a second poly tub where the process was repeated. After the third tub and washing, and a second Geiger scan, they were declared clean and told to remove their EVA suits, which the soldiers confiscated and bagged.

In the meantime, the lift had been decontaminated and reopened.

Zeke and Tanner were scanned again, and then finally allowed to venture into the Plaza.

When they'd left, the place had been in shambles. Wounded, impatient victims had been milling around the Sharp Shooter with shouts of injustice, incompetence, and every other slight the imaginations of desperate fools could conjure. Only a rare and stalwart few had been futilely searching the wrecked buildings for survivors.

Now the place buzzed with purposeful activity. Every able-bodied person—and there seemed to be hundreds, if not thousands, of them—cleared debris to rescue trapped survivors. The wounded lined up outside Simeon's casino, sorted according to the severity of their injuries. Most were in good spirits, despite their obvious pain, and were greeting loved ones who were being rescued from the ruins by the dozens.

More people entered the Plaza in sporadic, dust-covered groups and made their way, by foot, luggage cart, or improvised stretcher to the triage station.

Ana smiled briefly at Zeke, but as soon as she saw Tanner, her brow creased with concern. "What happened? You all right?" She reached up and touched his cheek gently with her palm. "You're burning up."

"Radiation sickness," Zeke answered for him.

"Come on." Ana began leading them into the casino.

"What—" Tanner croaked. The word was almost unintelligible.

"Get him some water." Zeke helped Tanner sit in a chair against the wall.

Ana disappeared inside and returned a moment later with a nurse and two crystal glasses of clear, lukewarm water. After handing one to Zeke, which he drank quickly, she cradled Tanner's head and held the glass while he sipped.

"What happened?" the nurse asked.

Zeke explained what they'd had to do to restore power. He finished by saying, "Tanner had already sustained some exposure in the tunnels before we went outside."

"How do *you* feel?" she asked Zeke.

"A little queasy. But not bad. We both took a dose of that Granulocyte stuff before we went out."

"Is he going to be okay?" Ana asked.

The nurse didn't answer. She gave Tanner another dose of Granulocyte and a sleeping pill. "That'll put you out for at least twelve hours. We'll have to check your white blood cell count to determine the degree of bone marrow damage." She drew some blood and asked Ana to assign him a room.

Ana consulted her thinpad and waved over two muscular civilians. "Room 417."

The men laid out a sheet, lifted Tanner onto it, and carried him away as though the sheet was a stretcher.

"That's all we can do for now." The nurse handed Zeke a Granulocyte pill and retrieved another blood-sampling vial from her pocket. "Your turn."

◈《○》◈

"I found it," Dana said. "The thing's as big as a refrigerator."

"Really?" Allistair scrambled over the lopsided stacks. He looked at the box, then at the door.

"Someone got it in here. It'll fit." Dana checked her suit's chronometer. They had just under ten minutes. "Give me a hand."

Together they moved another half-dozen crates just to get to the RI transmitter, and Dana braced herself against the wall of the cargo hold. "Take that side."

Allistair, with much less space on his side, curled the fingers of one hand under the lip of the crate and wrapped a dangling tie-down strap around his other wrist to hold himself in place. "Ready?"

Dana nodded and they both heaved upward. The crate moved slightly. The boxes around it shifted.

"Again." Dana put her back into it. This time the crate lifted free. Once it did, it seemed light for its size.

When they got it to the hatch, there was more room to spare than she'd expected. "Do we dare drop it?" she asked, only half joking. "We've only got a few minutes, at best." The ten-meter drop couldn't be any worse than the beating the crate had already taken.

"Here." Allistair grabbed a cargo net and threw it over the box. He hooked the corners to one of the longer tie-downs. Together they lowered the crate to the ground and scrambled down after it.

"How you doing, Miller?" Dana asked into the comm.

"I'm done. We've got three minutes."

"Get on board and get her fired up." Dana undid the corners of the cargo net and threw them aside.

By the time she and Allistair had manhandled the crate up the *Snow Leopard*'s cargo ramp, waves of heat pulsed from the ship's thruster ports. Several cases of ammunition that Miller had jettisoned to make room for the RI gear lay scattered on the ground.

154

Miller eased the ship off the surface. "I've got the Marauder on radar, about two hundred clicks out."

Dana gripped one of the handholds and prayed the fuel-line repair would hold, at least until she and Allistair could get themselves strapped into their seats, where they might survive a crash landing if necessary. "We're not sticking around to fight."

Allistair stumbled forward and thumbed the ramp control.

By the time the Marauder arrived, the *Snow Leopard* was about three kilometers up and climbing. From below, the ship's matte black exterior would hide her against the dark Mercury sky, and her stealth skin should help keep her off the Marauder's radar. Only the disruption caused by the missing cockpit door was likely to give them away now. Miller kept it turned away from the enemy.

The Marauder swept by beneath them and launched a pair of missiles into the *Taurus*. The remains of the freighter exploded, pulverizing everything inside. Then the Marauder began to systematically destroy the crates in the debris field with laser fire.

"Ready missiles?" Allistair asked, climbing into his seat and strapping his g-harness.

"No," Dana said.

Both of her crew turned to her.

"We're too fragile to fight, and Colonel Davis needs this transmitter. As much as I'd like to destroy that asshole, we can't take the risk of giving ourselves away. How much fuel do we have?"

"Enough to return to Deep West, or enough to achieve orbit—maybe. But not both."

"Establish orbit," she told Miller. Then she hailed the base.

CHAPTER 20

Ten hours after the detonation on Mercury, President Powers finally received word from Deep West. She immediately called her War Cabinet, along with Yates and the European team, into the Situation Room.

Dan Norton had not received a voice communication, which Colonel Davis was apparently too busy to provide, but a simple data dump from a mobile command station. Having reviewed the transmission with O'Leary, Dan reported what the logs revealed of the events unfolding on Mercury.

Though Davis had managed to land his ship with about two-thirds of his men, the robotic infantry were out of commission and the European soldiers weren't enough to stop the Chinese assault.

"Worse," Powers said, "I spoke with President Petrov this morning to discuss the inhumanity of nuclear weapons. I tried to convince him to refrain from their further use. Not only did he snub my request, he assured me he would use as many nukes as necessary to make sure the United States and Europe never use Mercury again—for either military or civilian purposes."

"Unfortunately," Norton said, "there's little we can do to provide aid from here. And with this kind of resolve from Russia as well as China, we can expect to lose communications again. Very soon."

≪《○》≫

A disheveled man wearing torn green pajamas tucked into rugged work boots ran into the Sharp Shooter and up to Ana. "Admin...is in...a pocket," he panted between breaths.

Zeke didn't recognize the man. He must have been a visitor to the base. By the dust on him, he was one of the men now working in the tunnels. Ana stared at him as if waiting for him to say more

"Admin's in a pocket," he repeated.

"Pocket?" Zeke asked. "What pocket?"

The man shot him a look, then continued speaking to Ana. "There's a pocket of air where the Administration complex used to be."

"Base Administration?" She glanced at Zeke, smiling. "They're alive?"

"Don't know," the dust-covered man said. "We found some old sounding equipment in one of the storage bays—from back when the base was being excavated, I guess. One of the guys on our search team, a mining geologist laid over on his way to Callisto, seems to know how to use it. He said there's a pocket of air where Base Administration used to be. The tunnels have collapsed, and there's thirty meters of rock to cut through, but the pocket is there. People may be alive inside."

"If we can get to them," Zeke said.

The man's face drooped. "Yeah, if we can get to them." Then he seemed to brighten. "There's more. We found some excavation equipment in the same warehouse. The roof has partially collapsed on it. We'll have to dig it out. And we have to find somebody who can operate it."

"I can," Zeke said.

"How do you feel?" Ana asked him.

"Better."

"You sure you're up to it?"

Zeke pushed himself to his feet. "Sure."

"All right." The Plaza had acquired a semblance of organization and the initial triage had been completed. Ana found a woman standing idle beside her husband, who had only minor injuries, and assigned them both to assist the nurse in keeping the patients in order. The medical staff would do the rest. She took Zeke's arm. "I'm going with you."

The man in the pajamas led them across the Plaza and into the tunnels of the base. Twice he stopped at an intersection. At the first, after a moment of hesitation, he selected a path and continued. At the second, he threw up his hands and turned to Ana.

"Are you trying to get to Administration, or the warehouse?" she asked.

"The warehouse."

"I want to see Admin first," Zeke said, "so I know what we have to get through."

"This way." Ana pointed.

The man nodded and led on. Within a few minutes, the three stood in front of a solid wall of rock, staring at a computer screen mounted on a tripod with some sort of scanner. The image was nothing more than a speckled mass of mottled grays. Two other men were there.

A stout, bearded man with black hair extended his hand to Zeke. "Ben Trollinger." He shook Ana's as well. "Planetary geologist for JUMP." The Jupiter Union of Mining Personnel had been the dominant organization in the Jupiter system for nearly two decades. "Someone's alive in there. We got a staticky comm a few minutes ago."

"That's great," Ana said.

"We can't make out much," Ben continued. "They're trying to transmit through this nickel-rich rock, but we got enough to know that there are survivors."

Zeke stepped up to the display. "What are we looking at?"

"Rock density." Ben reached for the controls. "Watch as I adjust the depth of the scan." Gradually the image turned from speckled grays to a solid black. "That's at about twenty-seven meters. There's no signal coming back from this depth, because there's no rock there for it to bounce off of. That's your pocket. I've been trying to refine the image."

Zeke frowned. "That's an awful lot of rock."

"You think we can do it?" Ana asked.

"Oh, we can do it. But it'll take time." He turned to Ben. "Any way to know if the ventilation ducts are still open?"

"Not directly. If you know where they're located, we might be able to tell from the density of the surrounding rock."

"Okay." Zeke studied the display. "Pan left? We need to go deeper too. See what's beyond the pocket."

The display shifted.

"Back that way." Zeke pointed to a corner of the screen.

The image brightened. "The rock looks loose," Ben said, "like a collapse."

"You sure?" Zeke couldn't see anything. It all looked the same to him.

"Yeah. I know it's fuzzy, but this would be a lighter gray, with white veins of nickel deposits, if it were solid bedrock." He looked Zeke in the eye. "If that's where your ducts were, that pocket's not getting any air."

"As many as thirty people work in there, even on night shift," Zeke said.

"Can we determine how much time they have?" Ana asked.

Zeke pulled a thinpad from his breast pocket. "We've got the plans for the base, which I should be able to access now. From that, I can look up the volume of the pocket and calculate how long the air will last. If I assume they're all adult males and all still alive, that'll give us a worst-case oxygen consumption rate."

He knew the layout and could probably estimate the dimensions with reasonable accuracy, but whenever people's lives were at stake, he always verified his assumptions. Within seconds, the schematic appeared on his screen.

In the meantime, an old man with a mousey mustache that twitched like whiskers was trying to communicate with the survivors in his frail, cracked voice.

Zeke grabbed the comm and thumbed the mike. "Clear the channel." The noise settled some, but one man continued talking. When he finished, Zeke pressed the mike again. "This is Deep West facilities manager Zeke Shepherd. I need everyone to clear this channel for the next few minutes."

The noise stopped, as did most of the static.

"Zeke Shepherd to Base Administration. Do you copy?"

After a moment, static filled the comm along with a garbled voice that said something like, "Mmfff you gambl."

Zeke looked at Ana and the geologist, then at the mousy old man.

The man shrugged. "That's the best we've been able to do."

"Zeke Shepherd to Base Administration. Do you read?" He thought he made out the word "yes" amid the burst of static that followed.

"How many survivors do you have?" Zeke said.

The reply was completely unintelligible, but the static stopped when the man on the other end stopped speaking.

"I can't read you," Zeke said. "But I get static when you key the mike. Key it once for each survivor."

The channel went silent for a moment, then sounded with a long string of static bursts, which Zeke counted. When it ended, he asked Ana, "Twenty-three?"

She nodded. "That's what I got."

"We read you," Zeke said into the comm. "Sit tight. We'll get you out."

Static filled the comm again as he handed the link back to the mousy old man and began an oxygen-consumption calculation on his thinpad.

When he finished, he turned the display so Ana and the others could see it.

∽⟨O⟩∾

"You see this?"

Colonel Davis wrenched his attention from his own display of the battle, and the orchestration of his troops, to glance at Brannon's screen. It showed a crablike robot lumbering out from a large port in the side of a lobate scarp, one of the exits from Gagarin Base. "What is that thing?" He tried to gauge its size against the cliff, but since he didn't know how big the door was, he had no reliable scale for comparison.

"Mining robot," said a voice from behind him.

Davis spun around. Major Ryan stood at his shoulder, battered and bruised, but his eyes were clear and he seemed steady. His wounds had been dressed. His uniform was clean and his salute crisp.

"You're late, Major," Davis said. It was a running joke between them.

Bill relaxed into parade rest. "As I recall, sir, so were you."

Ignoring the barb, Davis poked his thumb toward Brannon's display. "That thing? A mining robot?"

Bill nodded. "With a nuke on its back, just like the one that leveled half this base."

"Not on my watch." Davis scanned his display, looking for a resource to send against the thing before it got anywhere near Deep West. Both the *Siamese* and her captain were out of commission, and the *Cheetah* was busy refueling the *Jaguar* in orbit. Only the *Black Panther* was ready to go. He turned to Ryan. "You feel up to it?"

Bill had already fitted his link into his ear and was hailing his crew. "I thought you'd never ask."

"Hey, Ryan," Davis said as Bill walked away. "Aim for the miner. Try not to hit the nuke."

◈⟨ ◯ ⟩◈

Minutes after the *Snow Leopard* had taken off, the g force subsided and Dana went weightless in her seat. "*Snow Leopard* to Deep West," she called once she'd confirmed that her crew was okay.

"Davis."

"Mission successful, sir. We have the transmitter. But we're going to need some technical help bringing it online."

"Stand by." The comm went silent for what seemed like minutes.

Dana sent out a single radar sweep. No threats. No sign of pursuit. She cycled through her other scanners just to be sure. Nothing.

Finally, a voice came over the comm. "Major McCaughey?"

"Here."

"Major, this is Lieutenant J.G. Vance. I'm going to talk you through the assembly and startup of the transmitter. Are you ready?"

Dana glanced at the gaping hole in the side of her ship where the crew hatch used to be, then clipped a lifeline from her belt to a loop on her seat before unsnapping her g-harness. "Miller, keep an eye on that radar. One sweep every five minutes. No more. With that hatch open, we're more visible than we used to be."

"Aye, Major."

"Allistair," she said, "you're with me."

Together they moved to the cargo section—the ammunition hold, really. "All right, Vance. Go ahead."

"Okay. Step one: unscrew and remove the lid of the crate."

Dana strapped on her tool belt. She selected a head, inserted it into the battery powered driver, and set the torsion lock. Allistair did the same on his side. Eight screws later, the lid drifted free.

"We've got pretty cramped quarters in here," Dana told Vance. "Do we need this lid for anything? If not, I'm going to send it out into space."

"There should be a bag of fittings and fasteners. Make sure it's not taped

161

to the underside of the lid."

"It's not," she said. "They're in the box. I've got them."

"Then you may set the lid free."

Dana motioned for Allistair to check his lifeline and verified that her own was fastened securely before opening the cargo ramp. That alone would make them more visible, but they needed room to work. As for the lid of the crate, it was lightweight plastic and shouldn't create much of a radar blip. She and Allistair gave it as hard a shove as possible, so it would drift away from the *Snow Leopard* quickly.

Inside the box, the transmitter was packed in a translucent, form-fitting gel. The imprint of the packet of fasteners remained visible in its surface.

"All right," Dana said. "What's next?"

"Reach in and pull out the packaging," Vance said.

Dana placed her hand on the gel. It was spongy—elastic—almost like Silly Putty, but more pliant. "Cool stuff."

She and Allistair pressed their hands in around the edge, and together, lifted out the piece that covered the—

"Wait a minute," Dana said. The transmitter sat in the center of the crate, an oblong shape about the size of a yoga ball. Alongside it were two pairs of solar panels, a dish-style antenna, and several connecting rods. "This thing is a freaking satellite."

"Yes, ma'am. What did you expect?"

"I thought it was just a transmitter."

"Essentially it is," Vance said. "But it's also got a variety of space-to-ground sensors, mapping algorithms, and sophisticated command and control software."

"I thought this was a ship-mounted platform."

"No, ma'am. It's designed to function independently."

"Then we've got a problem."

In an instant, Colonel Davis's voice came over the comm. "What is it, Major?"

"Sir," Dana began carefully. "If we launch this thing, the Chinese will just send up one of their Marauders to take it out. It won't last thirty minutes."

"We're getting pulverized down here. We need that comm-sat."

162

Dana didn't have any fuel left to fight if a Marauder came after the satellite. The only way she could protect it, and her ship, was to keep it hidden, to keep it inside the *Snow Leopard*, and hope the open hatch wasn't enough to give away their position.

"What if we forgo the solar panels and piggyback on *Snow Leopard*'s power? We can point the dish out our personnel hatch and orient the ship so it's transmitting toward the planet's surface. That'll help keep it off Chinese radar."

"What do you think, Vance?" Davis asked, the comm channel still open.

"Umm…sure. I think we can make that work. But that'll only hide one of them."

"What do you mean, 'one of them'?" Dana said. "We only have one."

Vance's voice came back over the comm. "Oh, shit. Really?"

"How many are there?" Dana asked.

"Four. That's how many we need to maintain constant surveillance and communications over the battlefield."

He was right. Dana realized it as soon as he said it. Synchronous orbit was impossible over the pole of a planet. With only one satellite, they could maintain RI control from orbit for maybe an hour at a time.

Dana checked the orbit chronometer. "We'll be over the northern pole in forty-eight minutes."

"Then you've got that long to get that hardware online," Davis said.

CHAPTER 21

Zeke eyed several cracked support beams warily before stepping into the cavernous warehouse, which was illuminated by several overhead solid-state lighting panels, only half of which were working. There must have been a dozen people there already, most of them working to excavate a full-sized earthmover with a backhoe shovel on the visible end and who-knows-what on the buried end.

"Wait a minute," Zeke shouted. "Hey, guys! Wait a minute!"

Nobody responded. A grunting, swearing, fat man who reminded Zeke of a walrus gestured to his companions to keep digging.

"Guys!" Zeke shouted. "Wait a minute!" He began jogging toward the men.

The blubbery man turned to confront Zeke, sweat dripping from his shining, shirtless chest. The rest continued to work.

Ana emitted a shrill, ear-splitting whistle, and everything in the cavern became still.

"Guys!" Zeke yelled again. "You're thinking too big. Look at that thing. We *might* get it into the passageway, but we'll have to turn it sideways to attack the wall with it. What we need is a drill of some kind. Something small that can cut through rock."

"If we can drill a few holes," Ben Trollinger said, "and find some explosives, we might be able to blast our way through."

"Would that be safe?" asked the mousy old man.

Zeke gestured to the damaged support pillars. "Is anything safe in this base anymore?"

Before the men could reply, a woman with short black hair and the athletic build of an aerobics instructor shouted from the far end of the warehouse. "Over here!"

Two men, working with a pickax and shovel from one of the emergency-response cabinets, were trying to uncover a piece of equipment near her. Zeke and the others walked over. It turned out to be a Kubota tractor about the right size for backyard landscaping on Earth, small enough to maneuver in the tight passageways of Deep West.

"Perfect," Zeke said. "Let's dig it out."

Zeke called several of the search-and-rescue teams to the warehouse. In all, about twenty-five additional people showed up, many of whom brought pieces of metal, rigid plastic, or sections of piping and rebar to dig with.

"Let's begin with the little Kubota." Zeke set several men to digging. "The rest of us need to locate the assortment of front-end attachments. We'll probably need a variety before this is over. They should be somewhere in this corner."

The remaining men followed him over.

"Bring those," Ana told them, pointing to a row of wheelbarrows leaning against one of the warehouse's unburied walls.

"Good idea," Zeke said.

"I have them from time to time."

He smiled, thinking of the many adventures she'd introduced him to without ever leaving her own bed. "Don't I know it."

She shoved his hip with her tiny hand. "Get to work, cowboy."

He did. They both labored silently for a few minutes amid the grunts of the men around them, Zeke's massive arms straining to heave shovelful after shovelful of rock. It felt like he was doing rep after rep of bicep curls.

"How's the gym?" Ana asked, as if reading his thoughts. "Do you know?"

Zeke grunted. "Buried, along with the laser tag arena. Like most everything else." The gym and the nearby laser tag court had been Zeke's primary source of diversion whenever he wasn't working or spending time with Ana. The gym had kept him in shape—fit, if not small—and strong enough to shoulder the loads necessary to maintain the various facility systems that sustained life at Deep West.

The laser tag was just for fun.

He'd need no such diversions for quite some time, however. There was too much to rebuild. It would take years to restore some semblance of normalcy of operations.

"That's too bad," Ana said, about the gym and laser tag court. She smiled suddenly. "Now what are you going to do for fun?"

He blew her a kiss. The woman never let up. She was, he'd long ago discovered, insatiable. Sex was her release. She wouldn't be in the business if it wasn't. There were so many other things she *could* do, so many things she was capable of, like the things she'd accomplished in just a few hours on the Plaza, amidst people who, for the most part, didn't even know her. Those who did, saw her only as an object of sex. Yet she *had* done it.

He watched her for a moment as she heaved dirt into the nearest wheelbarrow, keeping up with the best of the men around her. The woman had stamina, he'd give her that.

He shook his head. He'd been hanging around her so long she'd even gotten him thinking in innuendo.

She glanced up. "What's the smirk for?"

"Nothing. I just love you."

"Do you?"

It was her standard response whenever he told her that. She'd probably heard it from most of the men she'd slept with. It wouldn't be fair for her to say it back if she didn't mean it, and it could lead to uncomfortable circumstances if her client took the words seriously and decided to "save" her from her life of debauchery.

Zeke knew better. Ana, of all people, didn't need saving.

"Yeah. I do." The thick air finally forced him to take a break.

Ana stopped too. "I could always teach you to paint." That was her hobby.

He'd asked her once how she got into watercolors, which seemed somehow out-of-character for her.

"No," she'd said. "It makes perfect sense. The materials are cheap and lightweight, and I can do it in my room."

He'd understood then. With the disdain Ana endured from the non-client residents of Deep West, she couldn't really take up a hobby that involved a social circle. He'd also understood, only then, how lonely her life must be. At the time, the realization had broken his heart.

The sudden roar of an engine broke his reverie. With a cloud of pearl-colored smoke and the french-fry smell of bio-fuel, the little Kubota clawed its way out from under the remaining dirt and rubble that tumbled from its back. The front-loader would significantly speed up their progress in exhuming the variety of attachments they'd eventually need.

Zeke thought again about Ben's idea to blast through the wall. The problem was, there hadn't been any mining at Deep West for at least a decade. As far a Zeke knew, all of the explosives had been removed in the name of safety.

∾❰◯❱∾

"Oh, shit," Davis breathed as another nuke-toting miner appeared on his screen, this one much closer than the last. He'd been so focused on the ground battle with China, he'd forgotten about Russia.

Somehow they'd slipped this miner past the Raptor surveillance. But because one of the Raptor crews had happened to catch the nuke coming out of Gagarin, Davis had demanded a scan of every square meter of surface north of seventy degrees. And there it was, crawling across the surface with a load of inexorable destruction on its back.

Brannon's Raptors were either engaged in scans of the northern latitudes—a tedious and time-consuming, though obviously necessary, task—on the opposite end of their orbits, too far away to intervene, or were providing tactical surveillance over the still-raging battle, which Davis and Brannon were systematically losing. Now Davis would have to pull either the *Cheetah* or *Jaguar* away from that battle. Both had just arrived, in a desperate attempt to counter a Marauder that had recently joined the fray, and to stall the Chinese for the time it would take the *Snow Leopard* to get the RI command-and-control transmitter into position.

"Davis to *Cheetah*. Engage critical target at the following coordinates." He sent the longitude and latitude of the incoming miner.

"Acknowledged."

On the display, the *Cheetah* veered sharply north. The Marauder banked hard in pursuit.

Bill Ryan spotted the first miner lumbering across the arid, sun-drenched waste of the northern Mercury expanse. It wasn't headed toward Deep West, exactly, but it was there, and it toted a nuclear bomb. "Ready missiles."

A low hum suffused the cabin as the missile doors slid open. "Ready."

Bill smiled back at Townsend. "Two ought to do it."

"Firing missiles."

As soon as they cleared the ship, Carter pulled hard on the controls, up and to starboard. The robot below disappeared, out of Bill's line of sight from the window. He watched it on his monitor. Seconds later, the missiles exploded. The miner collapsed and lay still upon the rocky ground. It was almost too easy.

When Carter completed her banking maneuver and g returned to a comfortable level, Bill brought up a map of the planet surface. "Now let's find out where that thing was headed."

As soon as the Marauder turned back toward Shenming, probably for want of fuel, the *Cheetah* rolled hard, mere meters off the ground, toward the Russian crawler approaching the planet's pole.

At first, as they neared the target, Captain Duval saw nothing. "We're here," he reported over the comm. "Approaching coordinates. We don't see any crawler."

"She's there," Davis assured him.

An instant later, the *Cheetah* ripped over the top of a bluff that had been invisible moments before, camouflaged perfectly against Mercury's pock-marked terrain. When the floor dropped away, a few meters suddenly became hundreds.

Duval grabbed the joystick and swiveled the ventral scanner back toward the cliff. There, at its base, nearly out of sight in the deep shadow—visible only on infrared—lumbered the miner. "Got it," he told Davis. "Bring us around, Romero."

As they looped back, the scanner auto-adjusted its image to compensate for the shadows and Duval zoomed in. The thing was a simple bomb strapped by metal cargo bands to the back of one of Russia's early mining robots—something dredged up from decades earlier. The whole design was so rudimentary it would have been comical if it hadn't already proven its effectiveness.

"I thought humanity had grown beyond such horrendous contraptions," Lieutenant Jordan said from the weapons console.

"Apparently not. Get rid of it, will you?"

"With pleasure." Jordan began the sequence that would bring a missile down upon the thing, but he never got the chance.

A blinding flash from their target was the last thing any of them knew.

CHAPTER 22

Corporal Gordon stood beside his defense pylon, looking out over the ruins of Deep West and the convoy that littered the plateau beyond. It seemed absurd to think that the enemy would attack the solar array from this direction, but he manned his post vigilantly nonetheless, just in case the enemy deliberately picked the least-likely line of attack.

Suddenly a tremor slammed Gordon to the ground. The rumble lasted for only a second, but the intensity of it caused his joints to ache.

As soon as it stopped, he inspected his visor and checked his suit's vacuum integrity light. Blood welled in his mouth from where he'd bitten his lip. His tongue found a loose chip of tooth. Unwilling to spit the blood and tooth into his visor, he swallowed both, climbed to his feet, and hailed his lieutenant. "Gordon to Mansene."

"What the hell was that?" somebody said over the comm.

"Quiet!" Gordon snapped. "Mansene, do you read?"

No reply.

"All right. Check in."

"Oh, shit," said the same voice as before.

"Check in, damn it!" Gordon shouted.

"Dannish checking in. Gordon, you see this?"

Gordon turned toward the center of the solar array as only two additional members of the squad sounded off. Private Dannish stood on the horizon, looking away from Gordon. Beside him, a short section of the titanium solar research tower hung, like the melted wax of a candle, from the ten-meter stump that remained. The rest of the tower was simply gone.

Gordon unsnapped the quick-disconnect to his air supply on the defense pylon, relying on the smaller tank attached to his back, and ran. When he reached Dannish's side, he stopped and stared. A wide stripe of the solar panels had been stripped of paint. Beyond them, a swath at the extreme edge of the array had been melted into slag. About eighty percent of the solar array remained

"Mary, mother of—" one of the unit's four survivors said as he too crested the rise. "What happened?"

"Come on." Gordon suspected he knew the answer, and he feared the potential radiation levels. He grabbed Dannish by the arm. "It's not safe here. Get back to your posts."

He returned to his defense pylon. "Gordon to Colonel Davis. We've got a problem."

∽⟨O⟩∾

A flash of light caught Bill's eye from just over the horizon toward the pole. "What was that?" He spun the long-range imager in that direction. A dense wall of dirt and rock had heaved upward and now settled into a ridge, as if a meteor had struck.

"No. No, no, no," Townsend was muttering. But the blast hadn't come from the direction of Deep West. Or from Shenming or Gagarin, for that matter.

Davis's voice came over the comm. "Deep West to *Black Panther*."

"This is Ryan. Go ahead."

"Bill, we just lost the *Cheetah*."

"What—" His voice caught in the back of his throat. "What happened?"

"She went after a nuke crawler, same as you. The Russians detonated it as soon as the *Cheetah* got within range. They must be keeping an eye on the crawlers from a visual satellite."

Bill gritted his teeth and pounded the arm of his g-seat. "Any chance of survivors?"

"She was vaporized. I'm sorry." Davis paused, but his mike remained open, so Bill couldn't voice the thousand questions running through his mind. "You should count yourself lucky. Apparently your target was too close to Gagarin for the Russians to detonate. Either that or they didn't see you coming. I suspect the former."

Finally the comm light went green. "Any other casualties?" Bill asked.

"Unknown. We think the nuke was headed for the solar array. We saw a dip in power, but we're still online, so I assume the array is intact."

"What are your orders for us?"

"Come home. If we find any more nukes headed our way, I'll have Brannon take them out with Raptors from orbit."

Fatigue and pain ate at Bill all the way back to Deep West. When they arrived, Carter brought the ship down as close to the base entrance as Commander Davis's flight control designee would allow, and Bill hobbled out. The contamination control team scanned him and his crew, sprayed off the regolith clinging to the legs of their EVA suits, and cleared them to enter. Bill limped onto the lift. His body had, once again, had enough. Carter and Townsend stripped him, and themselves, of their pressure suits.

By the time they reached Colonel Davis's command station, he mustered some hidden reserve and walked the last few steps on his own. "Major McCaughey?"

"Don't worry, Bill. She's in orbit. She'll be back soon. Why don't you get some bunk time?"

Bill started to protest, but Davis held up a hand. "That's an order. I'll need you back in the cockpit soon enough."

After the second it took Bill to process the words, he nodded and headed back toward the Sharp Shooter.

"The colonel ordered us to find him a bunk," Carter told the triage nurse, who met them at the casino entrance.

"Sorry. We're full," the nurse said.

Townsend stepped forward. "Look at him. You haven't got a single room? You know, in case of an emergency."

If Bill had had the energy, he would have laughed. *Yeah. We haven't seen any of those lately.* Truth was, if he looked half as bad has he felt, the nurse would have found him a bed.

The woman shook her head. "You're on your feet. That means you're better off than many who have to sleep on the floor." She produced a pen-light from her breast pocket and shined it into each of Bill's eyes. "Wait here."

She rounded the corner and returned with a pair of little white pills and a cup of water. "Take these."

Bill held out his palm. "What are they?"

"They'll ease the pain and help you sleep. At least for a couple of hours."

He swallowed the meds, then let Townsend and Carter lead him away.

❧❨○❩❧

The work was slow. Zeke and his companions had no way to verify the sharpness of the rock-grinding drill they'd recovered, but if their progress was any indication, it was past dull, well on its way to blunt. Not that it mattered—they couldn't do anything about it.

In truth, he didn't know how fast he should expect such a drill to cut through solid rock. As it was, the thing ground away at the wall for twenty-five minutes before they had to stop and clear the rubble that had collected at the base of the tractor. By then, every nerve ending in Zeke's body was numb from the constant vibration.

Carefully, he maneuvered the tractor over the mound of dirt and loose rock. He turned it down the corridor to where they'd left the front-loader attachment. Zeke, the blubbery man from the warehouse, and the man in the green pajamas swapped the attachment. In two or three passes, Zeke swept the rubble pile down the tunnel.

The crew repeated the entire process three more times. Each time, it went a little faster than the time before, largely due to their increased proficiency.

Ben Trollinger measured the thickness of the remaining rock between them and the Admin pocket. "We're not going to make it," he stated flatly. "We haven't got enough time."

"How far have we got to go?" Zeke asked.

"About twenty meters. At this rate it'll take two hours longer than those people have." He nodded toward the wall and the pocket beyond.

"Maybe," Pajamas said, "but our time estimate was conservative."

"Do you really want to rely on that assumption?" Ana asked.

Pajamas shrugged. "What choice do we have?"

"There has to be something else we can do," Ana said. "Some way to speed up the process."

"And while you all discuss it," said the mousy old man, "we're wasting time we could spend drilling."

"No." Zeke shifted the tractor into park and climbed down. "I agree with Ana—"

"You would," said the walruslike man.

Zeke wheeled on him. "What's that supposed to mean?"

The walrus squared his nearly nonexistent shoulders. "What do you think it's supposed to mean, 'John'?"

Zeke balled his fist, but Ana grabbed his arm. "It's okay."

"No," Zeke said. "It's not."

Ana put a tender hand on his chin and turned his face toward hers. "Now's not the time." She waited for his breathing to slow before continuing. "You think we have other options?"

"Maybe." He sighed. "There's a laser drill back at the warehouse. I didn't mention it because it's designed for drilling narrow holes to insert explosives, which we don't have."

"Fat load of good that'll do us," Mousey spat.

Just then, a small robot rounded the corner, skittering its way toward the workers. It looked like a little oblong spider, about the size of a football, with a brick of C-4 on its back.

CHAPTER 23

By the time the command-and-control transmitter kicked on, Colonel Davis's soldiers had all of the American RIs lined up several hundred meters from the bottom of the nearest lobate scarp, draped in camouflage netting.

"Ready," Dana reported.

Davis switched frequencies on his command console. Instantly, a visual image supplied by the satellite aboard the *Snow Leopard* replaced the similar display he'd been receiving from the European Raptors. The new display included a coordinate grid for the purpose of targeting enemy units. All Davis had to do was touch a target in the image and the satellite's algorithms would instruct an RI to eliminate it.

The Chinese undoubtedly had similar capability, but the camouflage netting would make it nearly impossible for the Chinese commanders to pick out their targets visually.

As the Chinese machines appeared at the lip of the ridge, where they could threaten Deep West and nearby convoy ships, Davis had them entered as targets. His own RIs were already firing. Any enemy that came within range was destroyed before it could do substantial damage.

The sudden activation of control capability that China thought it had eliminated, and that the Europeans had clearly lacked, allowed Davis to wipe out half the enemy troops before the Chinese commander realized a change of tactics was warranted.

❧《◯》❦

"Nobody move. Not a muscle." Zeke stared at the strange explosive robot. His first thought was that Tanner would've declared it to be a delivery from God—they needed explosives, and God had provided. But this was not from God. It came from Shenming.

Everyone near him swung their heads around—their bodies all but immobile—and watched the thing approach.

Though the robots Zeke had interacted with in the past had sensors sophisticated enough to keep them from running into stationary objects, most couldn't discern a human form unless it actually moved. His experience was with industrial robots, not military robots, but this particular model looked pretty basic. It was too small to have numerous bio-sensors on board. And if Zeke's suspicion was correct, this was a suicide bot, something upon which the Chinese wouldn't waste a lot of expensive hardware.

Of course, there was always a chance that they had programmed it with complex software algorithms to make up for shortfalls in data complexity. But software of that sort was notoriously unreliable; it required the programmer to make too many assumptions about human behavior.

The spider stopped just before the section of corridor that was constricted by the bulk of the tractor. Small servos in what would have been the head of an actual spider spun and whirled.

Pajamas, taking a turn in the Kubota's seat, reached for the lever that would move the tractor out of the way—pull it into the alcove it had dug into the wall. Zeke raised his hand to stop him.

Instantly, the spider spun toward Zeke. Servos whirred. He held his breath, waiting for the explosion that would send them all to oblivion.

After a moment, the robot returned to its original heading and skittered around the tractor without giving the pile of loose rock a second's consideration. It continued about fifty meters down the corridor, where it turned into a dead-end passage—one that had collapsed in the original blast.

About a minute and a half later, the corridor shook, the explosion pounding in Zeke's ears. A cloud of dust and a shower of gravel spewed from the dead-end tunnel. So much for explosives from God.

"Was anybody down there?" Ana asked.

"I doubt it," Pajamas replied. "I haven't seen anybody come through here in the last hour or so."

"I don't get it," said the mousey old man. "That thing clearly knew we were here. Why didn't it kill us?"

"They were sent en masse," Zeke said. "I saw a whole field of dead ones on the surface. Their purpose must be to bring down the base, one tunnel at a time."

"But—" Walrus began.

"Think about it," Ana said. "If it had blown up here, it would have blocked access to the rest of the base for any coming behind it."

"Now there's a comforting thought." Mousey glanced nervously down the corridor.

"It does give me an idea, though," Zeke said. "You guys get that laser drill and bore some holes as far into the rock as you can. I'll be back shortly."

◈⟨O⟩◈

Dana was not surprised when she got the recall order from Colonel Davis. She'd been watching the battle on the surface. Few Chinese remained. Several of their robotic infantry held a defensive line to stall any pursuers, but most—along with the handful of remaining human troops—retreated toward Shenming. One man stumbled and flopped to the ground. His companions left him behind.

Dana zoomed in on the man. Based on the puffed-out appearance of his pressure suit, his vacuum integrity was good, but a small red LED blinked from his regulator. Apparently, he'd run out of air. Had his companions bothered to check, they probably could have saved him by sharing an oxygen tank.

The American and European soldiers—what was left of them—were returning to Deep West. Unlike the ground troops, however, Dana couldn't comply with the recall order.

"We've got a problem," she told Davis. "We don't have enough fuel to land."

"Roger that, *Snow Leopard*. I'll send up a re-fueling ship. While you're waiting, finish assembling that comm-sat and get it launched. Stand by for Corporal Vance."

"Yes, sir. Thank you."

At Vance's instruction, Dana and Allistair maneuvered the core of the satellite out of the *Snow Leopard*'s cargo hatch, tethered to the ship by a slender cable. From there, it took two hours of EVA to get the solar collection panels and receiver antenna mounted to the small-by-comparison computing and transmitting core.

Halfway through, a European Raptor drifted into view. The ship closed slowly from a higher orbit for nearly an hour before it touched off its thrusters, adjusting its orbit to match that of both the *Snow Leopard* and the comm-sat.

Dana reached up from a solar panel she'd just finished securing and pressed the comm button on the collar of her pressure suit. "*Snow Leopard* to unidentified Raptor."

"*Snow Leopard*, this is *Condor Four*."

"I'm Major Dana McCaughey." She waved to identify herself. "Are you here to offer us fuel?"

"No, ma'am. We're here to relieve you, to provide protection for the satellite once you depart. Best intelligence indicates the enemy has only two Marauders. Davis is keeping a close eye on Shenming Base. If they launch one, our forces should be able to intercept it before it gets here. If not, we and the *Blackhawk*, which is still en route, ought to be able to do the job."

"Leaving is going to be a little difficult," Dana said, "until we get more fuel."

"I can't speak to that, but we'll watch your back until Colonel Davis works out your fuel problem for you."

When Davis did, his solution appalled Dana. She'd expected one of the other CATS or Raptors to show up, or maybe the *Siamese*. For a mission as short as a rendezvous and return, any one of those ships could have split its complement of fuel and still had plenty to spare. But Davis had sent up an entire tanker. The amount of fuel he'd expended just to get the thing off the ground spoke of how strapped Davis must be for ships—specifically small fighting craft. She'd seen what had happened to the *Cheetah* and knew Bill had returned to Deep West, but she hadn't heard from Etre, in the *Jaguar*.

She almost ordered Miller to contact Davis and ask, but that would have been an inexcusable breach of communication protocol in such a hostile environment. As it was, she had to wait until she reached the base to find out in person.

Fortunately, the refueling went without a hitch, and the repair to the fuel line seemed to be holding. As soon as the incoming *Blackhawk* appeared on the long-range scanner, Miller calculated a descent vector and nudged the ship toward Deep West.

As they passed over the pole, Dana noted the damage to the solar array and choked back a sob. Captain Duval and his crew had died well. If that nuke had gotten any closer, Deep West would be once again—permanently this time—without power. China and Russia wouldn't need to wage a land battle then. They could simply wait for Deep West to run out of air.

Dana didn't breathe easily again until they were on the ground with Bill's ship sitting beside them, apparently undamaged and draped with camouflage netting.

The *Jaguar* was there as well.

On the way down to the Plaza, the lift was crowded with surviving soldiers, none of them wounded—the wounded had all died of asphyxiation in their damaged pressure suits.

Dana and her crew hustled through decon, shed their gear, and reported to Colonel Davis.

He glanced up. "Sorry. No sleep tonight. Your comm-sat will be back over the pole in four hours. Whatever we're going to do next, we need to do it then. See to the repair, restocking, and refueling of the *Snow Leopard*. Be back here in one hour."

Dana heaved a heavy, fatigue-laden sigh. She'd been up for at least twenty-four hours already, but as long as the adrenaline kept pumping, she would continue.

"Bill?" she asked.

"I ordered him to find a rack. Don't know if he did."

"And the spider bots?"

"I've deployed snipers to the extremities of the base, covering all entrances—I hope. Civilians have been evacuated from the outlying areas. We've had to bring down a few more tunnels to block out the creepy things, but I think we're safe here now."

"Come on." Dana led her crew away from Davis and ordered them to oversee the refit of the *Snow Leopard*. Then she went to find Bill.

CHAPTER 24

Zeke returned to the Plaza and tried to march directly up to the man who seemed to be in charge of both the US and EU troops. A lieutenant stopped him.

"I need to speak with your commander," Zeke told the man.

"He's busy."

"This is an emergency."

"Everybody's got an emergency right now. This whole mess is one big emergency. Colonel Davis is handling it as best he can."

"Twenty-three survivors are trapped in the Base Administration complex," Zeke said.

"And you need help digging them out."

Zeke pursed his lips for a moment. "In a manner of speaking."

The lieutenant shook his head. "We haven't got the manpower right now. Or the equipment. There are plenty of able civilians. Recruit them to help you dig."

"It's not a matter of manpower. We need explosives to blast through the rock."

"Can't help you," the lieutenant said. "We need everything we have for the military effort."

Zeke took a deep breath before starting over. "You don't understand. I'm not asking for explosives. Several hundred of those spider robots went dead in the radiation zone on the surface. They have plenty of explosives, if we can get at them. I thought maybe your commander could spare a ship—"

The lieutenant was shaking his head again.

"Lives are at stake, man!"

One of the American airmen stood nearby, still in his flight uniform. "What's going on?" He had a petite black woman with him, similarly dressed.

Zeke extended his hand to each. "I'm Zeke Shepherd, facilities manager for Deep West."

"Lieutenants Carter and Townsend, of the *Black Panther*," the airman said. "You're the guy responsible for restoring base power, aren't you?"

"One of them."

"I couldn't help but overhear," Townsend said. "What did you have in mind?"

Zeke repeated the spiel he'd given to the obstinate lieutenant. "It doesn't have to be a military ship. Any ship will do, as long as it'll fly. It won't take but a few minutes to recover a couple of the robots by grapple from a safe altitude."

"If the robots are dead, what good will they be?"

Zeke took a deep breath and let it out slowly. "Even the most hardened of electronics are subject to failure if the radiation level gets high enough, but that shouldn't affect the brick of explosives each one carries. Knock out the electronics and the robot stops working. That should make them safe to recover and dismantle. The explosive itself should still be good." He shrugged. "I would think."

"Hold on. I'll see what I can do." Townsend walked up to Colonel Davis's command station.

Instantly, Davis gave him his attention. Zeke couldn't hear their conversation, but after a moment, Davis turned back to his console. He placed his hand to the comm link in his ear, spoke for a moment, and then nodded.

Townsend returned to Zeke. "You're in luck. It looks like the coast around the base is clear all the way back to Shenming and Gagarin. Davis gave us the okay to take the *Black Panther* up and recover those explosives for you."

"Shouldn't we check with Ryan before we take the ship?" Carter asked.

"He's got orders to sleep. I'm not going to wake him. Besides, we have authorization from Colonel Davis." Townsend led them both to the surface, past a load of US and EU soldiers who emerged from the lift, into the Plaza.

The *Black Panther*, which had looked small from the ridge top, was actually quite large, with a length nearing twenty meters. A ladder extended up to the cockpit door, which Carter opened.

Zeke followed the two inside.

In his bulky pressure suit, the cockpit seemed impossibly cramped. The two front seats faced a dashboard crowded with displays, keypads, and lights. Of the two back seats, one had only a monitor in front of it and a simple comm board at one hand.

Townsend climbed into the other rear seat, which swiveled toward an elaborate workstation along the wall opposite the cockpit door.

Carter took the pilot's seat and pointed to the vacancy beside her. "Sit there."

Zeke did. Two massive joysticks with red buttons sat prominently in front of him.

Carter entered an access code and the displays came to life. She and Townsend suddenly became very busy.

"Should I be doing something?" Zeke asked. The panel before him looked immensely complicated.

"That's the command console," Carter said. "Don't touch anything. I'll cover both portions of the preflight checklist."

"Time is of the essence. The air in Admin is running low, even as we speak."

"This won't take long."

Zeke let them work. His fingers drummed his armrest for what seemed like forever. The chronometer on his display claimed it had been only seven minutes.

"Strap in while you're waiting," Townsend told him.

With a nod, Zeke fastened the various latches of the five-point harness that would hold him in his seat for what he hoped would be an exceedingly brief flight.

"Ready?" Carter asked at last.

"Ready," Townsend said.

Zeke parroted the reply, in what he imagined was proper military protocol.

The roar of thrusters ramped up and, with a slight wobble, the *Black Panther* rose from the ground. Keeping one eye on the external radiation readout, Carter brought them to maybe half a kilometer above the field of demolition robots. Once there, the ride remained stable while Townsend unstrapped his harness and clipped a lifeline to a hook near his seat. With the push of a button, a hatch at the back of the cockpit opened into a small cargo bay with naught but a few boxes of high-caliber machine gun rounds strapped to the bulkhead.

He snapped his boots into clips on the floor, in front of a small control panel, and began to operate a variety of oversized knobs and buttons. A cargo ramp opened and a framework of struts motored out over the edge, toting a winch, cable, and grapple.

"All right, Shepherd." Carter reached over, activated a monitor in front of him, and then cycled through several images before settling onto one that showed the robot graveyard beneath them. She pointed to a joystick near his hand. "This operates the vid-scanner. You're going to direct Townsend to whichever robots you want. I'll maintain our position here."

"Got it."

Within a few minutes, the *Black Panther* had recovered half a dozen of the tunnel-delving spider bombs, and Carter nudged the ship toward the base's makeshift landing field.

≪(O)≫

Some areas of the Plaza had been substantially cleaned up since Dana had last seen it. Some of the buildings, once the debris had been cleared away, actually had some intact rooms. The ground floor of the Sundown had about half a dozen of them, in various states of disrepair. Based on directions from Townsend, Dana found Bill in one of these.

The electricity in the building was out, but this particular room had no door, and the restored lighting from the Plaza proper lit the area well enough for her to see Bill's face for the first time since she'd left Earth. It looked awful—beaten to a shapeless purple mass, torn, and then patched with dermaplast—but relaxed in sleep.

He'd been in worse shape after crashing his CATS on the Moon during

183

the China Dominion Affair five months before, but back then all the damage had been internal. At the time, he might have been sleeping, rather than comatose. Dana preferred this—knowing he would be okay, regardless of what he looked like.

Her arms ached to embrace him. Her body yearned to lie down next to his, to feel his arms around her. She set her gear down, wiped a tear from her cheek, and resisted the urge to touch him. He looked so much like he needed the rest, she was unwilling to risk waking him.

Beyond him lay a bathroom. Dana went in and tested the water. It was running, albeit cold. Still, she welcomed it.

She left the door open to give herself a little bit of light, stripped off her sweat-fouled flight suit, and sponged herself clean with a cold, wet towel. Then she dressed in a fresh uniform. With thirty minutes left before she had to report for duty, she sat on the side of Bill's bed and just stared at him. After a few minutes, he opened his eyes.

"Good morning," Dana said softly.

Bill smiled, then winced. "Oooh. That hurts my face."

"Yeah." A soft chuckle. "It looks like it hurts. Are you all right?"

"Just beat up. What time is it?"

Dana consulted her wrist chronometer. "Twenty-three thirty. Not actually morning. I have to report for duty at midnight."

He tried to smile again, this time more carefully. "That gives us half an hour."

"Hmmmm." Dana smirked, then lifted his blanket and looked beneath. He was wearing underwear. "Besides your face, is everything okay?"

"A little sore."

"Too bad. I guess we'll have to take a rain check." She paused. "What happened to your wrists?"

"Simeon's thugs put me in metal shackles and shot me repeatedly with a Lancaster."

"Ohhhh. Bill, I'm so sorry. Are they burned bad?"

"Yeah. That reminds me." He tried to sit up.

She pressed him gently back down. "I haven't seen you in twenty-three days. I'm not about to let you out of my sight now."

"I have to go to the Sharp Shooter. The doctors asked me to come back."

He held up his hands to display his bandages. "Dermal regeneration."

"In that case, I'll go with you." She helped him dress. Despite the damage to his face and wrists, and the generous display of bruises covering the front half of his torso and thighs, he seemed to be moving okay, with nothing more than an occasional wince and a groan or two.

Ten minutes later, the nurse smeared regeneration compound on Bill's burns and put them under a combination of deep purple light and gentle ultrasonic waves to induce the biochemical reaction between the salve and his skin. "How's that feel?"

"Better already."

Dana sat against the wall nearby, close enough to observe but far enough to be out of the way. More patients were now leaving the casino than were coming in. There were numerous dead, but nobody else seemed to be dying. In the sixteen hours since the first nuke had exploded, the base had shifted mode from "disaster" to merely "crisis."

A European officer came in, saw Dana there, and approached. He didn't salute and she didn't stand. Instead, he gestured to the wall beside her. "May I?"

She looked at the vacant spot, hoping he wasn't hitting on her. "It's still a free base."

With a nod, he settled himself next to her—a little too close for her liking, but not close enough to be an overt come-on. "I understand you and your crew are responsible for deploying the RI comm-sat."

Dana grunted. "Just doing our job."

"Well, we're all grateful." He offered her a pocket-sized flask, from which wafted the smell of strong liquor—whiskey maybe.

It was all Dana could do not to take the drink and down it all, though in the end it would probably just make her sleepy. "No thanks. I'm back on duty in a few minutes."

He took a swig. "Captain Kamieniechi."

She'd heard of him. His heroic defense had been the subject of several partially overheard conversations throughout the base since Dana had returned. His men, when they were being polite, called him Kamikaze. More often, they used the word *asshole*. But by all accounts, on this day, the man was a bona fide hero.

185

"You saved our necks out there. We were getting our asses plowed." He stood. "Anyway. I just wanted to say thanks." He raised his flask as if toasting, took a swig, and capped the bottle.

Now Dana did smile. She stood and shook his hand. "You did a good thing out there yourself, Captain. Don't sell yourself short. This whole base..." She gestured with a vague nod. "Everybody here. We all owe our lives to you and your men."

Before she released his hand, the comm-link in her ear chimed. Kamikaze reached for his own link. "Report in," Colonel Davis said simply.

"Hear that?" Dana asked Bill, who had inserted his link when he'd donned his flight uniform.

"Yeah. I have to go," he told the nurse, pulling his hand away from her.

"Oh no. You don't leave my care until I'm finished." To Dana, the nurse said, "I'm almost done. You can tell his commanding officer he'll be there in a few minutes."

CHAPTER 25

Dana followed Mike until they reached the ring of security around the command station, which now seemed unnecessary, as the civilians no longer crowded the military post. There, Mike slowed and let Dana go first. When she did, he placed his hand on her back, as if to guide her through the sentries. She twitched her shoulders in an effort to shake his hand off, but he left it there until they stopped in front of Davis.

Though he dropped his paw then, he continued to stand closer than necessary.

"Major," Davis began in a low voice. "As soon as the RI comm-sat passes over the pole again, we're going to use it to assault Shenming Base."

Dana nodded. She'd come here for combat. She wasn't surprised that Davis was deploying her crew again so quickly, despite the fact that her ship's cockpit door was still lying on some distant stretch of Mercury's surface.

"Lieutenant." Davis flagged down the ranking officer in his security detail.

"Sir?"

"Tell your men to take a break."

"Yes, sir."

With that, the sentries dispersed. They didn't go far, however. They merely lounged along the boardwalk or stood at parade rest, near enough to respond if Davis called them back, but far enough that they wouldn't overhear the conversation if Davis kept his voice low. Nobody below the rank of captain remained. Even the remainder of the CATS squadron hadn't been invited.

In the meantime, Bill arrived with fresh bandages on his wrists. "Excuse me." He nudged Mike aside and stepped between him and Dana.

Thank you, Bill.

Mike scowled at him and squinted at Dana as though trying to determine if she and Bill were together. She leaned into Bill's shoulder so Mike would have no doubt.

"According to our best intelligence, we figure whoever's running the show over there has just about spent his wad. Therefore, Brannon is going to lead an all-out assault on Shenming with virtually everything we have, more as a diversion than because I think we need that much force."

"I wouldn't underestimate them, Colonel," Dana said. "We know they have at least two Marauders left. They've got it all over us on speed and maneuverability. And without Earth's gravity to contend with, they can carry enough fuel for a sustained battle."

"I'm aware of that. We're going to pull a few Raptors from orbit to handle those.

"You three, however—" Davis pointed to Dana, Bill, and Kamikaze—"will be going to Gagarin."

Dana exchanged glances with Bill.

Kamikaze cracked the knuckles of his right hand. "Gagarin?"

"In a covert op." Davis nodded to Kamikaze. "Somebody needs to neutralize the Russian nukes. Brannon tells me you're the best man for the job."

"The only man for the job," Brannon said, "if it's a nuke. Kamieniechi's our expert. And he speaks Russian."

"Problem is," Davis continued. "Our intelligence on that base shows no facility appropriate for the security and storage of nuclear weapons. Wherever they're hiding them, it's not on the plans. And with all the civilians that come and go from Gagarin, the storage facility must be well hidden. There will only be seven of you, but you'll need to locate the nukes, bypass or disable the security, and neutralize the weapons. All of them."

"Anybody know anything about base utility systems?" Kamikaze asked.

"What are you thinking?" Brannon said.

"Obviously their nuclear facility is underground somewhere, presumably attached to the main base, but with labyrinthine underground structures like we have here—" he displayed a thinpad with a map of Deep West—"it could take days to locate. We won't be able to rely on architecture or logic to find it. Our best bet will be to follow the utilities."

"Yeah. So?" Brannon said.

"That will require someone who can distinguish between the normal facilities a base like this needs, and those that would be deemed unusual. So I'll ask again. Do we have anybody who knows anything about the utility systems of a base like this?"

Brannon looked at Davis. From their expressions, neither had a specific name come to mind.

The silence hung in the air for a long moment, and then Bill said, "I know someone who does."

All eyes turned to him.

"Zeke Shepherd, the facilities manager here. Problem is, he's a civilian."

Both commanders glanced at each other again, then back at Bill.

"I'll start checking dossiers," Davis said finally. "There must be somebody within the military ranks. If not, we'll have to learn what we can from Shepherd before we leave." He turned to Dana and Bill. "Wheels up in ninety minutes."

❧❦(◯)❦❧

Colonel Davis sat with Bill, Dana, and Mike Kamieniechi at a booth in the Sharp Shooter. The casino still housed about a dozen patients whose condition required constant monitoring, but the restaurant had been cleared. And because Davis had to wait for the comm-sat to return to a position over the northern pole, they were all taking advantage of the rare opportunity to eat something. While they were there, two privates arrived, escorting a large, square-jawed man in a dusty flannel shirt and blue jeans.

"Zeke Shepherd?" Davis asked.

Zeke took them all in with a slow, wary eye, then nodded.

"Please join us."

He examined the name patches that adorned each uniform, and then he slowly smiled. "War heroes all." He pulled up a chair to the end of the booth and sat down. "To what do I owe the pleasure?"

"We need your help," Davis told him.

"Anything I can do."

"We need a download of everything you can tell us about the utility systems on bases like this one."

"Bases *like* this one?" Zeke asked. "Or *this* base?"

"Like this."

"There are no bases like this one. Every base and habitat—and every space station, for that matter—is different. Each is unique, with its own quirks, its own needs, and its own systems." He paused. "Which base are we talking about? Shenming or Gagarin?"

The man was astute. Davis had to give him that. He frowned. This was to be a classified mission. Nobody was even supposed to know it existed. The troops who would be assigned to the simultaneous assault on Shenming, which was just about everybody, would be told that Bill Ryan and the *Snow Leopard* were staying behind because they were both unfit to fly.

Nevertheless, they couldn't succeed without picking Zeke Shepherd's brain for anything that might help them. "All right." Davis turned to Dana and Mike. "Clear the dining room." He waited several minutes while the two did so. Fortunately, almost everybody on the base was finally sleeping. There were only a few people to relocate.

Finally Davis said, "Gagarin."

Zeke nodded. "You're going after the nukes." He kept his voice low, conspiratorial.

"I can neither confirm nor deny—" Davis began, the required response to any inquiry regarding sensitive mission-related information.

"Oh, come on." Zeke swept his hand through the air. "Look around you. Everybody knows what happed here. And we know there was another detonation on the surface. Somewhere near the pole, I was told. It's no secret what's going on, and we're all hoping you can stop it."

Davis set a large thinpad onto the table. "This is the schematic on public file for Gagarin. We're looking for a secure warehouse that won't show up on the public record."

"A secret section of the base," Zeke said.

"Yes. Obviously we can't just walk around with this in hand and start looking for doors that don't appear on the drawing."

"But the secure section will need utilities: air, heat, water, electricity."

"Right. Presumably, those systems will tie into the existing base utilities at some point. Our plan is to locate those tie-ins and follow them to the Russian weapons cache. We need you to tell us what we should expect to find in a base this size, so we can recognize the discrepant systems when we see them."

Zeke frowned at the schematic. "This blueprint won't help you."

"Why not?"

"Look at the date. It's over ten years old. The base will have changed, likely expanded, since then. Just look at Deep West. I can't count the number of new tunnels and chambers that have been created or discovered in the sixteen years I've been here.

"The worlds become more populated every year, what with all the expansion going on in the Jupiter System. The workers' union there has grown nearly fourfold in the last decade. With Mercury as the transportation hub, we've had to expand accordingly. And since Russia is the biggest stakeholder in the Jupiter system, their base has probably seen the most rapid expansion of all."

"What if we can come up with a current schematic?"

"That'll help, but schematics almost never represent the actual as-built condition. Changes always occur as problems are encountered during construction and installation of the systems. The blueprints are supposed to be updated once construction is complete, but they almost never are."

"We're only looking for a ballpark estimate. Could you tell us, for example, what kind of electrical load the as-designed facility would need? We'll locate the power distribution node and compare the number of transformers with what you tell us to expect."

"Ultimately, it will depend," Zeke said.

"On what?"

"On a lot of things. On the vintage of the equipment, the rated capacity of the transformers, the electrical load of the systems they feed. Electricity is a hard system to gauge because the load varies from moment to moment. It's hard to say what excess capacity, or backup capability, the designers may have thought they needed, or how much of that excess the expansion of the base has already consumed.

"This base, for example, began as a simple unmanned solar research tower. Then the bunker at the northern pole was built to house a whole science team. That was later converted into a backup battery for the entire base. That one system alone could be used to power a hidden facility the size of the one you're talking about. And ours was idle for years, until Tanner and I restored it yesterday." He paused. "What you're asking for is *not* a simple thing. There are no easy answers."

Davis let out a heavy, defeated sigh. The whole mission was going to have to go back to the drawing board. They needed another answer.

Then Zeke supplied one. "I'll have to go with you."

∽⟨○⟩∾

Forty-five minutes later, Zeke stood among the military officers. All wore disguises that were somewhat makeshift but would be reasonably convincing if they could avoid detailed scrutiny. Zeke had managed to scrounge up several pairs of men's coveralls in approximately the color used by the pipefitter's guild that supplied contract journeymen for all three Mercury bases. He and each of the soldiers held a hardhat and had a pair of safety glasses in one pocket. With these, they should be able to infiltrate the civilian society on Gagarin, even to the extent of accessing at least some areas that housed the base facilities.

They had been unable, however, to find a pair small enough to fit Lieutenant Carter. After being around Ana, Zeke didn't see Carter as petite, but the smallest set of coveralls they could find looked ridiculously baggy on her.

Fortunately, her grey flight suit was similar in color to those of the Russian company contracted to do the electrical work on Gagarin's power system. If she turned her suit inside out to hide the military patches and insignia, and clipped a fake badge where the Russian company patch would normally be, Carter might pass for an electrical worker. Ryan volunteered to wear his flight suit the same way, so that if Carter was questioned and detained, at least she wouldn't be alone.

Zeke suggested they include someone in a business suit, with a large thinpad tucked into the crook of one arm and a stylus ready to jot notes.

192

If the Russian workers thought it was some sort of inspection, they would more likely make themselves scarce rather than raise a challenge.

At that point, the only clean business suits available were Simeon's. Short and scrawny as he was, Dana was the best fit for them, though she had to wear one of her own shirts beneath it to make it fit through the chest.

Various hand-carry toolboxes had been packed with equipment they might need—everything from bolt cutters and wire strippers, to a Geiger scanner, handguns, and thinpads packed with the latest in military encryption-cracking software.

In the scramble to get everything together, Zeke's mind had been occupied and he'd remained fairly composed. But now the soldiers were packing a duffle bag half again as large as a man's torso, which Townsend would carry over his shoulder and across his back. Zeke had cautioned that the monstrosity would betray them—there was no reason a pipefitter would carry a military-green bag of that size while on the job. But Davis, Kamieniechi, and Ryan all insisted it was necessary.

Into it, they packed several flight suits, half a dozen Lancaster pistols confiscated from the Plaza jailhouse, a number of automatic assault rifles—partially disassembled to make them fit—eight sets of infrared headgear, several bricks of military-grade plastic explosive, and he'd lost count of how many hand grenades. The thing must have weighted 30 kilograms, even in Mercury's gravity.

As each piece of gear disappeared into the bag, Zeke became more and more cognizant of the opposition these brave men and women were expecting—as well they should, given the nuclear nature of the weapons cache they were hoping to infiltrate—and how inadequately he himself was prepared for what they would meet. They couldn't possibly succeed.

Zeke swallowed hard. He could back out, he supposed, but that didn't seem quite like an option. The nukes were too much of a threat, and Russia would keep sending them until one slipped past Davis's defenses—until everybody at Deep West, including Ana, was dead and very well buried. Davis had to try, and his team's slim chances dropped to none without Zeke's help. That was the only reason Davis had agreed to let Zeke, a mere civilian, a liability to the mission in many ways, go along.

And it was the only reason Zeke had agreed to go with them, his only condition being that Davis provide a single demolitions man to help Ana free the survivors in the Administration complex.

"Ready?" Major Ryan said, finally, after all the packers had settled into a comfortable stillness.

"Yes, sir," they all responded in unison. All, that is, but Zeke.

"Ready?" Ryan asked him in a less-commanding, almost compassionate tone.

Zeke took a deep, settling breath, picked up his own packed toolbox, and nodded.

"Then let's move out." Ryan spun and marched toward the pressure suits hanging near the airlock.

His legs weak, Zeke moved to follow.

CHAPTER 26

It had taken the crews an hour to secure a layer of camouflage netting over the tops of the *Snow Leopard* and the *Black Panther*. With no atmosphere, there'd be no wind to rip at the straps or cause the netting to flap. Nevertheless, they had to make sure it didn't interfere with the thruster ports, missile doors, machine guns, or sensors. The netting, made primarily of nylon thread and bits of fabric, shouldn't cause an appreciable radar signature and might keep their black exterior from being spotted against Mercury's pale surface by one of the Chinese or Russian orbital vid-scanners.

"Ready?" Dana asked as Miller and Allistair secured the final strap on the *Snow Leopard*'s netting.

Together, she and her crew climbed into the cockpit with Kamikaze Mike. It felt odd, somehow, as though she was going out with too many blouse buttons undone, not having a hatch to seal the cockpit. When they'd launched from the *Taurus* with the RI comm-sat, they'd had no time to consider it. But now they were deliberately launching for enemy territory with an incomplete ship. "Sorry, girl." Dana patted the command console. "We've got to do this. Then it'll all be over."

Each of her crew checked in with a green board. Mike took his seat directly behind Dana, and he signaled "ready" as well. As soon as Bill launched the *Black Panther*, she gestured for Miller to follow.

Halfway into the twenty-minute flight, a heavy hand pressed on her shoulder. She turned and found Mike standing over her, looking out the windshield.

195

Dana keyed the intercom. "Back in your seat, Kamieniechi."

He didn't move.

"Sit down, Captain," she said more firmly, emphasizing Kamieniechi's rank. "We may need evasive maneuvers at any time."

"Worried I'll fall out?" he asked jovially, flirtingly.

Her voice hardened. "Get your hand off me and sit down. That's an order."

Allistair unsnapped his flight harness and stood. Though Kamieniechi outranked him, he was ready to support Dana if necessary.

She held up her hand to forestall him. This was between herself and Mike. It had to be, if she was to gain Mike's respect as his commanding officer.

He stood, unmoving, for far too long before finally resuming his seat. *Great*, she thought. *That's just great.*

⚫❨◯❩⚫

Gagarin Base looked vastly different from the sprawling surface footprint of Deep West. From the outside, it was nothing more than a row of enormous rectangular doors in the face of a 300-meter-high lobate scarp.

Miller and Carter brought the ships in high to prevent the thrusters from churning up regolith from Mercury's surface. The cloud of dust upon landing, however, was unavoidable. It sprayed upward, clearing a stretch of bedrock beneath the ships. But once they were on the ground, the camouflaged CATS should be virtually impossible to spot from space.

Dana lowered the cargo ramp and Kamikaze flew out, propelled by a jet pack of the type normally used on space walks. He waved back to the CATS crew, then sped toward one of Gagarin's smaller entrances.

On Earth, breaking into a civilian-run facility would have been child's play for a European special forces team, because all such facilities relied on external sources of power and air, whose conduits could be breached. Gagarin, on the other hand, presented an entirely new challenge. Its systems were designed to separate the base from the void around it. It produced its own power from a fusion reactor buried deep inside, and recycled its air and water. The only way in or out was through these doors, which Mike couldn't breach without setting off some sort of environmental alarm inside.

196

One way or another, he was going to have to convince them to let him in. He gave that the same response he gave to any mission challenge. "No problem."

He turned his comm to the Russian frequency, took a couple of deep breaths, and pushed the call button beside a small personnel entry door, which stood near one of the huge freighter entrances.

A scanner above the door swiveled. Mike waved at it. There was no way the scanner's operator could see him through the polarization of his faceplate. All he would see was a man in a civilian space suit with the logo of Deep West Base.

"May I help you?" a voice said in English, with a heavy Slovak accent.

Mike replied in fluent Russian, panting. "Open, please. I've just escaped from Deep West. My air is almost gone."

"Deep West?" the voice said, this time in Russian. "I didn't think there were any survivors."

That told Mike much of what he needed to know. The civilian population of Gagarin Base was apparently being lied to about the events occurring around them. Their media over the past twenty-four hours must have been censored.

"I was at the pole, doing calibration tests on the solar array. The whole base has collapsed upon itself." That statement, at least, was almost true. "I tried to hole up in the old science bunker, but even that is leaking slowly to space."

"Where's your—" the Russian began.

"Please! My air! I'll explain everything when I get inside."

An artificial chime sounded in his helmet, and the door panel began a slow slide to the left. "Come to Visitor Registration and scan in. We're marked on your left, about a hundred meters down the catwalk."

"Thank you." Mike stepped into the airlock, and the door slid closed behind him. As soon as the pressure equalized and the inner door opened, he unclipped his fishbowl helmet, tossed his gloves inside it, and clipped it to his belt.

From there, he stepped onto a catwalk, maybe two meters wide. Beside him, just inside the freighter entrance, sat a huge conveyor that looked like an enormous set of tank treads, which extended into the darkness of a cavern that made Deep West's Plaza look like a cubby hole. While Deep West Base had been constructed primarily for human traffic, including a significant percentage of the Russian and Chinese passenger ships, Gagarin had been built to accommodate the immense ore, hydrogen, and ice freighters that came in from Jupiter.

Mike walked as fast as he dared. If the Russian authorities were lying to the population about what had happened at Deep West, they were probably restricting traffic into and out of the base. A man in a pressure suit would draw attention. A running man in a pressure suit, even more so.

He turned the corner into a short alcove that contained only one door. A glowing green sign read, WELCOME. ALL VISITORS PLEASE SCAN IN, with the text printed in Russian, English, and a set of Asian glyphs—presumably Chinese. Beyond the door, a painting crew, a man and a woman, were spraying a lively shade of yellow paint on the wall.

When he saw Mike, the man began to reach for the comm link in his ear, then stopped. He scratched his shoulder, nodded to Mike, and turned his attention back to his work.

Mike returned the nod cautiously while scrutinizing them both. The yellow paint they were using had covered the entire left-hand wall from the personnel airlock through which Mike had entered, all the way to the registration center door. The crew had apparently been working for some time. The beige they were painting over, however, looked pristine. Their jumpsuits were genuinely paint-stained in several colors, but their boots— spit-polished combat boots—gave them away.

As casually as he could, Mike drew a Lancaster from his thigh pocket. The woman's eyes widened. From several rungs up on her ladder, she swung her paint sprayer at Mike. The man reached again for his comm link.

Mike spun to protect his eyes as a swath of canary paint soaked him. With his back turned, he shot a blind Lancaster pulse in the direction of the painters. The woman's sprayer clattered to the floor.

When Mike looked back, the man lay motionless on the catwalk. The woman had been caught by the edge of the Lancaster pulse. She appeared dazed—her eyes blinking, her expression confused. One hand rested, singed, on the top rung of the ladder. She blinked again, and her eyes began to focus. Mike's Lancaster whined, not yet recharged for a second pulse.

He grabbed a fistful of the woman's collar and slammed the butt of his gun into her temple. He could have simply thrown her over the railing, but her body would alert the authorities that someone had penetrated the base. As it was, he lowered her quietly to the catwalk floor.

With his fingernail, he popped the comm link from her ear and inspected it. Military issue. He unzipped her jumpsuit and rolled her over. Tucked into a pair of khaki pants at the small of her back was a Russian handgun, also military issue.

Mike smiled. If the base commander was hiding his military presence from the civilian population, that would make Mike's job easier.

He stood, leaving the woman unconscious on the floor. His own left arm and side were soaked in yellow paint. Though he'd hunched his head and the neck ring of his EVA had shielded him some, he found a patch of hair just behind his left ear that was sticky with paint. So much for not drawing attention to himself.

By then the Lancaster pistol had recharged. He tucked it back into his pocket, touched the door control, and stepped into the registration center.

Inside, a lone guard sat behind a counter lined with half a dozen computer terminals, all but one dark and silent. "What the hell happened to you?" He started to rise.

"Do you believe it?" Mike made a vague gesture toward the door. "Incompetent assholes. I'll want to file a complaint."

The guard sat back down. "All right, but you're going to have to scan in first."

Mike unclipped his helmet from his belt and glanced around for someplace to set it down and shed his cumbersome pressure suit. There was nothing but a few plastic chairs along one wall.

Across from the desk, a display showed a still image of Deep West Base that had been taken by satellite sometime after the initial blast, but before the US and EU convoys had landed. The base looked deserted.

A Russian news commentator reported that the image was actually a live vid-scan. "The cause of the blast is still unknown," the announcer said. "Radiation levels are too high to attempt any kind of recovery at this time. Experts speculate that one of the visiting ships must have been carrying some sort of volatile radioactive cargo. Or worse, the Western powers may have been transporting nuclear weapons, and suffered a catastrophic accident during landing."

"We felt the tremor all the way over here," the guard said. "And a secondary blast later."

"What?" Mike turned back to the guard. "Oh, yeah. You should have felt it at the solar array."

"What do you think happened?"

"No idea." Mike displayed his gloves and paint-splattered helmet.

The guard motioned to a standard thumbprint reader near the active terminal. "Once you've scanned in, the system will issue you an account number, which you can use to rent an EVA locker farther down the catwalk."

"Fine." Mike squatted to set his helmet on the floor, ostensibly to free his hands for the thumb scanner. While his movements were obscured by the counter, he slipped the Lancaster from his suit's thigh pocket.

Standing, he pointed it at the guard's head and pulled the trigger. The man, whose gaze had returned to the newsblip, froze. His eyes bulged slightly as his entire nervous system spasmed from the flood of microwaves. As he fell forward, his seat rolled back and deposited him onto the floor.

"Just a suggestion." Mike strolled around the counter. "You might want to consider some security."

As Mike had hoped, the guard's terminal was still logged in—his monitor displayed several images of the approaches to the base. He settled into the man's chair, adjusted the seat for his own comfort, cracked his knuckles, and began typing. Within minutes, he'd opened the visitor log, which contained a record for each time one of the base's exterior doors had opened.

He'd have to wait the prearranged five minutes, wondering now why he'd thought it might take him so long to gain entry. He used the time to pull the painters into the registration center and inject all three Russians with enough morphine to stop their hearts. He left the bodies in a heap behind the counter. Mike had time to create several locker assignments in the guard's name, which he read from the man's badge, before the rest of his team approached the airlock.

He cycled them through in two groups. By the time they reached the visitor's center, he had deleted any record of the airlock's having ever been used.

‹‹(O)››

As soon as he got inside, Zeke shed his bubble helmet so the tinting of the faceplate wouldn't hinder his vision in the dim interior of Gagarin Base. He ogled the massive, intricate network of lifts, ramps, conveyors, elevators, and bay doors that made up the enormous underground warehousing and ship-storage facility.

He leaned over the railing and peered down at a vast array of hangar doors, and then up at a single story of bays above them, carved out of the cliff itself. Giant pistons were poised to lift the entire conveyor, even with a freight ship laden with the heaviest Jupiter ore. Such a system would have been impossible on Earth, with that much weight to lift and with such elegant, though massive, mechanisms. But here, in the partial gravity of Mercury...

He emitted a long, low whistle at the hardiwork of the Russian designers and builders. Every base in the solar system, it seemed, could boast its own unique engineering marvel, from the first working fusion reactor of Lunar Alpha Base, to the frictionless lift collars of *Venus Rain*, to the vast solar array of Deep West—the only array in the worlds that was always in direct sunlight—to the enormous space elevators that launched ore from Callisto all the way to Mercury in a single massive throw... This lift system was the marvel of Gagarin Base. And the magnitude of it, as an accomplishment of man, was not lost on Zeke.

Major Ryan tapped Zeke's shoulder with the back of his hand. "Come on. We've got to keep moving."

Zeke took one long look back at the conveyors and followed the American airmen to Visitor Registration.

Major Ryan walked around the counter and checked the pulse at the neck of three casualties lying there. He rounded on Kamikaze. "You didn't have to kill them."

Kamikaze's expression was cold. "I believe I did." For a moment, it seemed he would add some justification, but he didn't. "There're lockers for our pressure suits down the catwalk."

Kamikaze led the way. They stowed their EVA gear and moved out quickly.

"The civilian guard had no idea what's been going on at Deep West," Kamikaze was saying, "or anywhere else outside the confines of Gagarin Base."

"That's good," Major McCaughey said. "It means this really is a predominantly civilian base."

"And that the general population has no idea their government is storing nukes here," Bill added.

"It means," Kamikaze said, "we can expect little in the way of any real security until we get into the concealed portion of the base."

At that, Major Ryan turned to Zeke. "You're up."

Zeke produced a thinpad from the pocket of his coveralls and pulled up the base schematic. He studied the floor plan for a moment, looked up to get his bearings, and then rotated the display to match the orientation of the base. "This way."

He turned left on the main catwalk and led them to a lift constructed of mesh on all six sides. They boarded together, and Zeke pointed to the Russian text near the bottommost button on the control panel. "What's that say?" he asked Kamikaze.

"Physical Plant."

When Zeke pressed the button, the lift lurched downward with a clatter, leaving his stomach to catch up. Fortunately, the motion smoothed as the lift descended.

Two stories, perhaps two hundred meters down, the lift stopped and two Russian workers got on. From the grease stains on their coveralls, they looked like maintenance personnel, though Zeke couldn't discern from their patches whether they serviced visiting freighters or the elaborate conveyors and lifts of the base's stacked-hanger system.

Casually, he hoped, Zeke pocketed the thinpad.

Kamikaze greeted the men perfunctorily in Russian. Major Ryan and several of the others nodded. The men turned toward the lift's control board, noted that the "Physical Plant" button was already lit, and settled in for the ride.

Zeke exchanged worried looks with Lieutenant Carter.

Kamikaze carried on a brief, unintelligible conversation with the men. One pointed to the paint in Kamikaze's hair. He said something and they all laughed, until Major McCaughey frowned and began taking notes on her thinpad. The Russians glanced at her and punched the button for the next available floor. Thankfully, both men got off there.

At the bottom. Zeke led his party through a series of populated hallways.

At one point, they passed a pub, small and dark, with cheerful Celtic music emanating from it. The inside, visible through a durapane window, was decorated with pipes and utility conduits, one of which extended through the wall and along the base of the pub's facade. When Zeke touched it, the pipe felt warm and vibrated gently against his palm. This wasn't faux decor but genuine base infrastructure.

Moving on, they nodded or waved as people passed. Kamikaze, now walking beside Zeke most of the time, replied to the few verbal greetings they received.

Nobody challenged their presence.

Finally, consulting his thinpad once more, Zeke stopped in front of a heavy metal door. He glanced both ways down the hall and tried the handle. Locked. "Now what?" They couldn't exactly shoot their way through without attracting a freighter-load of unwanted attention.

"What's inside?" Major Ryan asked.

"Facilities control room."

McCaughey pointed to a thumbprint reader beside the door. "And likely, base security."

"Which means," Ryan said, "as soon as we breach this door, the whole base is going to know we're here."

Kamikaze held out his hand, palm up to Townsend, but looked straight at Major Ryan. "Can't be helped."

Ryan hesitated for only a moment. "No, it can't."

At that, Townsend dug seven Lancaster pulse guns from his duffle bag and handed them out to the CATS crews.

Kamikaze set his toolbox down and extricated a cutting laser. Within seconds, he seared through the deadbolt. Then he and Ryan kicked the doors wide.

They blasted two men and a woman who sat at monitors along the far wall.

A guard inside shot a microwave pulse through the doorway. Ryan, Kamikaze, Carter, and Allistair all went down in a sprawl of blank stares and disobedient limbs, Lancasters clattering to the floor.

Zeke flattened himself against the stone wall.

Major McCaughey whipped her arm around the jamb and fired. A faint sigh and a whump followed from just inside. She swept her gaze and gun in an arc that covered the remainder of the room. "Clear."

Miller and Townsend strode in behind her. Zeke followed more cautiously.

"You better get moving," Major McCaughey told him. "We've only got a few minutes."

CHAPTER 27

Viktor Batkin, the commander of Gagarin Base, sat at the desk he'd had carved from a single slab of Mercury bedrock. A solid desk, a representation of the solidity that made things matter. A desk more solid even than his country or its government—more solid than it had been even at its peak. But not more solid than it would be when President Petrov's pact with China came to fruition. Russia would own half of terraformed Venus and hold a monopoly on the solar system's ore, ice, and hydrogen markets.

Then his country would be solid.

He commended Petrov for having the courage to take this bold step and the foresight of Petrov's predecessors for rebuilding their nuclear stockpile so Petrov could take advantage of this opportunity now that it had finally arrived.

He commended them for storing the stockpile here, buried beneath a kilometer of that same solid bedrock, on a planet bathed in solar radiation—an environment that had prevented their enemies from detecting any hint of the bombs' radioactive cores. From this planet, at the hub of interplanetary travel, Russia could deploy the arsenal anywhere, within a matter of days or weeks. Or hours, in the case of Deep West.

Finally, he commended them for assigning military personnel as the police force, chief administrator, and senior staff of Gagarin Base.

The whole arrangement was absolutely brilliant. With a single bomb, Russia had essentially crippled American and European ability to do so much as supply any of its extraterrestrial assets.

The electronics console imbedded in the top corner of the desk chimed. The comm channel lit up, as did the URGENT light beside it.

Batkin keyed the link. *"Da?"*

"Sir," the familiar voice of his security chief said in Russian, "we've received an alarm from facilities."

Batkin sat up and replied in the same tongue. "Report."

"Not sure, sir. Our panel is showing unauthorized entry of the control room. It could be a door sensor malfunction."

"Hold on." Batkin tried to contact his perimeter teams. One didn't respond.

"Check out facilities," he told his chief. "And check on our team outside the registration office. Find out what's going on."

It was probably nothing. There hadn't been a serious security breach at Gagarin in the history of the base. Furthermore, an overreaction at this point could be catastrophic. It could reveal the base's true nature to the civilian population, who knew nothing of Russia's nuclear weapons program. They would likely rebel. Batkin didn't have the personnel to handle that scale of crisis. Not yet. He must keep it contained, at least until the current conflict between Shenming and Deep West played itself out, and until Petrov received additional military troops from Earth. "Send security teams in civilian dress. Report to me as soon as you know more."

He rose and paced a path around his desk, like a satellite in the stone's orbit, waiting for word.

◈《○》◈

Miller and Townsend pulled their stunned friends into the control room. They bound the incapacitated Russians with flex cuffs and pumped enough morphine into them to render each senseless as well. That way they couldn't report any of the team's activities even when the Lancaster pulse wore off.

While Major McCaughey guarded the entrance, Zeke headed straight for an active computer terminal. Unfortunately, everything was written in gibberish. He glanced at Kamikaze's prone form. The man was supposed to be able to help him with this. "Any of you read Russian?" he asked the others.

All three shook their heads.

"Figures." He returned his attention to the terminal and began keying the incomprehensible icons, hoping beyond hope to locate some sort of schematic. There had to be a current one in here somewhere.

"You've got maybe ten minutes," McCaughey called from the doorway. "If we're lucky."

"Not gonna happen," Zeke called back. Each time he hit an icon, text appeared. He was looking for something he could understand—a picture—something that contained a diagram of the facilities.

Another screen of gibberish. "Crap. Where the hell are the schematics?" He had Russian-to-English translation software on his thinpad, but it would be too slow, and in any case it would translate only text files, not the operating system. If the directory tree had any organizational structure, he couldn't decipher it.

"Then we're going to get trapped in here." Without taking her eyes off the corridor, McCaughey pointed to the laser torch Kamikaze had dropped. "Hand me that. We may need to barricade ourselves in."

Miller picked up the pen-shaped torch and tossed it to her.

"How you doing, Shepherd?" she asked.

"Nothing yet."

"Then dump the whole core onto your thinpad and have Kamieniechi sort it out later. Just hurry."

"Major," Townsend said.

McCaughey took her eyes off the hall long enough to glance at him.

He pointed to a vent in the four-meter-high stone ceiling.

She nodded. "Get Ryan and the others up there, if you can." She paused. "Shepherd?"

"There's too much data. The memory core's too big. I need to narrow it down somehow." *Damn.* He wasn't used to this kind of pressure. Hazards, yes. Lives in his hands, sure. Time constraints, always. But not like this. Learn to read Russian in ten minutes? *You've got to be kidding me.*

Miller and Townsend pushed a heavy aluminite table under the vent. Together, they upended a filing cabinet that sounded like it weighed at least a hundred kilos on top of it.

Miller assembled an assault rifle from Townsend's duffle bag, climbed the stack of furniture, and pounded the padlock on the grate to failure with the butt of the gun. The appearance of the rifle brought home the danger of what they were trying to do, and despite the cool temperature maintained for the benefit of the equipment, Zeke's face dripped with sweat. Where the hell were the schematics?

McCaughey snapped her fingers twice, stepped out of sight of the hallway, and slashed her hand across in front of her throat. Instantly, Miller and Townsend went still and Zeke stopped his muttering. The only remaining sound was the soft drumming of Zeke's fingers on the keypad.

And the sound of voices from the hallway, gradually drawing nearer.

McCaughey rounded the doorframe and sent a Lancaster pulse down the corridor. The voices died and a few small items plinked on the stone floor.

"Help me haul them inside," McCaughey ordered Miller and Townsend. "I just bought us some time, but now they'll send the military. In force."

Miller and Townsend finished lifting Major Ryan into the air duct, where they'd already placed Allistair and Carter. They jumped from the table and disappeared into the hallway.

"I can buy us some more," Zeke said, surprised he hadn't thought of this earlier.

"How?" McCaughey asked.

He pointed. "See those blue wires along the wall, just above that computer rack? Cut them."

"What'll that do?"

"In a base like this, with so much rock, especially rock laced with nickel and iron, transmissions are spotty. Communications have to rely on hard lines. That box—" he pointed again—"is the comm router. Take that out, and the whole system goes down."

McCaughey plucked a pair of wire cutters from a workbench just as Miller and Townsend dragged the last two security guards into the room and dumped them along one wall.

"They'll repair that." Townsend cut a piece off a brick of C-4 from his bag. He slapped it on top of the router, shoved the detonator into it, and backed away. "Stand back."

"Oh, sh—" Zeke grabbed the monitor—as if that would somehow save the data he was trying to locate—and dove beneath the desk.

"Major?" Townsend's thumb was poised over the detonation button.

McCaughey thought for a moment. She looked up at the hole in the ceiling, nodded, and then ducked behind an equipment rack.

The blast left Zeke's ears ringing for the third time in twenty-four hours and produced a rain of shrapnel.

Townsend smiled. "That ought to slow them down."

"Or bring them running," McCaughey said. "We need to clear out. Let's go, Shepherd. Now or never."

Zeke dumped as much data as he could to the thinpad and climbed into the rough-cut stone duct. Miller and Townsend manhandled Kamikaze in behind him. McCaughey shoved the filing cabinet onto the floor and kicked over the table, so it all looked like wreckage from the C-4 blast. Then she leapt up to the hole. Miller and Townsend grabbed her wrists and dragged her through. She pulled the grate closed, then tack-welded it with the laser torch.

Together, they pulled the four Lancaster victims about ten meters back from the hole. "Go with them," McCaughey said. "And find that weapons cache."

Zeke nodded. If he'd gotten the files he thought he had, he should be able to decipher something. He moved down the duct and brought up one of several diagrams he'd located.

Townsend sat down next to him, looking over his shoulder. "That's not the electrical schematic."

"No."

"I thought you were an electrical guy."

"I manage all of Deep West's facilities." Zeke panned across the layout.

"We're going to have to shut down power to the weapons cache," Townsend said. "Security hasn't been that tight so far, because they have to maintain the illusion of a civilian base. But as soon as we get into the hidden section, electronic surveillance and entry countermeasures are going to get brutal."

"I know, but I can't count on finding the hidden warehouse that way. They may be running off an isolated battery system."

"Then what—"

"Air. It's the only other utility an underground warehouse absolutely needs. And if it's of any size, they'll have to pump in a lot of air. There's got to be a duct, and a pumping system."

Townsend gestured to the display. "But if that's a public file, it won't show what you're looking for."

"Not the duct, but the fans." He tapped the icon on the diagram. "Fans this size need a lot of maintenance. And systems that need maintenance need parts. They'll have to admit the fans exist in order to justify the purchases. I'm comparing the drawing with what the base, as shown, should need. Sooner or later I'll find a discrepancy between what they need and what they're supplying. That's where we'll find their undocumented duct."

McCaughey snapped her fingers, a soft sound that got both Zeke's and Townsend's attention. She cut her fingers across her throat, and everything fell to silence. Only a soft hiss remained, coming from somewhere in the room below.

In the next moment, Zeke heard a sharp crack, and then several voices speaking in Russian. He pressed the illuminated display against his chest to block out the light.

Townsend tapped his shoulder, pointed to the thinpad, and then made forward circles with his finger in a "keep going" gesture.

Reluctantly Zeke continued his silent search.

CHAPTER 28

As Dana watched, six people flooded the facilities control room, each sporting a military-issue automatic pistol. Instantly, the man in charge keyed the link in his ear. He tapped it, tried it again, and then stopped.

The comm router existed only as so many bits of shrapnel littering every horizontal surface in the room. Adjacent equipment dangled from the wall as ragged metal shells, waiting to cut the flesh of unwary repairmen. Beyond that, however, much of the room was still intact, the equipment operating.

The lead soldier issued an order to a man beside him, who tucked his weapon into his waistband, pulled the tails of a greasy work shirt over it, and darted from the room. Obviously, they were still trying to conceal the military presence on the base. So much the better. It would slow any armed response and limit the scale of the counter-operation.

The rest of the men swept the place, making sure it was clear of intruders.

"*Voht*," one said, coming upon the incapacitated guards who'd been dumped into one corner. He checked each for vital signs.

The sergeant took a long look at the vent in the ceiling. When he shined a flashlight through the grate, Dana leaned backward, bracing herself with one hand on the stone behind her, until she was out of range of the powerful beam.

After a moment, the soldier moved away. He sent a second man out with some unknown orders.

◄⟨ O ⟩►

The stone duct appeared to have been bored out by a small mining robot, with a central drill, surrounded by four smaller bits that, together, carved out an approximate square. Boring the ducts out of Mercury bedrock, rather than installing conduits in existing personnel tunnels, was not the way Deep West was constructed, but it made sense for Gagarin. Though it probably took longer, it might actually have been cheaper in the long run than shipping manufactured ductwork from Earth.

Besides, drilling the ducts out of the rock made it impossible for some sharp supply clerk to notice a discrepancy in the inventory every time materials had to be diverted for the classified warehousing facility.

Zeke glanced at Townsend to get his attention, then pointed at the thinpad's tiny screen. He'd located the base's excess blower capacity.

Townsend only nodded and put a finger to his lips, then glanced at the Lancaster victims.

Lieutenant Carter began to stir. Allistair put one hand on her arm and the other across her legs to help keep her from twitching as she regained control of her muscles.

Carter shifted slightly as her eyes fluttered open, but that was it.

Major McCaughey's head snapped around. She gestured "quiet" before turning back to the men below.

Carter raised one hand in a gesture of understanding and agreement. Shortly thereafter, Lieutenant Miller, Major Ryan, and Kamikaze recovered as well. McCaughey continued to watch the hole for several minutes, until the facilities control room filled with another round of surprised voices.

She chose that moment to move. In a squat, she worked her way to the others, her boots making no more sound than a soft scrape on the stone. Townsend handed out some infrared headgear that included an IR lamp— invisible to the naked eye—and goggles that could detect the IR's reflection off the stone. It gave the pitch-black tunnel an eerie white glow, like that of moonlight, as they moved away in the direction of Zeke's excess blowers.

The more Zeke had studied the schematics, the more it seemed this whole base was designed for a single purpose: to house the covert storage facility for Russia's nuclear weapons. That meant the need to store them, and to hide them, had been on the mind of the Russian government for decades. It meant that they probably had a lot of weapons to hide. And it meant that they were probably *all* here.

"We're looking for an awfully big warehouse," he whispered to McCaughey once they'd moved beyond earshot of the facilities control room.

"Good," she said. "That'll make it easier to find."

"But more heavily guarded," Townsend added.

"Maybe not," Major Ryan said. "If they've been successful in keeping it hidden, they won't need or want many guards. At some point, more guards just means a greater chance of discovery."

Zeke rounded a corner, and before him, exactly as it was shown on the schematic, lay a grate to a room below. A stretch of high-density polyethylene electrical conduit had been run through the grate and along the stone duct. He loved it when the drawings were accurate. It would make the covert facilities easier to recognize when he found them.

A little further on, he pointed to a duct that wasn't shown on the plans. A second electrical conduit ran through it. "There's the power feed for the weapons warehouse."

Settling in next to him, McCaughey pulled out the laser torch and tried to cut the pipe. Nothing.

Zeke tapped on it. Though it had been painted to appear identical to the plastic conduits, it rang like metal, probably tungsten, which had a melting temperature in excess of three thousand degrees centigrade. The torch simply wasn't hot enough to cut through. A grinding saw would do the job, but even if they had one, it would take time and cause far too much noise. "We'll have to follow it back. Shut it down at the source."

Ryan nodded. "McCaughey, take Shepherd and your crew. Find the power source and shut it down."

"Here." Townsend gave Allistair a brick of C-4 and a handful of detonators. "You may need these."

"They'll figure out what we're after and send troops to intercept us," Ryan continued. "So we don't have much time. The rest of us are going on ahead."

"Oh, no," McCaughey said. "Every time I let you out of my sight, you nearly get yourself killed."

"Sorry, honey." He pecked her on the mouth, a breach of conduct for which McCaughey looked immensely grateful. "That's an order."

Kamikaze gave both of them a distasteful scowl, which turned into a glare full of hatred as his gaze landed on Ryan.

"Be careful," McCaughey told Ryan.

Zeke followed the metal conduit until it dropped through a vent grate into a dark room. Shining his flashlight, he could see a power distribution panel and a bank of electrical disconnect switches. "This is it."

"All right," McCaughey said. "Stand back." She maneuvered closer and kicked the grate several times. Each kick deformed it until the hinges finally gave up and it hung by its padlocked latch. After checking the room, she scooted back and gestured Zeke toward the opening. "Show time."

"We'll cover you," Allistair added.

His heart pounding, Zeke lowered himself through the hole. There wasn't much to grip inside the duct—the electrical conduit was flush with the rock, so he couldn't get his fingers all the way around it. By the time his chest reached the lip of the hole, he just slid the rest of the way through. Fortunately, the ceiling was only three meters high and the space below was clear.

As soon as he hit the floor, the lights came on. Zeke spun. The door was closed. Except for himself, the room was empty, the light apparently on a motion scanner.

"I think it's safe to assume somebody knows we're here," McCaughey said. She was right. If the lights were on a motion sensor, so was security.

Wasting no time, Zeke traced the conduit from the vent hole, through which McCaughey was aiming her combat rifle at the room's only door. The pipe led to a high-voltage disconnect. He couldn't read Russian, but he understood the numbers and the universal symbols for Voltage and Amps. This was an extremely high-current system, which meant this one disconnect probably fed the entire nuclear warehouse.

Allistair dropped Zeke's toolbox into his waiting hands.

Without stopping to consider the risk of an arc flash, Zeke yanked the lever down, opening the switch and shutting off power to everything downstream. He removed a welding laser from his toolbox, along with an insulated Gauss driver.

214

"What's he doing?" Miller hissed to someone else in the duct.

"I'll be quick," Zeke assured them. If he didn't disable the switch, some-body would simply turn the power back on. He removed the front panel from the box and began to slag the switch contacts with the welding laser.

When the security panel by the door began to emit a string of electronic beeps, Miller and Allistair appeared on opposite sides of the vent, extending their hands through the opening.

Zeke dropped his tools and leapt for the vent. The airmen grabbed his wrists and pulled him through the hole.

Just as he disappeared, the door flew open and half a dozen armed men flooded in, all in full military uniform. Apparently the Russian commander was through pussyfooting around and trying to hide the military nature of the base.

The game was on in earnest.

CHAPTER 29

Major Bill Ryan scrambled down the long, straight duct for what must have been half a kilometer before he finally saw light streaming up through a vent in the floor. Immediately beyond the opening, at the end of the duct, a security scanner stood sentry. Other than a meter or so around the opening, the duct was pitch black, so the scanner wasn't a vid camera. And the temperature-controlled air streaming down the duct would make a thermal sensor nearly as useless.

"Probably a motion scanner," Kamikaze said, just as Bill came to the same conclusion. He produced a pair of hand grenades and whispered, "These'll take care of any guards below."

"Wait for the lights in there to go out," Bill said. "We don't want the security system lighting up."

Mike patted him twice on the shoulder and moved a little closer to the hole. For ninety seconds, Bill watched both his wrist chronometer and Kamikaze. "Come on, Shepherd. Any day now."

Then the light winked out. Bill expected Mike to scramble forward to beat the grate open and drop the grenades. Instead, the man skipped one down the duct.

"Oh, shit," Bill called. "Get down!" He threw himself to the floor, feet toward the grenade. When it exploded, a wave of heat and pressure washed over him. His ears felt like they'd imploded. Shouts rose from the room below.

He heard the second grenade, skipping like the first. *Son of a*...It dropped through the now-open vent and exploded in the room. Then everything was silent.

In the ghostly infrared image, Kamikaze was crawling on his elbows, rifle before him, toward the hole. The son of a bitch was out of control.

"Come on," Bill screamed to his crew. He scrambled forward and dropped into a simple stone-box room, half a dozen meters square. Two men lay dead, one of the bodies mangled as if he'd been standing near the grenade when it fell, or had been killed by the first grenade and the second had landed beside the body.

If not for the IR headgear, the place would have been completely black, without even emergency lights. Backup lighting would have required a redundant power supply, redundant disconnects, redundant conduit...It would have made hiding the facility that much harder.

Large steel doors, now pockmarked from the shrapnel, were embedded in two of the walls, a dead control panel beside each. One door would take them back in the direction from which they'd come. The other had a row of small fans above it, apparently as a means to get air circulating from this guard station to the rooms beyond. From here in, everything seemed to pass through this room. And though all of the electronic security systems seemed to be down, all of the physical barriers would be locked tight, the loss of power forcing them to their default—most secure—positions.

⊷⟪○⟫⟞

"Wait here," the Russian lieutenant told Corporal Krayev. He glanced at the toolbox and open disconnect panel. "Find out what they've done, and undo it." Then he and three of his men climbed into the duct to pursue the intruders.

Krayev was more than happy to follow the order. Just about anything suited him better than following a special forces team—who else would try to infiltrate a nuclear weapons facility?—into a stone air duct. Talk about ducks in a barrel. The lieutenant and his men would have nowhere to hide from the gunfire.

But Krayev didn't have to examine the equipment to determine the intruders' motives. The room itself told him why they had come here. This was where the power feed for the entire classified wing tied into the base's main power bus, and it did so through the only disconnect whose panel had been removed—the only disconnect the intruders had turned off.

He keyed the comm link in his ear. "Lieutenant?"

"What have you got?"

"They shut down power to the classified complex. Including all the security systems."

"Can you repair it?"

One of the contacts was scored and discolored, but intact. "They just shut it off. I think we got here before they had time to do any real damage."

Gunfire erupted from the lieutenant's end of the link, followed by a scream. Krayev thanked the stars he wasn't in the duct with them.

"Krayev, can you hear me?"

"I'm still here."

"Get it back on. Now."

"Yes, sir." Krayev closed the comm, grabbed the handle, and heaved the switch into the ON position. It moved easily but failed to click into place. As soon as he let go, the switch sprang partway back to OFF.

He tried again. It popped back out, as if something wasn't catching that was supposed to hold it in place. "Shit." He moved his face closer to get a better view of the mechanism and tried again. This time he held it for a second. It seemed to stick momentarily. When he let go, a small blue spark arced between the separating contacts—a dangerous sign. Yet the contact had almost held, and the classified wing needed power.

Against his better judgment, he tried it one more time, throwing all of his strength behind the switch. A metal chip shorted the contact to the grounded case, shunting all the available power through itself. The resulting arc blast turned the air in the switch box into expanding plasma that blew the whole panel apart. Molten fragments of shrapnel shredded Krayev and half the equipment in the room.

⊷⟨O⟩⊷

Kamikaze Mike slapped a whole brick of plastic explosive against the latch on the heavy steel door that barred their way. Their supply of C-4 was limited, but this door looked thick. He stabbed the brick with a radio detonator. "Take cover!"

The flyboys with him dove behind the desks and cabinets that littered the room. Mike himself ducked behind an overturned aluminite table. The table wasn't thick, but from a door that solid, shrapnel wouldn't be an issue.

Without waiting for Major Ryan's approval—as far as he was concerned, he didn't need it—Mike touched off the switch. The blast made the air in the room bulge. Dead electronics panels, and the table Mike was using for cover, warped inward, giving the whole place an odd sensation of concavity.

The heavy door hung on one hinge, a wedge of darkness visible beyond.

As if Ryan wasn't actually in charge, Mike waved the others forward. He ran in a crouch to the wall beside the off-kilter door.

Ryan moved up along the other side. Carefully, he peered through.

Gunshots sounded from somewhere in the duct behind them, muffled by distance and stone. Dana and her team had apparently run into opposition.

Suddenly the lights flickered on. The room became awash in white, like a vid-screen with the brightness turned all the way up. But the effect was momentary. Before Mike could strip his optical gear, the lights went out again, and his IR vision returned.

Gunfire poured out the hole in the doorway. If Mike had had another hand grenade, he would have used it now. He could have tossed in a brick of C-4, but he had only one left, and he'd probably need that for the next door they came across.

Moments later, the lights flashed on and off again.

Bill Ryan hooked one arm around the doorframe and shot a blind spray of machine-pistol ammunition into the equipment beyond. He missed the men, though, or someone would have cried out.

In the darkness, Mike grabbed the door and shoved it out of the way. He dropped to his belly and crawled through the opening.

The men inside, when he found them, had no dark-vision gear. They huddled behind a desk, listening.

Mike continued to inch forward, watchful for anything on the floor that might cause noise if he disturbed it.

He glanced back at the doorway. Bill Ryan appeared. Standing. Stepping as cautiously as Mike was crawling. As long as the men behind the desk didn't hear him…

Something inside Mike snapped, like a spring breaking under too much tension. The malicious streak in him, the one that hated all authority except his own, took over. It allied with his need to complete his mission and his desire for Dana McCaughey. He hooked his foot around the leg of a metal chair and tugged it just enough to make a scraping sound against the floor.

The Russians fired in the direction of the sound, the direction of the doorway.

As soon as Ryan went down, Mike popped to his knees and sent a spray of bullets across the top of the desk. One of the guards' heads exploded. The other ducked back down to safety.

The lights came on again, and Mike's vision became a blast of white. This time they stayed on. He could just make out the silhouette of the desk and other furnishings in the wash of white.

He lunged forward, beyond the desk, and fired two shots into the guard. "Clear!" he yelled to the others.

Carter and Townsend stopped beside Major Ryan, who lay in a pool of his own blood. Carter was trying to staunch the flow from a wound in Ryan's chest. With the major out of action, Mike became the ranking officer until Dana returned. And by the time she did, her boyfriend would be out of the picture.

"Leave him," Mike said. "We'll collect him on the way out. Right now, the mission comes first. We need to keep moving."

The room went black once more.

CHAPTER 30

Dana lay prone at the mouth of the long duct that led to the classified ware-house, her assault rifle pointed down the adjoining duct behind them. As soon as the Russians rounded the corner, she put a bullet into the head of the lead pursuer, which suddenly made the others more cautious. Behind her, Allistair prepared a brick of C-4.

As far as Dana could tell, the cramped tunnel before them was straight all the way to the end. The concussion from an explosion in such a confined space could knock them all out, so Allistair cut the brick in half before insert-ing the radio detonator.

Dana had hoped there would be another corner to round, but the duct was what it was. They had to block it here.

"Ready," Allistair said.

A wave of gunfire flooded the adjoining duct. The Russians would try to move forward under its cover. "Just a second." They might reach and disable the C-4 before Dana and her crew could retreat to a safe distance to detonate it. "Stick a detonator in the other half of that and give it to me." Dana fired a few sporadic rounds to try to slow the enemy.

Allistair did as she ordered.

When he was done, Dana tossed the brick down the tunnel and ducked back behind the wall. "Blow it."

They were too close. Allistair stared at her, his mouth wide.

Dana would have snatched the trigger and blown it herself, but she didn't know which frequency detonated which brick of C-4. "Blow it!" She scrambled past him toward the classified complex.

One of the Russians appeared at the intersection and pointed a machine pistol straight at her and her team. He never had the chance to pull the trigger. Allistair thumbed the detonator and a shockwave blew the Russian, in pieces, past the opening. A rumble filled the duct, followed by a cloud of rock chips and dust.

Several minutes later, after donning their IR headgear, Dana, Miller, Allistair, and Zeke Shepherd dropped into the grenade-trashed room at the far end of the shaft. Allistair, having been closest to the blast, had a dozen small cuts on one side of his face from a peppering of stone fragments.

"Blow the other one," Dana said.

Allistair wiggled his pinky in his ear on the damaged side of his face, as though trying to clear up his hearing. Dana jabbed her finger toward the radio-trigger in his hand. With a nod, he adjusted the dial and thumbed the switch again.

A rumble, lower and more distant than the last, sent a cloud of dust billowing into the room. With that, he had sealed off their only exit, but in the end, that didn't matter. They all knew when they came in that none of them would make it back out.

Another blast roared from somewhere ahead. "Stay behind us," Dana told Zeke, as she waved her crew forward.

They caught up to Bill and the others as they hauled aside an enormous steel door, the second such door they'd passed. Bill leaned on Townsend. The top half of his jumpsuit hung in tatters from his waist. A blood-soaked bandage circled his torso, just below his armpits.

"Oh, Bill. What happened?"

The cavernous space beyond them was dark. Their IR lamps couldn't begin to illuminate the space. Mike and Carter swept inside, weapons ready. Dana nodded for Miller and Allistair to go with them.

"Your klutz boyfriend here stepped into the way of a bullet," Townsend said.

Dana breathed a sigh. Though the news sounded bad, she'd figured that much out already, and Townsend's flip tone told her Bill was going to be all right.

Bill smiled weakly. He looked deathly pale, but some of that was caused by the IR lighting. "The bullet passed cleanly through. Missed the lung. Hurts like hell, though, and I can't move my arm."

"He wouldn't let us give him any morphine," Townsend said.

"I need to keep my head clear," Bill added.

"Looks deserted," Kamikaze called from inside the cavern.

"All right," Dana said, with one more critical look at Bill. "Sure you're okay?"

He nodded.

"Then let's go."

They all extracted flashlights from their various bags and toolboxes and shined them ahead, the beams extending significantly beyond the range of their IR headlamps.

Zeke gasped after they'd covered about a dozen meters of empty floor space.

Before them, on motorized racks, sat row after row of bombs, each easily a meter in diameter and twice as long, hunched in the darkness as if waiting for Armageddon.

"There must be over a hundred of them," Miller said.

Dana made a quick count. Six rows, each with warheads lined up side by side as far back as their flashlights could penetrate.

Kamikaze snatched up his toolbox and trotted toward the nearest of them. He swept a Geiger scanner down the length of the bomb. About a third of the way back, the reading jumped. "This is them, all right."

"Cover him," Dana said.

Immediately, Miller and Allistair fanned out to search the darkened recesses of the room. Dana tapped Bill's arm and gestured to the blasted doorway behind them. With a nod, he and Townsend backtracked to cover the entrance. Dana, Zeke, and Carter walked up to where Kamikaze was fitting a bit to his battery-powered screwdriver.

Carefully, he removed a dozen screws that secured a small access panel on the side of the bomb. Dana took a deep breath in a futile effort to still her slamming heart. The sheer destructive power of the device before them was unfathomable...especially with a hundred or more beyond it.

Beneath the access plate lay a simple control panel—a numeric keypad, an old-fashioned LED display that looked suspiciously like a countdown timer from a classic terrorist-drama vid-file, a crude knob with a white arrow and unlabeled tick marks all the way around, and four exposed screw heads.

"Looks antique." Zeke's voice shook.

"The design is," Mike said. "Nobody can do nuclear testing anymore. Detonate one of these babies anywhere in the solar system and we'll detect it."

"You'd think they'd at least require a Gauss driver to access them."

Mike shook his head. "Since they can't test any design changes, it's safer to keep building them to the old spec." He began to unscrew the panel, which would expose the guts of the weapon. "They had to go all the way back to a 1950s design, from before the thermonuclear era, because the tritium required for hydrogen bombs can't be manufactured without its being detected. Good thing too, otherwise Deep West Base would no longer exist at all."

Mike was rambling—nervous, maybe. Dana's heart was almost too jumpy for her to breathe. Her mind catalogued all the possible outcomes of a single wrong move. She could think of only one. At least that one would destroy every bomb in the warehouse, and probably collapse a substantial portion of Gagarin Base. It wasn't the way she wanted to die, but at least it would accomplish the mission.

Miller and Allistair returned. "We're alone in here," Miller said.

Dana nodded. "Good."

They all huddled around Kamikaze, staring over his shoulder, breaths held, as he lifted the electronics panel out of its socket.

As soon as it popped free, the bomb exploded.

CHAPTER 31

Ana planted her feet, crossed her arms, and stared up at Private Metzner, the one soldier Colonel Davis had spared to help with the explosives work needed to reach the Administration complex before the air ran out. "Can we do it or not?"

The mousey old man standing next to Metzner shook his head vigorously. "It's too dangerous. The whole ceiling could come down on *us*."

"He's right," said the man in the green pajamas. "We could bring the ceiling down on the victims in the pocket too."

Ana tried to keep from scowling. Until now, Pajamas had been a proponent of the plan. Where was this sudden caution coming from? "Scared?"

"No. I…" He paused, looking first at Metzner and then at Ben Trollinger. "I just think we should be careful. That's all."

Over the years, working for so many different personality types—especially male personality types—Ana had become adept at assessing moods and needs, tendencies and insecurities. Now, after a good ten minutes of arguing about the risks and benefits of using these explosives, for this application, in this potentially unstable tunnel, she thought she just about had these men pegged.

The old man wasn't a coward, just a pessimist, but one who didn't recognize the trait in himself. He valued the opinions of those he perceived as smart or likable. Apparently, he didn't think the man in the pajamas fell into either of those categories. He didn't seem to think Ana did either.

Private Metzner was a grunt in the absence of a superior officer. He was capable and willing to do whatever it took to save the trapped administrators, despite the risks. He'd packed and primed the explosives, but he seemed unwilling to make the decision to detonate them. As soon as the decision was made, he wouldn't hesitate. The problem was, nobody was in charge. Ana wondered briefly if she could offer him a freebie later if he'd just do it. But he seemed too professional to accept any proposal that so closely resembled a bribe. Metzner was waiting for consensus.

The geologist, Trollinger, wanted to do the job, as long as it could be done safely.

"What do you think?" Ana asked him.

He eyed the tunnel ceiling. "It's a valid concern. If these were mining explosives, I'd say we're okay. Packed properly, they'd bring down only the wall they're intended to. But you saw what a single brick did in there." He gestured to the dead-end corridor the demolition robot had collapsed earlier. "That tunnel is at least fifty meters shorter than it used to be. If these bring down fifty meters of *this* tunnel, we may never reach the pocket. That said..."

Ana finished for him. "If we don't try, the administrators are going to die anyway."

"Exactly."

The man in the pajamas was harder to read. He seemed to be most comfortable in a position of service. He liked someone to tell him what needed to be done, and as long as the task was something he knew how to do, he was all set. Now, though, the only thing they needed was to blow this damned wall out of the way.

Pajamas had just returned from moving all the other workers back to a safe distance, which he'd done at Metzner's request. Apparently the hundred and fifty meters Metzner had insisted upon as a "safe" distance had shaken him.

Ana had stated initially, as though she was actually in charge here, that they were just going to move back and blow it. "Do it and be done with it," as Zeke would have said. But unlike the milling sheep that populated the Plaza, these four men seemed unwilling to leave the decision to her. If Zeke was here, his title as Facilities Manager would establish his decision-making authority. But Zeke hadn't returned with Metzner. Metzner had refused to say why, stating only that Zeke was "busy elsewhere." And Tanner was still laid up in the Sharp Shooter.

So it was up to Ana. She took a deep breath. "According to Zeke's estimates, we're about out of time." The old man wasn't going to budge. She had to get him out of the way without pissing him off—that would just make him more obstinate. "We need Zeke Shepherd," Ana told him. "He's the only one with both the expertise and authority to make this decision."

The private nodded. Without a consensus, Zeke was the ticket, but it would take half an hour round-trip to get him back here. There was no time.

"Could you go to the Plaza and bring him?" Ana asked the old man.

"How will I find him?" he said. "The Plaza's a big place."

"I'll go." Pajamas turned to leave.

Shit! Ana should have seen that coming. "No!" *Damn!* "I need you for something else." She turned to the old man. "Try the Sharp Shooter. If he's not there, he's with Colonel Davis. Any soldier you see will know where Davis is."

"It'll take time to get there and back."

"Then you'd better hurry."

"I'll go," Pajamas repeated. "I can probably move faster. No offense," he added to the old man.

"No," Ana said again, a little too quickly. She had to come up with a job for him that the old man couldn't do—not just because she needed the old man to leave, but because she needed Pajamas here. He'd taken a turn in the tractor. He'd learned how to drive it. "I need your strong back. We're going to shore up this tunnel while he's gone.

"Go," she told the old man.

With a huff, he shuffled off down the corridor.

Ana turned to Trollinger. "Now, Ben, you and I both know we don't have the materials to shore up this tunnel. And we don't have time to wait for that old naysayer to get back. We need to save some lives. Get on the comm and tell the survivors in the pocket to move as far away from this wall as possible."

He hurried to the transmitter, from which he'd run a wire deep into one of the laser-drilled holes. With that as an antenna, they'd been able to clean up the static and talk to the trapped survivors.

To Pajamas, she said, "Fire up the tractor. In a minute, we're going to have a lot of rubble to move."

He trotted away.

That left only Private Metzner. "You got a problem with this?" Ana asked him.

"No, ma'am."

"Then let's get as far down the corridor as that detonator will allow and hope for the best."

Thirty seconds later, Metzner blew the wall away. The ceiling held, and a cheer reached them from the survivors in the pocket. They had a lot of debris to move before they could get the people out safely, but at least there were ample air gaps near the top of the rubble pile that now sat where the wall had been.

"Well," Ana said finally, "that wasn't so hard."

⋘○⋙

Everything was dark. Dana was dead; she must be, because there was nothing. No sights. No sounds. She didn't seem to have a body. If she did, she couldn't will it to move. But this was nothing like what she thought death would be. Nothing like the heaven she imagined, assuming she had actually gone to heaven.

Maybe she hadn't. Where then? Hell? Maybe. But where was the pain? The torment? Wasn't there supposed to be some sort of judgment first?

Slowly, a red-orange glow penetrated her consciousness. It didn't seem to come from anywhere. It was just there. Just beyond seeing. At no specific distance, with no apparent source. Her heart, if she still had one, sank. This must be hell.

Then she heard laughter, harsh and maniacal. She recognized the voice, though she'd never heard him laugh before. The smell of brimstone reached her nostrils.

Shit! This *was* hell, and Kamikaze Mike was there with her.

Others laughed as well, joining the eerie chorus one at a time. Miller, Allistair, and the others, including, apparently, Zeke Shepherd.

"Dana!" A harsh whisper. Miller's voice.

228

She didn't hear Bill. Maybe he'd made it to a better place.

Someone shook her shoulder.

Miller spoke more loudly. "Dana!"

She opened her eyes and a white blaze shot into them. "You all right?" Miller moved the flashlight he'd been shining onto her face.

Then she saw it, the warhead she thought had exploded, vaporizing body and soul. It was still there, still sitting on its rack, its belly now distended from some contained explosion that had apparently slagged its innards. Smoke billowed from the open hole where Kamikaze had removed the crude control panel.

"What happened?" she managed.

Mike chuckled again. "Tamper control measures. If anyone ever steals one of these babies and tries to muck with it, it self-destructs—prevents anyone from using it without the proper authorization code."

"Did you know that was going to happen?" Allistair asked.

For the first time Dana had ever seen, Mike looked a little sheepish. "I suspected. But, no. And if it did, I wasn't sure the explosion would spare the person doing the tampering."

"And anyone else nearby," Dana said.

Mike shrugged. "We're here to destroy them, not use them, so this actually makes our job easier." He swept the length of the bomb with the Geiger scanner. His mouth pursed as if he were both surprised and greatly impressed. "It's still clean." Not that it mattered. They would do the job, regardless.

Dana took a deep, steadying breath. Nothing to it, she told herself. "All right. Everybody pick a row. We haven't got much time before the Russians force their way in here." She swallowed hard as she reached into Mike's toolbox. Even Townsend joined them, starting at the far end and working his way back.

Dana stepped up to the next bomb in line and checked her watch. She had to remove sixteen screws. The twelve securing the outer cover slid out easily. Then she removed the inner four and tugged gently on the corner of the control panel. When the charge inside the bomb detonated, she jumped. For a moment, her heart felt as if it would stop in her chest. Then it was over. The bomb was disabled. She took a breath—her first since she'd started working on the bomb—and checked her watch again. Forty-eight seconds. The next one would be quicker.

Ultimately, it wasn't as bad as she'd feared. The first few were nerve-wracking, but it got easier and she became faster—less than two seconds per screw, with the power screwdriver. The precise, consistent way in which the bomb casings bulged spoke of how meticulously designed the self-destruct mechanisms were. That gave her the confidence to finish the job.

Twenty minutes later, just as they were completing the last of the demolition, an explosion erupted from the direction of the base proper.

"We're out of time," Bill yelled. "As soon as you're done, get changed." He himself was already in his flight uniform, though he had turned what was left of it right-side out. The effort had caused his wound to bleed again.

Dana triggered the last two bombs in her row, then reached for a uniform from Townsend's bag.

This was the part she was really dreading, even more than the prospect of being killed by the Russians.

Because it was a civilian base, they'd needed civilian clothes to infiltrate it. But now, in order to don her uniform, she actually had to disrobe, at least down to her underwear, in front of Mike Kamieniechi.

Mike, who'd been the first to complete his row of nukes and had already changed, was fastening the last few buttons on his shirt. He leered at Dana while she stripped. She turned her back, which hid some of her shape but made her feel no less self-conscious. If that asshole ever had the gall to bring this up with her...

When she turned back around, most of the others were changing as well, Carter last. Mike, Dana noticed, didn't even glance at Carter. Apparently his attentions were solely for Dana. *Great. That's just great.*

Zeke was a problem. Because he actually was a civilian, he couldn't rightly don a military uniform. Whether he did or not, he would likely be executed as a spy or terrorist. Dressed as civilians, they all would have been.

Townsend gathered up the discarded clothing and ignited them in a two-hundred-liter trash barrel in one corner.

"Freeze!" A Russian soldier called in English from the doorway.

As one, they all spun around, revealing their insignia of military rank, arms raised in surrender.

As military officers, undertaking a military operation—in military uniform, during a time of open conflict—they might actually be treated as prisoners of war, according to the requirements of the Geneva Convention. Not that Dana expected the Russians to do so—they'd broken every treaty that had gotten in their way so far. By now, though, there would be too many Russians and too much distance between her team and the civilian population they might have otherwise lost themselves in. This was the only chance any of them had.

CHAPTER 32

Davis received a comm from Colonel Brannon at Shenming Base.

"Report," Davis said.

"Shenming is ours. General Chou in custody. Several casualties. The civilian medical staff is tending the wounded from both sides. Those two Marauders were just about all Chou had left. I plan to leave the bulk of my men here to secure the base. I figure since most of the team that went into Gagarin are yours, you'd want your men available to bring them back."

That was true enough, though Brannon was probably more concerned about keeping his remaining men out of harm's way in the event that it became necessary to storm the Russian base. "Acknowledged. I think your men have done more than their share. We can handle the rest."

"Any word from Gagarin?" Brannon asked.

"Not yet, though I don't expect to hear anything until Batkin learns that we've taken Shenming. And I think he should hear it from both you and Chou via whatever channel those two have been using to communicate. Then I'll contact Batkin and give him an ultimatum: surrender or we'll take Gagarin by force."

"That sounds like a plan," Brannon said. "I just wish we had some way to know if those nukes have been neutralized."

"I have faith in our team," Davis said.

"So do I. Still…"A static-laden silence hung for a moment before Brannon said, "I'll make the call."

Davis killed the link. He figured he'd wait an hour before contacting

Gagarin. That would give the Russian commander a chance to think through his options. Forty minutes into the wait, however, his link chimed. "Colonel Davis."

"This is Comrade Viktor Batkin of the Gagarin Command. It's my duty to inform you, under the terms of the Geneva Convention, that we have captured eight prisoners of war."

"Excellent." The count was correct, and all were apparently alive. Now that Batkin had disclosed the prisoners, he couldn't execute them as spies. In essence, they were as safe as if they were back at Deep West. Even Zeke Shepherd was apparently being treated as a military combatant.

Davis had expected no less. He'd given Batkin ample time to learn that Shenming Base was under attack before sending Major Ryan and his team to infiltrate Gagarin. Batkin would have been foolish to make any decision regarding his prisoners until he knew the outcome of the Shenming battle. Because the Americans and Europeans had won, Batkin had only two choices: execute his prisoners out of spite and face a trial for war crimes, or treat them according to the Geneva Convention.

Batkin spewed all the required information about his prisoners: name, rank, serial number, medical condition…The next words out of his mouth would tell Davis if his team had been successful before they were captured.

"I would like to discuss terms for the surrender of Gagarin Base," Batkin said.

Davis smiled. The nukes, if there had been any more, were out of the picture.

⨯⟨◯⟩⨯

Two American soldiers frog-marched Simeon Tuck onto the Plaza, bound with flex cuffs, his feet shuffling. He shot Ana a withering glare.

Ana returned an easy smile, with a touch of pity. She took no pleasure in the breaking of a man, even one as despicable as Simeon, but to free the Plaza from his grip was a sweet prospect indeed.

Beside her stood Marcus Anderson, the director of Deep West, or what was left of it. He shook his head in disgust at Simeon. "Honestly, I had no idea."

That was probably true. The administrative aspects—all the logistical bullshit that came with the comings and goings of ships and cargo—was more than a full-time job without worrying about passenger lodging and law enforcement. The reservation clerks of the Plaza's various hotels had always handled passenger lodging. Base Administration got involved only if there was an influx that exceeded Deep West's capacity. As for law enforcement, that's what the sheriff's office was supposed to be for.

From here on out, Davis's men would handle every aspect of Simeon's incarceration. Because of Simeon's influence, none of the base residents could be trusted with it. The way he'd threatened his way out of his first jailing had proven that well enough. And nobody but Simeon himself knew for sure who had been in his employ.

The man Ana thought of as "Pajamas" approached, though he was now dressed in respectable day clothes. "We've completed hanging safety signs to mark the unstable tunnels and radiation areas, as you requested."

"Thank you," Ana said.

"And we've unearthed the entrance to one of the facility storerooms. It's marked P-17 on the base layout. The storeroom itself is intact, with a variety of spare-parts cabinets and several huge water-recycling filters."

"I'll inform Zeke Shepherd as soon as I see him," Ana said.

The man smiled and hurried away.

"What should we do with the sheriff and his deputies?" Davis asked Anderson. Since this was an international base, the US military had no jurisdiction over such matters, unless Anderson specifically requested their involvement, which he'd done in Simeon's case.

Anderson thought for a moment. "Haul them out with Simeon, I guess."

"Actually…" Ana said, tentatively. She would never second-guess Anderson in front of any of his people, but at the moment, only Colonel Davis stood within earshot. "I don't think any of them had a choice."

"Are you saying I should pardon them?" Anderson asked.

"I don't know what the right answer is, but I can tell you this: Simeon had them by the balls."

"Everybody has a choice," Davis said, his jaw set.

"Not with Simeon."

"You had a choice. You defied him, and you came out okay."

"That's different. Simeon didn't need me. And I didn't have a family for him to threaten. If the deputies hadn't cooperated, he would have had them killed, along with their families, and then coerced their replacements into his service."

"They could have notified me," Anderson said.

"Then you would have turned up dead."

"Nevertheless…"

A woman approached this time, one of the base's computer technicians. Ana didn't know her personally, but she'd been active in the rescue efforts ever since Deep West had collapsed. She made her report to Ana, not to Anderson. "We've gotten the Administration network up and running. We now have access to the ship manifests and stores inventories."

"Good," Ana said. "Go through them all. Make a single list of everything that might be useful. You're looking for medical supplies—especially antibiotics and Granulocyte—food, construction materials, anything we might need to survive until help arrives from Earth." That wouldn't be for at least eighty-eight days. "Don't take or move anything yet. Just make a list so we know what we have for when the time comes to make a decision. With your permission," she added quickly to Director Anderson.

He nodded. "Of course."

"Include the location of everything," Ana told the computer tech. "We'll need to know what we have access to and what warehouses and hangars we need to excavate."

Davis watched her. "Looks like you've got quite a bit of influence yourself."

She smiled. "That just cropped up in the last thirty-six hours."

"But you seem pretty plugged into what's been happening on this end of the base."

"Believe me, in my line of work, I learn more than you can imagine."

"Very well." Anderson turned to Davis. "Consider the sheriff and deputies pardoned. But I'd like you to escort them off the base, even off the whole damn planet when you can. I need law enforcement I can trust one hundred percent, and those three no longer fit the bill."

"Consider it done," Davis said.

"Now, if you'll excuse us, Colonel. I need a word alone with Miss Davenport."

◦◈❨ O ❩◈◦

A week after Zeke returned to Deep West, he joined Ana in the restored lounge of the Sharp Shooter Hotel, which was now on the market and being run by Ana, the interim manager appointed by Director Anderson until a new owner could take over.

In the meantime, any remaining patients had been stabilized and relocated to the base hospital, along with a variety of medical supplies commandeered from the relative surpluses at Shenming and Gagarin.

Ana had removed all of the gambling equipment and turned the entire floor into a dining room, furnished with a mishmash of tables salvaged and repaired from the wreckage of other buildings or constructed from pieces of debris. "Gambling," Ana had said, "served only the greed of the casino's owner."

In addition, many salvageable rooms in other hotels had been cleared, inspected, and declared safe to occupy, if not altogether comfortable. Ana was managing those rooms as well. Those who had lost their rooms had been set up in temporary quarters—sometimes nothing more than blankets and pillows in whatever patch of Plaza floor could be secured for them.

Aside from the buildings themselves and the large percentage of the base's tunnels that were still inaccessible—many of which would remain permanently buried because of radiation concerns—the routine of Deep West had been more or less restored. Zeke had worked tirelessly to make sure the air and water were both clean and reliably flowing. The vast majority of the solar array remained intact and had been swept of the layers of dust the bombings had deposited on them.

And, just that morning, Tanner had returned to work, having responded well to bed rest and Granulocyte. He credited God with his recovery, and maybe he was right. He had a high probability of acquiring cancer later in life, but that too could be treated.

Zeke could finally slow down, yet he shifted uncomfortably at the table.

Ana sat with one leg under her bottom to boost her height in the chair, her red silk dress a little too formal for her current clientele. She cocked her head at Zeke like a curious puppy for a few seconds. "Still shaken up over your covert op?"

"It's not that," Zeke said. It was unlike her to miss the mark when it came to assessing the moods of men. This, though, she was ill-equipped to see coming. "I...I want to give you something." He reached into his hip pocket.

Ana held up a forestalling hand. "If you're going to try to pay me for the other night—"

This had been an awkward issue for them ever since they'd started sleeping together. She was a prostitute. When she slept with a man, she got paid for it. It was that simple. If Zeke didn't pay when it was his turn, he felt like a cheat. On the other hand, he didn't think of her as a whore, so he didn't want to treat her like one.

Tonight, he chose a third option.

He opened a black velvet box to reveal a shining diamond ring—not a large diamond, but the best he could afford. Ironically, he'd bought it at the jewelry shop right here in the Sharp Shooter about a month before. Pay Ana for sleeping with him? No. "I think we're past that. Don't you?"

Her smile could not have been more radiant. The glow in her shining eyes rivaled that of the tiny gemstone glittering in the box. For the first time Zeke had ever seen, she didn't seem to know what to say.

"Will you marry me?"

"Yes." Ana's chest heaved as she labored to control her breathing. "Of course, Zeke Shepherd, I'll marry you."

He slipped the ring onto her finger and, for a long time, they just stared into one another's eyes. Then Ana got up, walked around the table, and plopped her feather-light body into his lap. She wrapped her arms around his neck and gave him a kiss so passionate he wanted to take her right there in the bar.

Finally, she said, "I'm getting out of the business. So I'll be all yours."

"What are you going to do? Buy the Sharp Shooter?" He was half joking. Though she had proven herself an able manager, he didn't think she could get the credit she'd need to purchase it.

But Ana's reply seemed to be well-considered and serious. "I thought about it. Lord knows I've got enough money."

Zeke's brows shot up, but he said nothing.

"Actually," she continued, "I have a better offer."

"Really?" He sat up straighter now and studied her face.

She shoved his shoulders playfully. "Don't look so surprised."

"Okay. What's the offer?"

"Director Anderson lost his executive assistant in the blast. He wants me to replace him." She rushed on when she saw Zeke's skeptical look. "This is strictly professional. He'll handle the budgeting and traffic approvals, and make all the major decisions. I'll help manage the people." She paused. "Did I mention I'm good with people?"

CHAPTER 33

A few days later, Colonel Davis received a military relief convoy, one that had departed from Earth's moon three days after the Freedom Flight, with three additional squads of American marines, munitions, foodstuffs, and other supplies. Though the Mercury battle was now over, the next jaunt would likely be to Venus in a couple of months. The supplies would be needed then.

Following that, an unscheduled ship arrived. Like the relief convoy, it had left its departure point after the standard launch window to Mercury had closed, thereby taking longer than usual to make the trip. What made this particular ship of interest was that it had come from *Venus Rain*, and had launched *after* China had hijacked the station. The ship, the *Eclipse*, settled into orbit based on a pre-programmed trajectory. Deep West's traffic controller had to send a descent vector that would bring it down on autopilot to the landing field south of the station. Fortunately, the three occupants—a teenage girl who introduced herself as Kelly Baker, her older boyfriend, and her nine-year-old brother—had pressure suits onboard for the walk to Deep West proper.

Colonel Davis was waiting for them, with several of his marines, when they stepped off the lift. His men helped the young trio out of their EVA gear.

When Kelly turned to Davis, she stared at the US flag on his uniform. "You're US military?"

"That's right."

"And that insignia." She pointed to the bird emblem on his shoulder. "What is that?"

"Colonel," supplied the young man with her—Mark Torben, Davis had been told.

"That's a high rank, right?" Kelly asked.

Mark laughed nervously. "Yeah. It's high." Then, to Davis, he said, "Sorry."

"It's okay."

"Can we speak to you, Colonel?" Kelly glanced at the other uniforms, some of which displayed the blue-and-gold flag of the European Union. "In private."

∞《○》∞

President Powers invited the European delegation back to Washington.

"We've stopped shipments to *Venus Rain* from going through Mercury," Dan Norton was saying. "That'll slow the flow of hydrogen to the Project, but if we want to stop it all, we'll need to stop the shipments at their source."

"Jupiter," Mariano said.

O'Leary nodded. "But we can't do so until we get an orbital launch window.

"In the meantime, we've gotten something of a break." Powers gestured for O'Leary to explain.

O'Leary didn't activate any of the fancy holograph or video displays the Situation Room offered. Instead, he spoke quietly from his seat. "A small transport arrived at Deep West yesterday with three civilians on board. One of them, Kelly Baker, gave Colonel Davis a data card she claims to have received from one of your agents—Doctor Dennis La Roche." He turned to Andrew Yates. "Do you know La Roche?"

"Not personally, but he does work for EU intelligence on *Venus Rain*. If this Baker girl knows that, the data card is probably legit."

"*Worked* for EU intelligence," O'Leary corrected. "According to Miss Baker, La Roche gave his life to get the card to her."

"Then that card belongs to us," said Wolfgang Das, the intelligence officer in Yates' delegation.

"Perhaps," Dan Norton said, "but Miss Baker gave it to Colonel Davis. Be thankful we decided to share the information."

"Easy, Dan," Powers said. "They've done their share of disclosing. And we're all in this together."

"Well then, by all means," Yates said, apparently unperturbed. "What's it say?"

O'Leary produced a data card from his inside jacket pocket and handed it to Wolfgang. "This is a complete copy of the original. What we know so far is that it contains a list of Colonel Chang's resources." He turned to Powers. "That's the name of the man now in charge on *Venus Rain*." Until they'd received the card, they hadn't even known that much of what was happening on the hijacked station.

"We have troop counts, defense satellite information—types, quantities, deployments—and strategic resources, including food, water, hydrogen. It's all very detailed, right down to the amount of toilet paper on the station."

Norton stood and addressed President Powers directly. "It'll take us some time to sift through it all and see if it suggests a strategy."

"One more thing of importance," O'Leary said. "As we suspected, the explosion we observed on Venus's surface thirty-seven days ago was indeed a terraforming processor. According to La Roche, without that processor, the terraforming project doesn't have enough gas-conversion capacity to keep up with the greenhouse effect caused by carbon dioxide in the Venusian atmosphere. The terraforming process is no longer moving forward. It's slipping backwards. Time is now on our side."

Mariano's head snapped up. "That's great! Now we might be able to get them to negotiate."

Powers shook her head. "We're way past that. I'm no longer willing to negotiate with Muyou or Petrov, not after what they've done to Deep West."

"At least not until they relinquish control of Venus and reveal their nuclear weapons plant," Yates said.

Powers nodded, conceding the point. If they did that, she'd be willing to talk. "That brings us to Russia. Any luck locating their weapons factory?"

"Possibly." O'Leary rubbed the back of his neck. "We've gone through a process of elimination." Now he brought up a hologram over the middle of the table—an image of Earth and its moon. "We know they're not building on Earth. When the complete nuclear disarmament treaty was implemented, every nuclear weapon was accounted for, as was all fissile material. Because there aren't any fission plants left on Earth, and because all known radioactive waste has been disposed of in deep space, the background radiation signature is low enough that we would detect any significant quantity of fissionable uranium or plutonium on the planet."

"Unless it was deep underground," Norton interjected.

Wolfgang was already shaking his head. "Refinement of radioactive isotopes to fissionable purities requires enormous facilities. The inspections provided for in the treaty would prevent such an operation from going unnoticed."

"They couldn't build the facility, even underground, without our surveillance satellites spotting the construction activities," O'Leary added. "It's just impossible."

"Okay," Powers said. "It's not on Earth. I think we already knew that, but I appreciate your thoroughness. Where else?"

"Russia has no significant bases on the Moon. So that's out." O'Leary touched a button on the control panel in front of his seat. On the hologram, an eight-pointed, three-dimensional X crossed out both the Earth and Moon. He expanded the image to include the entire solar system with the planets enlarged enough to keep them visible. "Mercury was a possibility. High levels of solar radiation, and the depth of some of the underground caverns, would mask the radioactive signatures of uranium or plutonium. That's how they got away with warehousing the bombs there. But only three bases exist anywhere on the planet: Shengming, Gagarin, and Deep West."

"We now own them all," Norton said.

"Exactly." O'Leary crossed out Mercury. "We've combed every meter of Gagarin Base. There are no nuclear refinement or assembly facilities there. Only the warehouse."

"Venus?" Mariano guessed. "It would give them a reason to side with China and retain some control of the planet."

O'Leary shook his head. "*Venus Rain* is the only sizable station there, and until thirty-eight days ago, it was internationally owned. With the exception of a few small research labs and a couple of government offices, everything that happens on the station is completely transparent. It has to be, otherwise the terraforming project would never get the international and corporate sponsorship it needs to keep it running."

Wolfgang spoke up as well. "The atmosphere is such that a sizable base could be concealed on the surface, but temperatures there—even hotter than those on Mercury—prevent human occupancy for more than a few hours at a time."

He added a big X to Venus and continued, working outward from the center of the hologram "The Mars colony is, of course, independent." Because the orbit of Mars around the sun allowed for a launch window from Earth only once every two years—the longest interval to any planet in the solar system—and because the colonization of Mars had predated that of Mercury, which had reduced the transportation interval substantially, Mars had been selected for an experiment—an autonomous base that was unaffiliated with any Earth country. "It's entirely self-sufficient, but it lacks the material resources for an undertaking of the size we're talking about."

"And," O'Leary said, "although it's independent, it enjoys a large, rotating population from virtually every country on Earth—to attend Mars Tech, for tourism, or to study their unique ecology, politics, or culture."

Wolfgang tapped a key and crossed out the planet. "If they had something like this going on, it wouldn't stay hidden for long."

"Jupiter then," Powers said with certainty.

"That's where our concern has always lain," O'Leary admitted. "That's where the concentration of Russian activity is. With all the moons and mining activities, corporate facilities, union headquarters, and tourism, it's nearly impossible to keep track of all the comings and goings. Simply put, it's a nest of unregulated activities."

"Then it's got to be there," Norton said.

"Maybe. But I doubt it."

"Why's that?" Powers asked.

"Because Jupiter has always been the center of our concern, we've applied the bulk of our surveillance there."

"As have we," Wolfgang added.

"We have spies and satellites keeping track of the mines and accounting for a significant percentage of the ships and payloads. They may be smuggling uranium ore from somewhere in the Jupiter system, but I think we would have detected any refinement activities large enough to produce weapons-grade material."

Powers gripped her cane. If she'd had more strength in her hands, she might have snapped it in two. "You're saying Russia has nuclear weapons, yet they can't be producing them anywhere."

"Not quite." O'Leary shifted in his seat. "There's one more possibility. Unlikely, but feasible."

"Do tell." Yates gestured to Wolfgang with a flourish of his hand.

Wolfgang adjusted the hologram to zero in on Saturn's largest moon. "Russia has a small science station orbiting Titan."

"And," O'Leary said, "Nobody else has any presence there at all."

Mariano's brow creased. "But it's small. You said any refinement operation would have to be huge."

"Aren't we monitoring it for background radiation?" Norton asked.

"Of course," O'Leary said.

Then Wolfgang dropped the bomb, so to speak. "The orbiting station is small, but Titan isn't. And its methane-rich atmosphere obstructs virtually any form of surface surveillance."

O'Leary continued. "According to Russia, the space station is there to study the methane moon, but what if they're really there for another purpose? The location is ideal."

"All right," Powers said. "If all this is true, why do you say you consider Titan unlikely?"

"The methane in the atmosphere won't burn by itself, but add heat and oxygen from the exhaust plume of a rocket and you'll ignite huge methane clouds. Our surveillance would see that, even from Earth. Yet we never have. Small craft descend through the atmosphere on a regular basis—ostensibly science probes—but we've never seen anything launch *from* the surface."

"Then how would they get the weapons out?" Powers asked.

"We don't know. That is a technical puzzle, but I think we need to check it out."

∽(O)∾

Dana sat across the table from Bill in the makeshift mess hall at the Sharp Shooter. A waiter placed dinner in front of them.

"What'll you trade me for the burger?" she asked Bill.

He eyed it speculatively. This had been a daily ritual ever since the casino had begun to refit nonperishable MREs, the ready-to-eat meals that had arrived on one of the military freighters, as civilian fare. Dana was a vegetarian and most of the MREs contained something the label generously called meat. "Are we talking the whole burger, or just the meat patty?"

"Make me an offer."

He smiled. "Can I make you an offer later?"

"Yes, but I still need something to eat now."

"All right." He pursed his lips and pondered Dana's plate again. "What kind of meat do you think it is?"

She peeled the bun back and scrutinized it. "I'm not even sure it is meat. But it came from the Sharp Shooter's kitchen, so it's bound to be good." That was true. Considering what the chef could do with an MRE, Dana would have bet that Simeon had hired the best chef in the solar system—and he probably had.

Bill pushed the meatballs off his mound of spaghetti and marinara. "All my noodles and sauce for your meat patty."

"Deal." After transferring the patty to his plate, she scooped all of his noodles and sauce onto the bottom half of her bun and placed the other half on top. She picked it up, burger-style, and took a bite. In truth, the food could barely be traced back to the MREs. The chef had done a great job of disguising it with herbs, sauces, and who knows what other bits of his own culinary magic.

The two ate in silence for a few minutes, during which Dana savored Bill's company, knowing it wouldn't last.

Finally, he broke the silence. "You're being shipped out."

She frowned. "I know. I got the orders this afternoon." The United States had either discovered or surmised that Russia's nuclear weapon factory was hidden on Titan. One of the CATS had to check it out—find the base, verify its purpose, and if possible, disable it.

During the two and a half weeks since the battle for Mercury had been won, the *Snow Leopard*'s door had been located. When Dana had jettisoned it during her hasty retreat from the ground battle, it had hit the surface with enough force to bend it. Fortunately the maintenance team had been able to straighten it and restore her ship to vacuum-tight status. The bullet holes in the wing had also been repaired.

The crew of the *Jaguar* wasn't so lucky. Their ship had taken significant damage during the battle. It was grounded until the necessary parts could be machined locally or shipped from Earth. Bill's arm wasn't yet well enough to deploy the *Black Panther*. And the *Siamese* lacked the stealth cladding this mission would require.

"I'd go in your place if I could," Bill said.

"I don't want you to go in my place." She gestured to his left arm, which remained in a sling to keep him from tearing the healing tissues in his chest. "You've got a bad habit of not coming back in one piece." She gave him a rueful smile. It was an impossible mission for a single CATS if she'd ever heard one. Nobody expected them to return, let alone in one piece.

But Bill wasn't done. "You'll wish I was going, once you hear the rest of the bad news."

EPILOGUE

Thirty-seven days into the three-month flight to Saturn, the *Snow Leopard*'s decompression claxon began to blare. Miller silenced the alarm so the ear-splitting sound wouldn't cut through their concentration, while everyone else on board scrambled for their pressure suits. Protocol required him to remain at his station to prevent the venting air from pushing them irrecoverably off course.

"Status." Dana shrugged her suit onto her shoulders.

"We're losing point-six standard cubic meters per minute. The environmental system is compensating."

"Shut off the O_2."

Miller overrode the automatic bleed that was flowing into the cabin to maintain pressure while they donned their gear. With a slow leak like this one, they had time without the bleed. And they might need the air later.

"Course?" Dana asked.

"Autopilot is correcting."

"Begin pumping the cabin." That would conserve even more air. "And get into your gear."

Miller was halfway into his pressure suit by the time the others were suited up, and fully geared long before the pumps, pulling cabin air back into the reserve tanks, brought the pressure below safe limits.

Unfortunately, the door repair had failed. The constant pressure in the cabin had finally forced the hatch's shape beyond tolerance. It took less than ten minutes to realize the leak was too large to fix with vacuum tape, the only means they had to address such a breach in flight.

"I suppose it could be worse," said Kamikaze, who'd been the only person on Mercury who knew enough about nuclear weapons to assess and address the nuclear threat once they reached Titan.

He was probably right, though Dana wasn't sure how it could have been worse. They were flying a broken ship, on a one-way mission, to a moon whose very atmosphere could be ignited into flame by the *Snow Leopard*'s exhaust. This time she really was going into hell, and despite Dana's vehement protests to Colonel Davis, Kamikaze Mike would be there with her.

The story continues in:

METHANE MOON
WORLDS ASUNDER: BOOK IV

ABOUT THE AUTHOR

Kirt Hickman was born in Albuquerque, New Mexico. He earned a Bachelor's degree in electrical engineering in 1989 and a Master's degree in opto-electronics in 1991, both from the University of New Mexico. He began writing fiction in 2003. Kirt has also published the sci-fi thriller novels *Worlds Asunder* and *Venus Rain*, the fantasy novel *Fabler's Legend*, the writers' how-to *Revising Fiction: Making Sense of the Madness*, and the children's books *I Will Eat Anything* and *Purple*. Visit his website at www.kirthickman.com.

www.ingramcontent.com/pod-product-compliance
Lightning Source LLC
Chambersburg PA
CBHW050507260626
47157CB00004B/1230